Olly
& THE SPORES
OF OAK HILL

BY GLENN SOMODI

Glenn Somodi
Three Bobcats Publishing, LLC
3528 Abington Court
Brunswick, Ohio 44212
info@OllyAndTheSpores.com

DEDICATION

To my parents
for fostering my imagination and
supporting every endeavor I ever wanted
to explore. To my wife for putting up with
the time, expense, and space needed to support
my crazy ideas and hobbies. To my children for
making parenting so easy. To the late Mrs.
Nancy Chubb for opening my eyes to journalism,
advertising, and publishing.
To my large family
for each purchasing
a copy of
my book. To
all of you who
enjoy this book
and inspire me
to continue writing.

CONTENTS

ACKNOWLEDGMENTS

I have to thank my wife for proofreading drafts and giving me the validation to continue writing.

Thank you to Stacey Reynolds and Stan Himes for giving me tips and insight into being an author and dealing with the publishing world. They both provided me with words of wisdom at a time when I had almost given up writing.

Thank you to Dawn Thompson for being my first reader.

1. AN ENDING TO BEGIN THE STORY

Oren Appleton was walking back to his house on Oak Hill after his customary Saturday visit to downtown Littleton. Since the death of his wife, the walk into town offered him the chance to talk with real people after toiling away on his house projects all week. With his hands full of supplies from Sawyer's Hardware, he walked up Oak Ridge Road, the only paved road that led up to his house – which sat dead center atop Oak Hill.

It was a warm summer evening and the sun was setting. He stepped to the beat of a show tune he was whistling. A very quiet whistle, slightly off-tune and off-beat, accompanied Oren's – it came from the leather satchel hanging over his shoulder. This duet made Oren smile.

He was so focused on the tune and his whistling partner

1

that he didn't hear the engine of the vehicle approaching. It approached quickly, and accelerated as it got closer to Oren. It was the crunching sound of the gravel directly behind him that made Oren turn. It was the last thing he would see and hear, as his body flew through the air and onto the ground. The force of the impact threw his body off the road and into a gully 15 feet away. Life had instantly left Oren. Without hesitation, the vehicle shifted into reverse and drifted back down the road and out of sight.

After ten minutes, the leather satchel next to Oren rustled with some movement, and the leather roping that had been cinched at the top of the satchel started to unravel from the inside. Very slowly, a small creature pulled its body out of the bag, stood, and slowly looked around to see what had happened. The creature was about the size of a common salt shaker you would find in a diner, and resembled a mushroom, but with a slightly thicker stem. Just like a mushroom, it seemed to wear a maroon and white mushroom cap on top of its head. Its arms and legs fit so snugly into the stem, that if it was standing upright and perfectly still in the woods you wouldn't know it from a garden-variety mushroom. Its small black eyes and a hardly-discernible mouth gave it a childlike and friendly expression. The skin had turned a bluish tint from the accident but gradually faded back to its normal off-white color as it shook off the impact to its body.

With a slight limp, it stepped away from the sawdust-filled satchel and toward Oren's face. It knew instantly there was no life left in Oren, and it slumped with sadness before it started off into the woods with what sounded like a sniffle.

Five minutes had passed and the creature came back from the woods to Oren's body, dragging a large clump of pink and white clover flowers behind. It slowly plucked the flowers off the stems, and arranged them in a circle all around Oren's head while whistling the rest of the show tune that he and Oren had

2

started together. When the supply of clovers ran out, it stood silently for a moment and then walked off into the dark woods of Oak Hill. The forest was oddly silent and still.

2. THE CRAZY HERMIT ON THE HILL

The "crazy hermit on the hill" was dead. Rumors of the cause of his death had passed through town faster than the announcement of the fake Littleton gold rush of 1850.

"Crazy hermit" was just one of the many names the townsfolk in Littleton, Massachusetts used when describing Oren Appleton, my grandpa. It wasn't the kind of crazy that would scare people, because he was actually quite a peaceful soul... but he was always very awkward in his interactions with people, much like me. For that reason, people just seemed to want to steer clear of him... and that's exactly how my grandpa normally liked things.

Oren Anthony Appleton was his real name, but I had called him "Poppy" for as long as I could remember.

He had many other given names, all of them seemingly related to his strange behavior and appearance.

Mr. Carell, the postal carrier, called him "The Mushroom Man," because of the boxes my grandpa mailed out every first Saturday of the month. Mr. Carell only guessed that the boxes contained mushrooms because of the holes in the sides of the boxes and also because they were always stained with dirt smudges. They also smelled of sawdust, dank earth and moss. Each box had the word "FRAGILE" scrawled on all sides in bold red marker.

Mr. Carell assumed that only fragile mushrooms could require such careful packaging, and carry that pungent smell. The packages were addressed to be delivered to many different cities around the United States, but he distinctly remembered one city in particular was a popular destination for the boxes – Littleton, Colorado. He thought it was odd that mail would go from one town of Littleton, in Massachusetts, to another Littleton on the other side of the country. In similar fashion, with each box Oren shipped out, a heavier box would come back to Oren, but sent by registered mail.

I had heard from my dad that some of the meaner kids in town mocked my grandpa, calling him "Dorky Crocket" - because he always wore the same odd, handmade frontiersman-style hat when he strolled into town. But my grandpa's hat wasn't made of raccoon fur like Davey Crocket's... it was his own unique, nature-inspired creation that just screamed for him to be put in the looney bin.

He had crafted the hat out of the steamed and hand-shaped bark of a white birch tree. He adorned the brim with an abundance of small pine cones and it was topped with rust-colored pine needles perched straight up into the air. On the front of the creation was a dried pink flower from a rare American chaffseed plant. He tied all of this together with long

5

pieces of wild grapevine, wrapped several times around the hat. Out the back, falling down past his shoulders, was a bundle of dried brown fescue grass, which resembled a tail.

His clothes did not stray far from his creative hat theme. He always wore the same outfit to town. His pants were baggy and moss-green colored, barely held up with a belt made of grapevine. The knees seemed a lighter shade of green because they had been worn away — apparently from kneeling in the dirt.

His shirt was like a pajama top, light brown and always stained with dirt and sweat marks. Basically, he always looked as if he had been wrestling rabid animals in the dirt. I always imagined he looked like a peasant character taken straight out of a medieval storybook.

He also carried a handmade leather bag, which always hung at his side. Among other odd things (younger kids joked that he carried magical potions), it was rumored that he carried some of the mushrooms he had grown, because the pouch had neatly-punched holes around the top allowing fresh air inside.

His attire made him stand out like a sore thumb in town... but, you would need a keen eye to ever see his camouflaged outfit anywhere in the woods surrounding Littleton. It was just one more way he could achieve his goal of going unnoticed when he wanted.

He wasn't always this dirty and disheveled. When grandma was alive, she wouldn't have ever let him leave the house looking like this.

At one time, my grandpa was an esteemed professor of organismic and evolutionary biology at Harvard, which is a mouthful for me even now at 15. I started calling him by his nickname of "Poppy" because that's what Grandma said his college students had called him.

Their nickname for him, "Professor Poppy," made sense because back in the day Grandma always placed a bright red poppy in the lapel of his tweed jacket. It was the same tweed jacket, complete with leather elbow pads, that he wore every single day to class.

Poppy had grown up in Littleton, and he and Grandma decided to stay there when he earned his professorship. It was only a 30-mile drive between Littleton and Harvard, and Littleton offered a lot more nature and fewer people than the busy university town of Harvard.

Poppy and Grandma had been living in their small farmhouse out in Bumblebee Meadow, which is where my dad was raised. With Poppy's success at Harvard, he and Grandma were able to eventually buy a bigger piece of property, which the town called the "Oak Hill" property.

My dad was able to see the Oak Hill house for the first time when he helped Poppy and Grandma move there from Bumblebee Meadows. He came back and described the Oak Hill property to me and my mother.

Dad said, "There is a beautiful oak tree forest on one part of the property, and the oaks seem almost as large as the giant sequoia in California. It had all of the landmarks that I remember exploring when I was a kid." He went on to mention a few of the landmarks, and seemed rather excited about "a huge rock that jutted out of the hillside and looked over the entire town."

He said the townspeople call it Lookout Rock.

"The house itself is a nice two-tone green Victorian, with three stories, steep-gabled roofs, a big turret, and a nice porch that wraps around the lower floor. Pops is going to have to spend a lot of time keeping that thing from falling apart," Dad said.

My dad was a woodworker, so he was overly excited when talking about all of the decorative, dark oak trim inside the house. He was also enamored by the stained-glass windows wrapped in hardwood oak frames. He went on to talk about the grounds.

"There is a beautiful, white-trimmed conservatory-style greenhouse across a courtyard off the back of the house, with flower gardens. Mom is going to love working on those gardens while Dad is teaching at the university. There are walking paths around the property, one of which leads to an old, dried-up waterfall."

After Dad went on for at least another half hour, my mom said she wished she could see it. With Mom and Dad trying to make ends meet, and Mom's salon seeing most of her customers on the weekends, it would be hard for both of them to take time away to go back to Littleton to see the new house.

Unfortunately, just two years after moving into the new property, Grandma's health started to decline and she wasn't able to get out of her room, let alone into the yard to keep up or even enjoy the gardens. Her death was rather sudden after she had fallen sick, and we didn't even have a chance to visit her before she passed. It turns out Grandma and Poppy knew she had a very severe case of cancer that spread rather quickly. It was Grandma's wish that Poppy did not tell anyone, not even my dad, as she didn't want people to fuss over her, and there wasn't much hope of her getting better.

Poppy kept her wish, even though he knew it would cause issues with my dad later. Poppy was right in worrying that keeping this secret would cause problems. Dad was quite upset that Poppy didn't let him know the full details until after the funeral. I think that is why Dad and Mom had not gone back to Littleton to visit with Poppy since the funeral – they were both quite upset with him.

Of course, their anger meant that Poppy's visits to Medina also ended. Poppy and I had gotten closer every time he visited me. During his visits, Poppy would take me on hikes up to Whipp's Ledges, teaching me everything he knew about nature. He taught me about all of the plants I could eat and those I had to avoid (as if I would ever be stranded alone in the woods and would need to live off the land in Medina, Ohio).

He often emphasized this warning by pretending to eat the poisonous ones and then acting out the worst deaths I had ever seen acted out – floundering and lurching all over the ground, pretending to foam at the mouth.

He would quiz me on the names of all the different types of mushrooms hanging on the forest stumps. My favorite lessons involved looking closely at moss piles under a plastic microscope he always carried with him. He would push on the moss in the sunlight and have me watch all of the bugs come running out. I was amazed by these tiny magical kingdoms that comprised just one square inch of our huge world.

Even though I shared his geeky, nature-loving side, our hikes weren't all just nature lessons. He would take big, floppy leaves and fashion them around his waist and mine, and we would play "Peter Pan vs. Captain Hook" together. His favorite part was swinging on the grapevines, pushing from tree to tree, and landing on our pirate ship (which was just a large log covered in moss).

He would help me decorate the ship with all of the coolest pirate decorations. There was a ship's wheel he had crafted out of a vertical tree branch holding up a rounded piece of thick bark. The four cannons were simply rotted, hollowed-out logs – pointing from the ship in all directions.

There was a dead-man's walking plank fashioned out of a piece of wood leveled on a few large rocks he had rolled next to the log. My shirt would act as the pirate flag raised high above us on a tall branch. According to my t-shirt logo, my ship would be forever known as the "Adidas". We would play until one of us would fall off the ship during a sword fight and hurt ourselves.

3. PROFESSOR POPPY

Poppy was always young-at-heart and had an imagination beyond anyone I knew. This imagination definitely got him in a little trouble. Just after Poppy and Grandma moved onto Oak Hill, Poppy lost his teaching position at Harvard.

When it happened, my grandma called my dad out of concern for Poppy. After the call, I overheard Dad tell mom, "Poppy started claiming there were creatures living out in the woods that had never before been seen by human eyes. It would have been one thing to claim there were plants, or even insects that hadn't been discovered – that would be believable. But he claimed these newfound creatures talked to him, and had names and personalities like us."

"He became so adamant that they existed, he started to

make it the topic of almost every class. Some of the students felt he had gone off the deep end, and decided they were not getting a decent education from him, so they reported him to the dean of the school," Dad said.

I heard my parents talking about how the Dean and his colleagues always liked my grandpa, and they wanted to give him a chance to explain himself, to give up his crazy talk, and continue teaching. But when they asked him to stop talking about his "discovery", Poppy became angry that nobody would believe him, raving about how his peers were blind to his new discoveries.

Not long after this, they decided to ask him to present even the slightest proof of the creatures. In an odd twist, and only a day later, Poppy seemed to calm down and change his story, telling them it was all just a prank.

With this admission and a zero tolerance for lying, the university had no other recourse and they had to let him go – not just for the good of the students, but also for the reputation of the school.

I remember my mom and dad talking about it when it happened. In addition to the loss of grandma, losing his teaching position would surely be too much to handle.

They really thought Poppy would be lost without his prestigious title at Harvard, and he would miss the interaction with his students.

Although they were still mad about Poppy hiding my grandma's ailment, my parents kept tabs on Poppy by checking in with his old friend, Harry Sawyer, in Littleton. Poppy and Harry were of similar age and had grown up together in the small town. They were best friends for as long as my dad could remember. Harry reassured my parents that Poppy was just fine, and seemed to be even more excited about life and his field of work lately.

My parents were still concerned by Poppy's apparent lack of concern over grandma's death and his lost professorship. They were convinced that senility or some other brain-changing disease must be taking over. They also had no clue as to how he was still paying for the Oak Hill property with the loss of his teaching job.

Harry said, "Poppy comes into town on Saturday mornings to pick up food and other supplies. He always comes straight to my store. I'm there every Saturday morning to share a coffee, doughnut, and small talk with him. He seems to always have enough cash to cover his expenses."

Harry told them that mushroom farming seemed to be Poppy's new hobby. After grandma's death, Poppy seemed to be spending all of his time toiling away up on Oak Hill.

"Poppy's shopping list was usually comprised of boxes, burlap sacks, scrap wood, strands of lights, and nails," Harry said. "From these items and the matching stories from Mr. Carell, I can only assume that Poppy was simply building up a mushroom farming empire up on Oak Hill. I am so sure of it I never even bothered to ask Poppy about it."

Harry went on to say, "And the mushroom crops that Poppy mails out every week must be some darn good mushrooms because he never seems to be hurting for money."

My parents always ended their calls letting Harry know how happy they were to have a friend of Poppy's watching over him. My parents felt comfortable that Harry would let them know if anything changed for the worse. For another six months, my parents would call Harry weekly to get updates on Poppy.

It wasn't until last Saturday afternoon that Harry called

my parents, letting them know that Poppy hadn't been in the store for his regular visit.

Harry said, "I'll call back with news shortly. I am sure that it was probably just Poppy being absent-minded, or losing track of time while mushroom farming. I already called Sheriff Don McGough and asked him to check on Poppy. The sheriff is already on his way up to Poppy's house up on Oak Hill."

Sheriff McGough came back to Sawyer's Hardware Store almost two hours later, with a sad look hanging on his face. "Harry, I have some sad news about your friend, Oren," said the sheriff. "I apologize that it took me a bit longer than I had anticipated to get word back to you. On my way up to Oak Hill, on Oak Ridge Road, I found Oren laying lifeless in a gully. There was something odd about the surroundings, so I had to call in my deputies to tape off the area and investigate further. That's why it took so long."

"What was odd about it, sheriff?" asked Harry, with tears starting to well up in his eyes. "I can't think of anyone that would want to hurt Oren!"

Harry could see that the sheriff was still trying to analyze the accident scene in his head. "I am pretty sure someone hit him from behind," the sheriff said, "but there wasn't much evidence to surmise who or why they had done it. Oren had a large, black bruise on his back, and had been thrown a good 15 feet off the side of the road, down into the gully. His hat was laying back where I believe he was originally hit, so the car had to be going pretty fast."

"There were no witnesses, and it didn't seem like anything of any value had been taken from him. There wasn't any trace of a car braking before the impact."

The sheriff continued with a quizzical look on his face. "I did find something very odd, though. The bag he was carrying seemed to be filled with nothing but sawdust. And where the sawdust had spilled from the bag, there were small prints, as if something crawled out of the bag. Oddly, there were no prints going into the bag. I couldn't tell what kind of animal made the prints — they were nothing like any animal tracks I had seen before. The footprints were larger than a field mouse, about the length of my thumbnail."

The sheriff seemed almost embarrassed to tell the rest of the facts. "And I'll be darned if there wasn't a ring of small clover flowers, evenly placed all around his head. Whoever did this had a cruel and morbid sense of humor."

"I knew Oren pretty well, and aside from some mutual banter with the mean kids in town, he never had any grudges or misdealing with anyone that could have led to his murder," Harry proclaimed.

Sheriff McGough told Harry the investigators would need a while to come to any conclusions, but he was going to have his whole team assembled to look into it right away. The sheriff knew how close Oren and Harry had been. Harry bowed his head and extended his hand to thank the sheriff. In Littleton, foul play and murder didn't happen but every 50 years, so it was a big deal to the community. Harry knew the sheriff's office would put in every effort to get to the bottom of it.

Harry was kind enough to call my parents back right away and explain the details of Poppy's death. I was in the family room when I heard my dad in the kitchen get choked up on what seemed to be a very somber call. My mom was comforting him when I heard him hang up the phone. I walked into the kitchen to see what had caused such sadness.

I had never seen my dad cry before so I knew the news wasn't good. "Your Poppy has passed away," Mom said. "The sheriff is investigating, but it seems he was hit by a car." At that instant, all of the great memories I had of Poppy flooded into my head and I started to cry. There would be no more science lessons, no more fake deaths or pirates, or adventures on ships. I realized I was now 15 and probably wouldn't really have had any more adventure like we had when I was younger, but Poppy's visits always lit up my imagination and I would miss that. I went to bed with the plan to replay all of the memories of the adventures we shared. By the end of the first adventure, I cried myself to sleep.

4. THE APPLETON ESTATE

Two days later, my parents received a box via next-day mail from one Jacob Fitzgibbons, Esquire, of Littleton, Massachusetts. Inside was a variety of items, most importantly Poppy's last will and testament.

My parents read the letter out loud to me, as they thought I should hear my grandfather's final wishes.

The letter read:

Jacob Fitzgibbons, Esq.
Fitzgibbons & McCann Law Offices
32 Main Street
Littleton, MA
01460

Monday, August 10, 2020

To the family of Oren Anthony Appleton,

It is with great regret that I inform you of the death of Oren Anthony Appleton, of 25 Oak Ridge Drive, Littleton, Massachusetts. His passing was evidently due to a hit-and-run accident. The accident investigation is still ongoing through the sheriff's office. Upon notification of his death, I am executing Mr. Appleton's last will and testament per his expressed wishes. This last will and testament, along with the other enclosed items, are intended for his living relatives, Ronald Oren Appleton (son), Rebecca Ann Appleton (daughter-in-law), and Oliver Oren Appleton (grandson).

The settlement of assets of the Oren Anthony Appleton estate are as follows:

- Ronald Oren Appleton (son) and Rebecca Ann Appleton (daughter-in-law) shall receive all deeded property at 25 Oak Ridge Drive, Littleton, Massachusetts – inclusive of the house and its contents on Oak Hill, and surrounding wooded acreage and structures (deed and plat enclosed). The mortgage has been paid in full, leaving only yearly taxes to be covered.

- Ronald and Rebecca shall receive all savings held at Main Street Bank, 220 Great Road, Littleton, MA – under account No. 80-134223. (savings account transfer paperwork enclosed).

- Ronald and Rebecca shall receive all contents of safety deposit box 325, held at Main Street Bank, 220 Great Road, Littleton, MA (key and assignment paperwork enclosed).

Oren Anthony Appleton's final wishes are as follows:

- Ronald and Rebecca – please take great care of the property on Oak Hill. Since your mother's passing years ago, I have invested all of my time tending to it, making it a haven for all creatures. My wish is that the property is protected and passed on to generations of Appletons for years to come.

- I have enclosed a package addressed to Harry Sawyer. Please hand-deliver this package and the attached note to my friend at his hardware store on any Saturday morning.

- Olly – I know you have always shared my love for nature and adventure. I have enclosed a map showing all of the wonderful trails and places of interest on Oak Hill. More importantly – enclosed is a key. Please make sure you do not lose it, and please tend to my "special garden".

Legal copies of this last will and testimony and some additional items from Oren Appleton's estate can be picked up at our offices in Littleton at your convenience.

Sincerely,

Jacob Fitzgibbons, Esq.
Fitzgibbons & McCann Law Associates

----- end -----

My mom and dad told me they had spent the whole

night thinking through Poppy's last will and testament, and his wishes for them to tend to the Oak Hill property. It had just clicked in my brain that Poppy's wishes would mean we would have to leave Medina, Ohio... for good.

It hadn't taken long for them to make the decision... dad's job as a handyman and carpenter wasn't panning out in the fortune he thought he would make. My mom was a hairdresser and ran a small hair salon on Medina square. She said she had already heard all of the local rumors and stories from the ladies of Medina, so she had no qualms about moving and opening a salon in a different small town. It would give her the chance to hear some different stories and rumors, which was exciting to her.

As for me, I was up for the move. Although I liked Medina, I really didn't have any friends here. Much like Poppy, my eccentricities usually scared any would-be friends away. There were geeks at my school, but none that were geeky about plants like me. They were more of the Dungeons and Dragons types or computer geeks. I just didn't have much in common with either of those groups. I lacked many of the social skills shared by my peers, and they realized that I cared more about learning about nature than I did about making friends.

My science teacher, Mr. Harvey, was really the only friend I can claim I ever made at Medina Middle School. He and I shared an interest in plants and biology, and he would often ask me to help him during study hall and lunch. He knew I didn't have many friends and that I would jump at the chance to do anything other than getting hit in the face with a dodgeball at recess.

Mr. Harvey often brought in plants from his weekend travels, and my job was to press them and try to classify them. I would pick and then place the best leaves and flowers between two pieces of wax paper, and then set it under a stack of old books in the back of the class directly in the sunlight. The weight of the books and the heat from the sun would flatten and dry the plants and flowers exactly as I had arranged them. It was actually an art form to get them to look good when flattened – at least in my mind.

There were great resources online I used to classify the plants, but my favorite was an app that let me take a photo of the leaf or flower, and it would try to classify it against its database of thousands of plants. This app worked more than 80% of the time. The other 20% of the time Mr. Harvey and I would compete with each other to be the first to identify the plant. Mr. Harvey always seemed to win – I think he had a premium version of the plant app that he wasn't telling me about.

Once the leaves had flattened and dried, I would carefully take the specimens out, put a coat of transparent lacquer on them, let them dry and then pin them to a wall in the back of the class. On one busy day, I think I got a contact high from all of the lacquer wafting off the plants recently pinned to the back wall. I made a deal with myself that I would limit how many I lacquered in one day.

Under each pinned plant I would write the kingdom, division, class, order, family, genus, species, and also the plant's common name. It became a museum of sorts after a while.

The wall was called "Harvey's Herbarium" and it was quickly running out of space as Mr. Harvey kept bringing in new plants. I would spend any spare time I had working on the project with him.

As summer approached, I started to feel sad that I would be leaving middle school which meant I would not get to see or work on "Harvey's Herbarium" anymore.

On the last day of school, I walked into Mr. Harvey's

class and instantly felt an oddness... as everyone was staring at me with smiles on their faces. They weren't friendly smiles, but more like envious sneers and I had no idea why. I scurried to my chair wondering what I had done to deserve the unwanted attention.

Mr. Harvey walked in, gathered everyone's attention, and said, "I have an announcement to make. Due to the efforts of Olly Appleton, the wall at the back of the room has been populated with plants from almost 500 species."

500 species? I can't believe it.

We started with twenty plants at the beginning of the year, and I have no idea how I could have flattened and classified 480 more over the school year.

This had to be a record somewhere.

I started to turn toward the back wall and noticed my classmates chuckling at me. I was excited and embarrassed at the same time, excited that Mr. Harvey and I accomplished such a feat, but embarrassed that my classmates would never accept me and my passion for plants.

"This was a monumental task and I would never have done this without Olly's help. Therefore, in dedication to his year of work, and in honor of him graduating to high school, I have forever renamed the wall Olly's Herbarium," Mr. Harvey proclaimed.

I looked back at the wall again and realized why I received the stares when walking into class. Along the top of the plant wall was a new sign replacing the old hand-drawn sign. The new sign spanned the entire back wall, above the collection, and was made from a cross-section of a huge old oak tree. That piece of wood looked to have been at least 100 years old. For a second I felt guilty that Mr. Harvey would have killed an old tree like that, but quickly told myself it was probably an old tree that had fallen on its own.

The tree slice was shaved down to about one inch thick and still retained its bark on the edges. It had been sanded and lacquered to a nice shine, and etched in a serif font, in big letters, was the new collection's title "Olly's Herbarium."

I fought hard to keep back the tears because I knew that if I showed any emotion it would result in a barrage of hazing after school. I turned back to Mr. Harvey and mouthed a thank you. He grinned like a proud father and clapped his hands loudly, urging my classmates to clap along. The rest of the class gave half-hearted applause, but all I needed was my friend Mr. Harvey's acknowledgment – that was enough for me.

I still got a good hazing after school that day. There wasn't any violence involved because, although I was a bit odd, people still remembered that I could hold my own in a fight. Danny Bristle discovered that the day he decided to square up to me in the hall at the beginning of 8th grade.

I was walking to Mr. Harvey's class with a big Ziploc bag of plant specimens that I had been collecting that whole summer. Danny stepped in front of me and knocked my books out of my hands. The bag of plants fell with them.

When I bent down to grab the bag of plants, Danny dug his boot into the bag, making it pop. To make matters worse, he purposefully twisted his boot so that all of the plants mashed together into one big green pile that looked like a freshly tossed salad.

It only took two seconds for the beast to come out of me, and I don't think Danny was expecting it – he certainly didn't think I was brave enough to do what came next.

Before I could stop myself, I clenched my fist and it shot

straight up into Danny's crotch. I hit him so hard, I swear his body lifted off the floor a few inches and one of his boots came off during flight. As he fell to the floor, I noticed the entire hallway of students fell silent. It was so quiet, the only thing I could hear was the wind leaving Danny's lungs as he lay still on the ground. I must have hit him really hard because my fist became just as red as his face.

A few of Danny's friends tried to pick him up. Some of the cute girls that were watching nearby patted me on the head, helped me gather my books, and urged me to move along quickly in case Danny got back up.

I thought for sure I would be called to the principal's office that day, but I think that my new hero underdog status, plus Danny's inability to walk to the principal's office, saved me the punishment.

From that day forward, the bullies of our school decided to pick on the band geeks instead of the nature geek.

So, with middle school and Danny Bristle in the rearview mirror, the thought of starting fresh in a new town seemed like an opportunity for rebirth. Maybe I could re-invent myself and become the captain of the football team or the new class president at my new school. The thought faded away as I realized I had no athletic abilities, and finding even one vote for class president, let alone a majority, would probably be a monumental challenge. So, I settled for looking at the move as a big adventure in a new land.

I also knew that, even if I had disagreed with my parents' decision, they had already made up their minds to make the move and there wasn't much I could do to change that.

They let me know we would be moving fairly quickly. We would need to get to Littleton to take care of the final details of the estate and to make sure the Oak Hill property didn't fall into disrepair. They also wanted to get me enrolled in school before the start of the new year, to avoid any additional awkwardness.

So... I guess I would be starting my freshman year at Littleton High School... how could anything go wrong?

I let Mom and Dad know that I was fine – in fact, I was excited - to be moving to Littleton, which I think gave them a little spark of happiness.

My dad, relieved there was no argument from Mom or me about moving, went back to Poppy's estate box and began pulling out the items sent by Mr. Fitzgibbons. He pulled out a large manilla envelope, held it to his ear, and shook it in wonder. It sounded as if it was filled with 50 keys. He reached deep into the envelope, past all of the keys, to grab a small cardboard box he touched with his hand. Upon opening the box, he held up its contents - an old barrel key – the kind you see in old movies about castles or pirate treasures. The key was about 4 inches long, silver and tarnished, and looked like it had seen years of use. Hanging from the key was a string attached to a dirt-stained label that simply read, "Dearest Olly – Have fun. Love, Poppy."

Dad handed me the key with a shrug, letting me know he hadn't any idea why Poppy thought that key would have any meaning or importance to me. My dad continued rummaging through the other keys in the bag, guessing what they could be for – as they didn't all have labels.

As Mom and Dad argued over what the other keys could be for, I walked to the side of our couch and held my key under the light, to get a closer look.

Fizzy, my overly curious Siamese Tabby cat, woke from her nap on the edge of the couch, stretched for a second, and ran over to sniff the key with excitement. Fizzy always made me chuckle because she had slightly-crossed eyes, and when she looked at something she would move her head from side-to-side to try and focus on it. She seemed really excited about the key for some reason and her head jerked quickly from side to side as she tried to sniff it.

Holding the key closer to my nose, I did pick up the odd smell that Fizzy must have latched onto... it reminded me of a musty log or the smell of the weird antique shop next door to mom's salon. Sometimes I would go to that antique store just to look at all of the oddities while Mom finished up work at her salon.

That reminded me of a funny story... Mrs. Crosby, the old lady that owns the antique store, once scared the bejesus out of me. I was looking for treasures inside a wooden footlocker near an old rocking chair. I had no idea Mrs. Crosby was sitting in the chair because she was so still. When I opened the box, it made a loud creaking sound and Mrs. Crosby jerked awake, causing me to jump back and the footlocker to slam shut. She and I both screamed at the same time, and I was out of the store and back in Mom's salon in the blink of an eye. I never went back to check on her to see if I had accidentally scared her to death. I figured I would hear about it in the town paper if that were the case. I always laugh to myself when I imagine she is probably still sitting in that chair, dead, and people just shop the store while ignoring the sleeping old lady in her rocking chair.

After Fizzy had enough of that smell, she turned two full circles on the couch and plopped back down for her post-nap nap. Fizzy's day was full of naps. There was a morning nap after breakfast, one right before lunch, another right after lunch, and so on and so on. I think Fizzy was asleep more than she was awake.

The key was extremely old and looked like it would have

been a perfect prop for one of the many adventures Poppy and I would have shared. The shaft had three bits at the end, all different lengths. The bow of the key was quite intricate, with ornately carved leaves swirling around what looked to be a single mushroom in the center of the design. The mushroom almost looked like it had a face, although the fine details on the key had been worn away with time and overuse, so I wasn't really sure.

"WHACK!"

My key inspection was interrupted by a large, rolled piece of paper my dad had thrown at me. It bounced off my head, hit the lamp shade, and landed onto Fizzy's now-fluffed tail. It startled Fizzy from her second nap and she instantly started licking the spot where the rolled paper had attacked her. "Sorry, Olly – didn't mean to throw it so hard. I think that's the map Poppy wanted you to have," Dad said with a quiet chuckle.

The rolled paper looked like a yellowed ancient scroll, was torn and dirty on the outside, and wrapped with a few pieces of wild grapevine bark. On the outside was a handwritten note that said, "For Oliver."

There was no way to easily untie the grapevine, so I just snapped it off. The paper unrolled itself as if it had a memory of when it was last opened. I could tell instantly the map was created by Poppy, as the labels were written in his unique old-world-style handwriting. There was a title at the top that read 'The Spores of Oak Hill, Shrewsbury Ridge.' Below that, in all caps was written, "PROPERTY OF OREN ANTHONY APPLETON." The "OREN ANTHONY" portion was crossed out, and underneath was scribed, "OLIVER ASH." Poppy had declared the map my property, and that made me smile. I realized he must have thought about me as much as I thought about him, prior to his death.

Little icons of the landmarks drawn around the map

were not of Leonardo da Vinci's equal but were good enough to tell what things were. There was a drawing of a boulder outcropping titled "Lookout Rock," and an area called "Tophet Chasm." The chasm led to a swamp, and there were dotted lines drawn across the map that looked to be trails. These lines seemed to extend across Oak Hill in opposite directions, all leading from a sketch of a house dead-center of the hill marked as "Oak Hill Manor". There was a greenhouse marked a little way from the manor, and what looked to be a grouping of trees in a swamp labeled "Sporing Oaks" down a trail past the greenhouse. Between the greenhouse and the "Sporing Oaks" was drawn a small mushroom and the words "The Community / Grand Cavern" underneath. The drive up to Oak Hill Manor was titled "Oak Ridge Road."

Surrounding Oak Hill were two roads: Oak Hill Road and Harvard Road. At the edge of Oak Hill, close to Oak Hill Road, was a dashed line surrounding a third of the Oak Hill property with a scrawled note, "KEEP THEM OUT!!! Dalton's proposed mall." I had no idea what that meant, but it seemed very important as Poppy had added two exclamation points after it. When I figured out what or whom I would be keeping out, I would put my entire heart into it – just as Poppy had wished in his instructions.

I rolled the map back up and took it and the key to my room. I put the key into an old cigar box that Poppy had given me, where it would be safe for our move to Littleton. I put the rolled-up map into an old wrapping paper tube, and wrote, "IMPORTANT / KEEP / PROPERTY OF OLIVER" all over it so nobody would confuse it for trash.

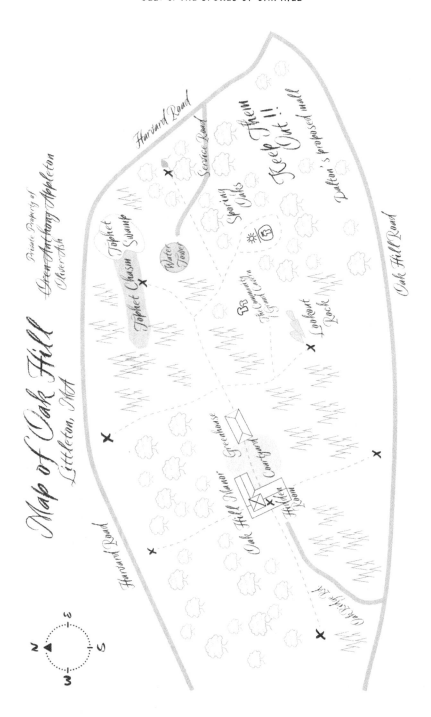

5. HARRY & THE HARES

Our old station wagon felt like it hopped a good three feet off the ground, bouncing down hard and jerking me from a good dream, a dream which immediately left my memory.

Dad seemed to always find the biggest potholes to run over while driving on our family trips. With each pothole, Mom would scold him and tell him he was going to have to buy a new car if he keeps tearing this one up. I heard this same argument no fewer than five times on this trip alone.

I am surprised that our 1966 Ford Country Squire station wagon was still in one piece, considering the torture Dad put it through. You would think he would treat it like the treasure he made it out to be. He washed that ugly car almost every other day, always reminding us that it was a valuable piece of history. He washed it so much that I wondered how the fake wood-grained stickers on the sides of the car had not been rubbed off.

When I woke, I could feel a thread of drool running down my chin. After over nine hours of sleep, my forehead was sweating and had somehow suctioned to the fake leather interior of the station wagon's door.

I lifted my head, straightened up, and realized Fizzy (my only backseat companion) was staring at me, cross-eyed of course. Fizzy seemed to be judging my napping skills rather harshly. After a look of disgust, she turned and laid on the blanket I had balled up for her, making sure to position her back to me, as a further insult. The sun had finally come up, and the long trip from my home in Medina, Ohio, felt like it would never end.

Dad had been driving through the night, as he wanted to get into Littleton as early as possible. He wanted to have a full day to settle in and deal with the business of Poppy's estate.

We started seeing signs for Harvard University and Boston, so I knew we were getting closer to Littleton. I could tell I would like Littleton because as we got closer, everything screamed of the outdoors and nature. I saw a huge Cabela's store off the highway... I wasn't into hunting (I actually despised it, much like Poppy did), but Cabela's had some cool camping gear and nature displays that made up for the hunting gear they sold.

As we got closer to Littleton, the signs pointing to the lakes, woods, and nature conservation areas made me chuckle – especially when I said them in a fake, over-exaggerated cowboy accent. There was "Butter Brook," "Bare Hill," and my favorite, "Holy Hill." Repeating "Holy Hill" a few times, with my childish giggle, made both Mom and Dad turn in disgust. I had to explain I was just pronouncing "Holy Hill" and not what

31

they thought I was saying.

My dad chuckled and reminded me that Littleton was once Nipmuc territory. He joked that my cowboy accent might get me in some trouble "in these here parts." His cowboy accent wasn't nearly as polished as mine. I looked over to find Fizzy staring at me in disgust, once again.

"Littleton had been home to the sixth Praying Indian village way back, more than 300 years ago. Praying Indians were a group that had been converted to Christianity. They owned about four square miles of what we now know as Littleton. I guess the land was really fertile, and the fishing and hunting in the area made for a good home. Unfortunately, the 'white man' realized the land had these great qualities, too, and took over their land. They even shot a few of them – mostly women and children. It is really a shame and inhuman, if you ask me," Dad said.

I stopped using my cowboy accent after hearing that story and noticed a big, white welcome sign that indicated we were just crossing into Littleton.

Just after the sign, I noticed a huge billboard that quickly contradicted my thought that Littleton was going to be a nature-focused town. The sign read, "Dalton Mall – Coming to Littleton 2022." On one side of the sign was a picture of a balding man wearing a pink shirt under a stark white suit. He was pointing at a concept picture of the future mall. My first impression was that this guy looked like he owned a used car lot or a seedy motel on the outskirts of town.

Even though I hadn't yet seen Littleton, I had heard enough about it from Poppy and my dad to know that a mall was the last thing Littleton's residents would want in their quiet town.

My dad also saw the sign and let out a loud laugh, "Hah!

Looks like old Henry Dalton is getting out of the used car business. Dalton Mall looks like the next big failure in his long list of crazy ideas."

He turned to Mom and said, "Henry and I went to school together. He was quite the bully back then, and Henry's dad thought his family was the royalty in Littleton."

"When Henry graduated, I remember he started a mafia-like landscaping company," Dad said. "He hired his friends, and just about half of the football team, to do the work around town. If I, or any other kid for that matter, tried to cut lawns for money, Henry's goon squad would push us around and threaten us. None of us would dare stand up to the defensive line of the Littleton High School football team."

Dad continued, "I remember it didn't take long for Henry's crew to realize how much of a cheapskate he actually was. He ended up either not paying them or paying them below minimum wage, and his entire crew left the business. He only had a few friends left after that endeavor."

"Last I heard, Henry started a small used car business out near Harvard University. He would sell beater cars to college students – he made sure the cars would last at least past the 30-day warranty. He knew full-well students didn't have the resources to sue him when their cars fell apart on day 31. The best part was that when his customers graduated, word-of-mouth of his bad reputation would leave the college town with them. Incoming students had no idea what a schmuck he was. It was an endless cycle."

"It looks like he swindled enough college kids to save up for his next venture," Mom said.

"A mall in Littleton will never fly – unless things have changed around here since I was a kid," Dad said as we entered the center of town known as the Littleton Commons.

It was Saturday morning, and even at this early hour, things were already bustling in downtown Littleton. We passed by the old train station, where a little farmer's market was already buzzing with excitement.

"Look at all of that awful hair! I am going to make a killing with my little salon here," Mom said with a big grin on her face. This, in turn, put a smile on my dad's face. I think that even though they both agreed to move to Littleton, my dad held some fear that he was forcing my mom into the move. Seeing her happy and optimistic made him visibly relax and settle into the luxurious fake leather seats of our station wagon.

Our first stop was Sawyer's Hardware, to visit Poppy's best friend, Harry Sawyer. As we pulled from the road and into the parking lot in front of the store, my dad slammed on the brakes causing the car to slide and fishtail through the gravel.

"What the heck are you doing?" screamed Mom.

"Didn't you see it? The biggest black rabbit I've ever seen just ran out in front of the car... tell me you saw it!" Dad said, slightly panicked that he had either run over the rabbit or damaged his car in the ordeal. My mom shook her head in disbelief and in relief that nobody was hurt.

I had to admit to Mom that I did see something out of the corner of my eye, but it moved so fast, I couldn't be sure what it was. I also had to admit that my dad was a great packer... because none of the boxes or furniture strapped to the top of the car slid an inch.

Just as my dad stopped his heart from racing, and finished a very cautious parking job, an older man walked out of the hardware store with his hands in his overalls, and a big white-toothed grin on his face. I wasn't sure if he was laughing at the looks on our faces after our close call, the green color of my dad's classic car, or the fifteen pieces of furniture strapped to the roof rack.

"Oh my gosh, it's Harry!" Dad said with a big grin on his face.

Harry looked like he could be anyone's perfect grandfather, with a warm expression on his face, wrinkles, white hair, and weathered hands. Although he was older, he was tall and very fit for his age.

My dad had hardly put the car in park before jumping out excitedly.

"Harry! You look great. How long has it been – at least 10 years?"

"I think it was when you bought that car new," Harry said jokingly.

Dad gave Harry a bear hug and then turned to me and Mom.

Before Dad had a chance to make an introduction, Harry belted out, "Nice to meet you, Rebecca. And you have got to be Oliver! You look just like your grandpa... even the way you walk reminds me of him," Harry said with a big smile.

I smiled even though I wasn't sure if that was a compliment or further reassurance that I was awkward like Poppy.

"Come in, I have fresh coffee and doughnuts waiting for you inside!" Harry said as he opened the big swinging screen door for us.

As I walked inside, I was taken aback at how much it looked like a hardware store from the old days, but it was filled with many of the newer tools of today. The floor was a little uneven, and it looked like it was made from wide planks of very old pine. It was a bit worn in certain places but still looked solid and worthy of lasting another hundred years.

It smelled of freshly-cut wood, an acrid odor of fertilizer, but also peppermint candy, which was an odd combination.

The shelves looked like they were the original dark oak planks. They were hand-hewn and looked to be original to when the store was built. There were steel metal bins on the floor holding all of the smaller necessities one might need: nails, screws, nuts, and bolts of all different sizes.

Bags of feed and fertilizers were stacked in the center aisles, and straw bales lined one wall near a shipping dock. There were some old three-wheeled wheelbarrows lined up near the entrance which I realized must have been used as shopping carts for Harry's customers.

In the front, there was a large bay display window showing three different rabbit traps and bags of rabbit food. A sign dangled from twine hung above the traps, and it read, 'SPECIAL: No Harm, Catch-and-Release Rabbit Trap plus FREE Bait. $29!'

Carefully placed around the rabbit traps were at least fifteen stuffed animal toys – rabbits of many colors and sizes, posed as if they were running in every direction. I thought it was ironic that Harry was trying to sell rabbit traps, but his display didn't have even one of the stuffed animals posed inside a trap.

All around the store, covering the wall down to about three feet below the ceiling were copper-colored tin squares. Each square had an ornate leaf design embossed on it. The tiles had a natural light green patina, which further highlighted the leaf's details. I immediately fell into geek mode and tried to classify the plant leaf that the craftsman had used as inspiration for the design. I gave up trying to identify them and decided what they were, laughing to myself when I said it:

The leaves must be from a "WALL" nut tree.

The original wooden checkout counter looked to have seen its share of sharp tools and was stained by years of fertilizer and feed bags making their way through the checkout area. It had a sheen that was almost fully worn away in spots.

On the counter, there was a bronze antique-style metal register, the type with the crank arm. The register was in great shape and looked like it had been recently hand-polished. The small wooden tray above the money drawer glistened as if it had been polished with oil. My dad was as interested in it as I was, and he ran his fingers over the detail work and bends of the machine, complimenting Harry on his fine antique.

"She still does all the work today, believe it or not! I just can't seem to move to one of those newfangled registers... it just wouldn't be right after 50 years of using her," Harry said with a proud smile, patting the old register.

The hardware store must have doubled as an ice cream shop at one point, as I noticed there were silver sundae cups neatly stacked on a mirrored shelf behind the counter, and long silver spoons sticking out of a glass jar. Underneath the shelf were about 15 clear jars packed full of all different kinds of hard candies, chocolates, licorices, peppermints, and rock candy sticks.

Harry must have seen me eyeing the candy, because he strolled behind the counter, grabbed a blue rock candy stick, and handed it to me. I felt like I was five years old again and Harry had instantly become my first best friend in Littleton. I knew now why he and Poppy had been such good friends – Harry just seemed to be an all-around great person.

He then gestured to the row of candy jars and offered

chocolate to Mom and Dad, but they were both pretending to be on a diet, so he closed the jar. He moved on to a white box on the counter, opened it, and offered them each freshly glazed doughnuts - which Mom and Dad were more than happy to dive into.

Hypocrites!

It was nice to see Harry and my parents eating doughnuts together, and I could picture Harry and Poppy having similar visits on Saturday mornings. My face must have expressed sadness as I realized Harry had been watching me with a concerned look.

It was then that I remembered I had the small, hand-carved wooden rabbit that Poppy wanted us to deliver to Harry.

"I brought something Poppy wanted you to have, Mr. Sawyer," I said.

"You best be calling me Harry as we are practically family," Harry corrected me with a warm smile.

I reached into my pocket and pulled out the rabbit, which I had re-wrapped in brown paper and closed with a piece of twine before leaving our home in Medina. I handed the small brown bundle to Harry.

"What's this?" Harry asked as he began to untie the twine. When the paper flopped open, Harry's expression turned to pure happiness and he let out a loud giggle, which made him sound like a little kid. Then he turned the rabbit over and let out an even louder laugh.

"Oh, Oren – you always knew how to make me laugh," Harry said to himself, under his breath. Harry held the gift out in his hand and raised it up to the light to show us why he was laughing. The oak rabbit had been hand-carved and stained by

Poppy. It wasn't very detailed, but there was enough artistry there to make out that it was a rabbit with floppy ears. Harry turned it over to show us the bottom. Inscribed were chiseled letters reading, "To Hare-y, my friend." Underneath the note was scrawled the number "1200+". I got the HARE-y pun because Poppy and I shared a love for puns and often had pun wars, but had no idea what the 1200+ meant.

Harry set the rabbit right on top of the old register, in a spot where everyone coming and going could see it. He adjusted it slightly and made sure it was facing out the door.

"I'm so sorry about your dad (and grandfather)," Harry said to us all in a serious voice, "You are probably wondering why this rabbit means so much to me. I have some great memories of Oren and our time growing up together – too many to tell. But I want to tell you one story that will explain why Oren and I got along so well, and how we formed such a special bond. Plus, now that you will be in Littleton for a while, you deserve to hear it."

I saw Mom and Dad perk up – I wasn't sure if it was the sugar from two doughnuts kicking in, or the chance to hear another great story about Poppy.

"As a teenager, Oren had earned a reputation in town for being the protector of all things in nature. It almost got him (and me) into some serious trouble with the farmers in town," Harry said.

"I can remember it like it was yesterday," Harry chuckled. "Oren was really wound up about the local farmers. He was in a downright tizzy one day. I guess the farmers were fed up with their gardens being destroyed by a growing brood of rabbits that were overtaking Littleton. The farmers had gathered together for the biggest rabbit hunt ever to be held in Littleton. They were bent on getting rid of every single rabbit, big or small, in and around town. And they seemed close to getting every single one, too. After the hunt, they hung all of the rabbits they had killed on a fence in front of the town hall - for all to see – almost as a sign to show their superiority over the rabbits."

Harry's mood turned quite serious as he looked down at me, shaking his head as he continued his story. "Now Oren loved nature more than just about any person I knew, and he had a spot in his heart for anything small, and with fur. He actually believed he was put in Littleton to be a furry animal guardian of sorts. The sight of all of those dead rabbits strung up on the fence set off a fit of anger I had never seen in him."

Harry's stern face slowly turned into a child-like grimace. "Your grandfather was usually quiet and reserved, so it would have been very unlike him to make a public spectacle about what the farmers had done. He also knew that if he had done anything in retribution right then, the farmers and townsfolk would know that Oren had a hand in it."

"This is where the story gets good, and where you will learn of your grandfather's brilliance and mischievous side," Harry said proudly.

"Oren and I were like brothers, and he confided only in me when it came to his master plan. I even had the opportunity to help him, although until this day I have never told anyone or taken any of the credit. I think it is a good time to tell the story! Can't imagine I'd get in any trouble telling the tale now... heck, half of the farmers here owe me their farm's worth in back payments for supplies bought on credit."

"Oren didn't tell me the whole plan at first. But he asked if I would help and, as he was my only and best friend, I just couldn't say no."

"After the hunt, Oren and I made up what sounded like old folklore. It professed that the death of an innocent animal is forbidden by the Nipmuc spirits. Oren added a claim that these deaths would result in a curse. The spirits would fight back with the goal of returning the animals in even more numbers. So, in essence, if you kill one rabbit, two will come back in its place."

"At night, Oren and I secretly took all of the dead rabbits off the fence and gave them a proper burial on the island in the center of Tophet Swamp. The next day, the missing rabbits were the topic of conversation in every corner of the town. The farmers were really upset that their furry trophies were gone. It was at that time Oren and I went about town, taking turns telling the other kids and townsfolk the contrived folklore. We also made sure to tell Margaret Betcher and Ruth Delany, the two ladies whose specialty it was to serve beer and local rumors at Betcher's Inn. We told them we had heard the folklore from some old-timer out walking on Willow Road."

"If you ever wanted a rumor to spread, you need only to tell Margaret or Ruth. After that, the story spread like wildfire, and soon it was the talk of the town and nobody had an inkling of where the folklore had originated. It was a stroke of genius!"

"While the folklore continued spreading, Oren and I would go out into the countryside every day after school. For two weeks, we scoured every square inch of Littleton – from Lake Nagog to Whitetail Woods, trapping every rabbit we could find. We actually made it a friendly competition to see which one of us could capture the most rabbits. We did this all with the utmost secrecy – never traveling on roads or going near any heavily visited areas of town."

"We took all of the rabbits we had caught to a makeshift pen we had built from dead tree branches out in Bumblebee Meadows, near your family's original home. We built it deep in the center of the meadow where nobody ever wandered. I swear we had caught over 50 rabbits – of all shapes, sizes, and colors."

"Once we had 50 rabbits exactly, Oren explained the next step of his plan to me," Harry continued with the story.

"Now Harry – you do know that rabbits love to have babies, right? And actually, they are able to have up to 12 babies at a time – and... they can get pregnant again in 31 days' time? So, by my calculations, these 50 rabbits will produce anywhere from 300 to 1800 offspring by the middle of summer."

"Right then, the sheer magnitude and brilliance of his plan clicked in my head and I was excited to complete our task. Summer came, and we were getting tired of hauling scrap veggies out to the meadow to feed the multiplying rabbits. It was time to complete Oren's grand plan. On a Friday afternoon, we commandeered my father's wagon without him knowing, covered it with a heavy tarp, and took it all the way to the center of Bumblebee Meadows. We laughed the whole time we were loading those rabbits, and we joked that it seemed like they were multiplying as we were loading them into the wagon. Loading those rabbits was a challenge as one of us had to corral them to keep them in the wagon, while the other ran around trying to catch the others in the pen."

"It was completely dark by the time we filled the wagon for the first run, which we had timed perfectly for the next part of our plan."

Harry looked like a little kid again, and he got even more excited as he told the rest of the story to me and my parents – who were equally amused.

"So... Oren and I unloaded two full wagon-loads of rabbits, in the dead of night, all around town. We counted at least 1,200 rabbits by the time we stopped counting. We started on the outskirts of the farmers' gardens and worked our way toward the center of town. We freed the rabbits strategically so that when the town awoke in the morning, there wouldn't be a single person that didn't see at least one if not three rabbits hopping around."

"We aren't sure how, but we made our special delivery and cleaned out the wagon – which was now filled with quite a few shovel-loads of rabbit poop - and made it back to our beds in time to safely avoid any suspicion of our involvement. Our parents hadn't even noticed our absence that night. As it was summer, Oren and I often spent the nights camping out or coming home late from our night swims at Long Pond. "

"We made extra sure our parents saw us the next morning before we headed off into town, so even they would believe we couldn't have been involved in the rabbit scheme. We now had our alibis."

"We timed everything so that we could make sure we were back out and walking the streets that morning just to see people's reactions. It worked out better than Oren and I had ever imagined. There were so many rabbits running around, the sheriff's deputies were in full force to direct traffic around the town commons. It seemed that nobody wanted to kill a single rabbit anymore – for fear the curse would cause that rabbit to multiply in front of their eyes."

"You know, I still get a warm feeling and have a good chuckle every time I see a rabbit in Littleton. And lord knows, my hardware store has made a good profit off all of the farmers buying rabbit trapping kits so they can peacefully capture and then relocate the rabbits outside of town. I do believe there hasn't been a single rabbit killed after the curse came true, due to us."

We all laughed about the story, and Dad turned to Mom and proclaimed, "It's a good thing I stopped for that black rabbit in the parking lot, honey!"

"Well, we have a lot of stops to make today, Harry, but I know I will be in the store quite often with all of the work I will have to do on the Oak Hill property," Dad said. "I may have to start a tab to cover it," he said with a grin.

Harry shook his head with a smile, "Actually, Ronald and Rebecca, you have a good balance of credit prepaid here by Poppy. Last I looked, he had credit on the books for over $4,000 in supplies still left to be used."

Dad and Mom were happy to hear this as the move to Littleton seemed to drain quite a bit of their savings. At least that's what they told me when I asked for a snack during a gas station break.

"Well thank you, Harry, but I have a feeling we will need to come up with more than that to help take care of that hulk of a house," Dad said. "Our next stop is the lawyer's office, the bank, and the sheriff's office to settle the estate. It's going to be a very busy day!"

"I know Don...oh, sorry... I mean Sheriff McGough, will make sure he gets to the bottom of Oren's death. Did he tell you they found Oren's body surrounded by a ring of wildflowers? Sick monsters aren't going to get away with anything like that in this town!" Harry said.

I was already sad enough about Poppy's murder, so I decided I would wait outside and crack my teeth on the blue rock candy while Dad, Mom, and Harry talked in-depth about the investigation the sheriff had started.

Just as I walked through the screen door, I saw a commotion out at the corner of the street, at the end of the hardware store's parking lot. Two boys were pushing a red-headed girl around, trying to take a poster out of her hands. One was quite a bit larger than me and had a military-style haircut – shaved so close I could barely tell if he was balding. The other kid had a mop of brown hair that was so long and uncut, it flopped over his eyes. He kept having to throw his head to the side to keep the hair out of his eyes.

I wasn't sure if they were playing, so I started toward them slowly to see if I could hear more about what was going on.

"END THE SPRAWL, STOP THE MALL," the red-headed girl yelled to the passing cars. She kept yelling and holding her sign high above her head – if she waved it any more she could have gotten a job as one of those sign spinners.

"I have every right to stand here with my poster," she yelled at the two boys. "It's my first amendment right, actually!"

The larger boy positioned his leg behind the girl as she was looking away, arguing with the smaller boy.

As the smaller boy advanced toward her, she stepped back, tripping over the larger boy's leg and falling onto her back with a hard thud. Her poster flew out of her hand and the larger boy picked it up and started tearing it into pieces.

Without even thinking about it, I had already started a full sprint toward the bigger boy right when I saw him put his leg behind the girl. I knew what he was doing and I wasn't going to sit around and do nothing.

By the time I realized it, I was in no position to stop my body's momentum. I fully launched, arms outstretched, straight into the bigger boy's upper body. His whole body left the ground and flew a good four feet, where he landed on the curb and rolled out into the street.

A passing car honked its horn as it swerved to miss his body. He rolled in pain in the street and I could hear him gasping, trying to catch his breath. I turned to see what the smaller boy was doing. The smaller boy's eyes were wide in disbelief that I had launched his friend, and I could tell he wasn't looking for a fight on his own. I stepped toward him and he reeled back, moving away from the girl on the ground.

As I took another step toward him and the girl, he made a wide berth around me and ran over to help his friend out of the street.

I knew I was going to be in for it when I looked back and realized the larger boy had caught his breath.

He crawled back to the curb and stood up, rubbing his ribs and arm. His face had a mixed expression – of pain and hate.

He had just started moving toward me with a deadly stare and both fists curled when I thought I heard an angel. It was my mom's voice, and she and Dad had just left the store and were making it over to where we were standing. The larger boy stopped his advance and dropped his fists when he realized there were adults coming over.

I turned and helped the girl up from the ground, and without even realizing what I was doing, I started wiping the dirt off her butt like a mom would do when her child fell off a bike.

My face turned bright red and started burning when I heard silence and I realized I was touching her butt. Everyone was staring at me in disbelief. I turned to the girl... "Oh my, I am soooooo sorry!" I said to her. "I wasn't even thinking, you had dirt... your butt was dirty... I mean..." I fumbled out loud until my dad interrupted, thankfully.

"Is everything okay over here?" Dad asked.

I could tell he knew the two boys were up to no good because he was talking firmly, and staring straight at them.

"Uhm, yes sir, we were just... uh... joking around," Buzz

said.

Both boys, almost on cue and without another word, turned around and ran back to the side of the hardware store where they had propped up their bikes. They rode away as fast as they could without a glance backward.

As I watched them ride away, I felt a smack on my butt, and a female voice whisper, "I appreciate your help." I turned around to see the cute red-headed girl with her hand outstretched, and my mom and dad chuckling quietly between themselves.

"My name is Ember... Ember Fein. But you can call me Em," she said as she forcefully grabbed my hand and shook it, "And those two idiots were Buzz Dalton and Trent McNabb – royal pains in this butt since third grade."

Although her face was slightly dirty from the fall, I was stunned by how naturally pretty she was. She had freckles around her nose and brilliant blue eyes. Her teeth looked naturally straight, and her smile showed a hint of trouble and fun at the same time. She had dimples and they perfectly framed her smile. She didn't seem overly conscious about fashion, as she was wearing denim overalls with a white t-shirt underneath. I assumed by her height and mannerisms that she was about my age, or maybe a year younger, and her ability to get up off the ground quickly and without crying told me she was scrappy.

"My name is Oliver Appleton... well... my friends call me Olly," I said. "I am so sorry I touched your butt. I wasn't really thinking with all of the excitement."

"Consider yourself lucky... Dan Welton touched my butt in fourth grade and nobody has seen him since," she said with a grin on her face, and then winked. I quickly realized she was razzing me, and my reddening face turned into a smile.

"Appleton? Are you related to Mr. Appleton who lived up on Oak Hill?" Ember asked.

"Yes, he was my grandfather. And this is my mom and dad." I said as I turned toward them. "We just got into town, and we're moving into the house up on Oak Hill today."

"I am so sorry about your grandfather's death," Ember said softly. "I had the chance to get to know him. I would see him at the hardware store every once in a while. He and I both liked plants, and he would bring me unique specimens from the forest and teach me their names."

She was friends with Poppy and also loved nature. I realized I already created a love/hate relationship with Littleton... I was convinced I loved this girl at first sight, but I knew I was going to have a rough time with those two bullies in the near future.

"Poppy (that's what I called my grandpa) used to always take me into the woods and teach me about nature, too. I'm going to miss that," I told Em.

"There is plenty of nature around here. I would be glad to show you all of the good, hidden natural spots here in Littleton. Many are even up on Oak Hill in your new backyard! Actually – that is why those two goons were giving me a hard time. My protest and that poster is intended to get the city council to stop the eminent domain process on one side of the Oak Hill property."

My dad's ears perked up and he said, "Wait... the new mall is going to be built near Oak Hill?"

"Not near Oak Hill... On Oak Hill. Yeah, Mr. Dalton seems to think that his mall would benefit Littleton – enough so that my mom believed he has somehow talked or bribed some of the city council to vote his way. They plan to vote to take over the eastern side of Oak Hill through eminent domain. My mom and I have been doing everything we can to stop it. We live directly across the street from Oak Hill and our house and land are slated to be flattened and turned into a parking lot," Ember said.

"Well, that's not going to happen if I have anything to say about it," my dad said, "I am on my way over to the bank and the law firm now to settle my dad's estate, and I am sure as heck not letting his property go to the likes of ole' Hank Dalton."

"Looks like my mom and I have a friend in this fight then," Em said as she directed a smile and a handshake toward me. I could tell I was still blushing, and I was embarrassed that my hands were sweating when I shook her hand.

"I assume you're starting school at Littleton High School this coming week?" Em asked, "I'm starting the 9th grade... back to being the 'little woman on campus' again!"

"Yeah, same, 9th grade. My parents had to sign me up over the phone – I don't even know what the school looks like, or what classes I am taking yet. The counselor just placed me in a homeroom that had an opening. They said I need to show up to a homeroom with Mr. Eggert on Monday morning, and he would have my full schedule."

"No way!" Em said excitedly. "I'm in Mr. Eggert's homeroom, too. We're doing this pod thing with the classes, which means the kids in the same homeroom go to almost all of the same classes – so we should be in most classes together. I guess I will see you Monday morning, bright and early. I can show you around the school once you get your schedule – the school is not too big, but it's easy to accidentally get stuck in an upper-class hallway – and that means having to learn to avoid getting your books slapped out of your hands."

It was at this time I realized that I had already made at least one friend at my new school – and a cute one at that. That's one more friend than I had at my old school. Things were looking good in Littleton already.

Em could tell my parents were anxious to get moving, so she said a quick goodbye to all of us, winked at me, and ran off across the street to the park to continue her protesting.

6. POPPY & THE CLOVERS

Our next stop in town was the Littleton sheriff's office. We wanted to meet with Sheriff McGough, to discuss the investigation into Poppy's death. They must have been expecting us because when my parents and I walked into the office, the deputies jumped from their desks and rushed to us like we were celebrities.

"You must be Oren's family, I'm Frank Bledsoe," a portly man with a big mustache said as he grabbed my dad's hand to shake it. Another female deputy was overly personal and grabbed my mom in a tight hug. As she pulled away, she introduced herself.

"I'm Deputy Ostran. We are so sorry about Oren. He was a real character in the community. We were all so sad to see him go, especially under the awful circumstances. We are spending all of our time trying to find out what happened and who could just hit a man with their truck and leave," she said.

I noticed she said "truck" and not car. This made me feel like they were looking into his death as this was a new fact we had not yet heard. The last thing we heard was a car that hit him.

I could tell my dad picked up on this too, and just as he started to ask a question about it being a truck that hit Poppy, the sheriff stepped out of his office and cut off the deputies with a loud greeting.

"Welcome, Appleton Family! We've been waiting for you. I don't want you to get any misinformation or rumors, just the facts. Step into my office and I will tell you everything we know and what we are working through to determine the cause of Oren's death. These fine deputies have plenty of work to do... don't you?"

The deputies all nodded and went back to their desks as if scolded by a parent. The sheriff led us into his office, which had a very odd smell to it. It had the smell of the inside of a car in the summer heat after you leave a fast-food bag in the back seat. I quickly noticed a few McDonald's and Burger King bags along with hamburger wrappers hanging out of the overstuffed trash can in the corner of the room.

The sheriff's office was covered in plaques – commemorations from mayors, citations of excellence, five and 10 years of service awards – everything a proud mom would tape on her refrigerator. You could tell the sheriff liked to be the center of attention in anything related to the sheriff's department.

Mom and Dad sat in the two leather-seated antique armchairs that were perfectly situated in front of the sheriff's desk. I looked around for a place to sit and realized the only seat left was behind the door to the office, placed in the only space a third chair could occupy - under an overloaded coat rack containing all of the sheriff's weather gear. My dad could see I was struggling with the decision of whether to sit or stand, and he winked at me and nodded toward the chair.

I pushed aside the sheriff's coats on the coat rack so there was room to sit in the chair. The coats fell back into my face and I had to endure the smell of old cigar smoke, body odor, and damp rubber for the rest of our visit.

The sheriff was a large man, and I could tell just by looking at him that personal hygiene took second place to his desire to impress people with his importance. He had a syrup stain on his shirt, which still had a piece of a waffle attached. I could only assume it was fresh from his breakfast that morning. I chuckled to myself.

If he had known it was there, he probably would have dipped the crumb in the syrup and placed it in his mouth.

The sheriff yelled out to the nearest deputy, "Deputy Ostran, go get me Mr. Appleton's belongings from the evidence room." The deputy jumped up and practically ran to an adjoining room as if this was the first real important job she had been asked to do in a while.

"I have your father's belongings. We've been through everything with a fine-toothed comb, and it's been photographed and cataloged... I see no reason to hold onto any of it anymore," the sheriff said.

Deputy Ostran practically ran back into the room with a large bag that looked like a clear garbage bag, striped with yellow tape and the words "EVIDENCE" written across it. She pulled off the protective strap that kept the bag sealed, and started to open the bag. Before she could get the bag fully open, the sheriff jumped from his seat and angrily snatched the bag from her.

"Mind your business, deputy!" the sheriff yelled. He pointed to the door and the deputy scurried away with her head down.

He threw the bag on his desk and walked back around to get in his throne. As he did, I could tell Mom and Dad were just as unimpressed with the sheriff as I was, because they turned to each other and shook their heads at the same time when he wasn't looking.

"Let's see what we have here, shall we?"

He opened the zipper and turned the bag upside down, shaking it violently so that everything fell to his desk with no consideration for the condition of any of Poppy's possessions.

"Here we have one odd, handmade hat," the sheriff said as he handed it over to my dad. My dad smiled, turned around, and tossed it to me. He must have known it would remind me of our adventures in the woods.

This must be the hat Poppy was wearing when he was hit.

My thoughts were interrupted by the loud sheriff.

"One leather bag, filled with... sawdust?" he chuckled to himself while holding it out for my mom to grab – without even looking at her. Just before my mom reached for it, he dropped the bag between her fingers and back onto his desk. The sawdust spilled across his paperwork and, unbeknownst to him, into the mayonnaise dripping from the side of his half-eaten sandwich.

The sheriff looked up and gave my mom a disappointed look as if it was her fault for not grabbing the bag quickly enough.

You big, clumsy oaf, I hope you choke a little on that sawdust when you eat the rest of that sandwich.

The sheriff looked back into the bag. "Here we have a simple house key – which I tried on the house on Oak Hill – it's for the front door," the sheriff said as if he did us a favor by figuring that out. He handed the key to my dad.

"And lastly, Oren's wallet – containing his driver's license, a debit card, and $43 in cash."

"Strangely, whoever hit him didn't take his wallet or try to figure out who he was – they just left?" my dad said.

"Look... all we've been able to figure out so far is that from the width of the treads and spacing of the tire marks in the gravel, plus the height of the point of contact on your dad's body – was that he was hit by a large pickup truck. We estimate the driver was going around 30 miles an hour – and that was going UPHILL. He was hit on a straightaway, so the driver would have likely seen him on the road with plenty of time to stop. We believe this person was either VERY distracted or was trying to hit your dad – and that's why he didn't stop. Do you have any clue as to whether anyone might want to hurt your dad?" the sheriff asked.

My dad replied, "He kept to himself and didn't spend enough time in town to make enemies. It just wasn't in his nature. From what I have heard, he went straight from his home on Oak Hill to stop at the hardware store, and then was on his way to return home."

"Do you know anyone that would have placed flowers near him without calling the accident into our office?", the sheriff asked with a quizzical look on his face.

"Is it possible the flowers were from the bag? My dad collected plants and flowers – it was one of his hobbies. Maybe they flew out of the bag when he was hit?" Dad asked.

The sheriff rudely snorted as he let out a chuckle. "No, I don't think so.... we found clover flowers in a perfect circle around his head – and nowhere else. They were placed by someone. It was the strangest thing."

I could tell my dad and mom were thinking the same thing that I was... why would someone take the time to do that, but not call an ambulance or report his death?

Just as my dad was about to ask another question, the sheriff looked at the clock and his attention seemed to drift to something else he needed to do.

"Well don't you worry, Mr. and Mrs. Appleton, we have the finest Littleton detectives still working on the case," he said loud enough so that the three deputies sitting at their desks outside his office would hear him. All of the deputies looked up and smiled as if this was the first time the sheriff had ever included them in the investigation or complimented them.

"I am sure we will find a clue or an eyewitness that will come forward with more information. It is the hot topic in the town right now," the sheriff said.

The sheriff jumped up from his desk, rubbed his chubby hands together, patted his stomach, and then grabbed my dad's hand and shook it. Then, as quickly as he dropped my dad's hand, he picked up my mom's hand to do the same.

"I'll keep you informed as we get any news or leads," the sheriff said as he motioned toward the door and started corralling my mom and dad out of their chairs and out of his office. In his rush, he almost forgot that I was sitting in the chair, covered in the clothes of his coat rack. He stepped back into the office, put his hand on my shoulder to yank me out of the chair, and then escorted me out, too. As I got up, I looked at the clock and realized it was almost lunchtime.

Looks like the sheriff has an appointment with another hamburger... what a terrible waste of that tasty sawdust.

Mom, Dad, and I stepped out of his office and headed for the front door. All of the deputies were looking at us, but they all seemed afraid to say goodbye for fear the sheriff would see them and reprimand them. They just offered small waves and head nods to us as we walked out the door.

"That had to be the oddest meeting I have ever been in," Dad said as he and Mom quietly chuckled at each other.

"Let's get over to the lawyer's office before it closes. It's noon and I know how lawyers like to cut their office hours short."

The lawyer's office wasn't far from the sheriff's department. It was across the park on the other side of the square. We decided we would leave Dad's 'collectible' car in front of the sheriff's office, knowing our cat Fizzy would be safe and quite happy to be left basking in the sunlight. I peeked in the cracked window and noticed she had spread out and seemed very happy to have the whole backseat to herself now.

7. AN UNCOMFORTABLE PROPOSAL

The Fitzgibbons & McCann Law Offices looked like your
typical small-town law office. It had a red brick front, with a
white sign swinging above the door. The only thing missing was
the little gavel icon you usually see on a lawyer's sign.

Equally spaced on either side of the door were two
sashed windows with white mullions. The glass was clean and
inside I could just make out dark oak shelves spanning from
floor to ceiling, filled with rows of red and brown-covered law
books. They looked to be organized by color, and the rows of
books were all of equal height. The only decoration on the shelf
was what I only guessed was a Native American Indian bowl
made of clay, painted in white, red, and black tones.

Dad opened the door for Mom and me, and followed us

in, instantly admiring all of the nice trim work and hardwood details found around the office. He was so busy looking up at the crown molding and tin ceiling that he didn't notice the balding man sitting in a leather chair in the corner. The man was dressed in an all-white suit, with white leather boots, holding a cowboy hat in one hand, and an envelope and unlit cigar in the other. He had a fake smile and I could tell right away that I didn't like him.

"Well, I'll be a monkey's uncle, if it isn't little Ronnie Appleton in the flesh," the man bellowed as he stood up from the chair. It startled my dad a little as he wasn't expecting someone to be behind him. My dad turned and his face revealed what I had already surmised – that the man in the white suit was someone he didn't like. My dad didn't stretch out his hand for a handshake right away – which was rare for my dad who was always getting on me about manners. The man practically leaned into my dad so that there was no choice but for my dad to shake his hand.

"Well, hello, Henry... it's been a while," Dad said.

"Awe c'mon, Ronnie... we've known each other since we were kids, and I consider you to be a friend – the least you can do is call me Hank!" the man said.

A quiet cough came from behind a bookcase further back in the office. A short man with wire-framed glasses, a plaid vest, and matching bowtie quickly stepped out toward us.

"Mr. and Mrs. Appleton... and Oliver, I presume?"

My mom and dad nodded and realized this was Mr. Jacob Fitzgibbons – Poppy's lawyer and the person they came to see.

"I see you've met Henry Dalton. He was just about to leave," Mr. Fitzgibbons said sternly while glaring over his glasses at Mr. Dalton.

Mr. Dalton chuckled, disregarded Mr. Fitzgibbons completely, and then handed my dad the envelope he had been holding. "I'm sorry about your father, Ronnie. I know the timing isn't the best, and I don't want to come off as rude, but I wanted to give you this before you got too busy fixing up that old house on Oak Hill. It's a very fair offer for the Oak Hill house and land — essentially ALL of Oak Hill. You've got quite a fixer-upper project up there, and this offer will be much fairer than the pennies on the dollar the city will give you when they take the property through eminent domain."

I know where I've seen this greasy slime ball — it was HIM on the billboard on the way into town — the one wanting to put up a mall on Oak Hill and turn Ember's property into a parking lot.

I could feel my blood boiling — and my dad could sense I was about to say something. Just before I could blurt out some choice words for Mr. White Suit, my dad reached his hand back and gently held me back.

"Well, Henry, we just got into town, and as you can tell we have quite a bit to do getting the estate in order and getting Oliver situated in a new town and school. Let me soak in your offer for a bit and we will talk again real soon," my dad said with a slight grin.

My dad isn't going to take the offer... he's just playing him.

I calmed down when I realized my dad was being smart, and that Henry Dalton isn't one to take no for an answer. My dad was going to buy some time and find a way to put up a fight on his terms.

"Well, I hope your boy Oliver likes the school here in Littleton. My son, Buzz, seems to have already befriended him out at the hardware store earlier today — said he looks forward to introducing Oliver to the gang. Imagine that... second generation Daltons and Appletons in school together... it will be just like us in the old days." Mr. Dalton said with a menacing smile on his face.

"Nice to see you again, Henry," Dad said as he directed his gaze to the front door, hinting for Mr. Dalton to leave. I noticed Dad made it a point NOT to call him Hank.

As Mr. Dalton started to leave, he leaned in awkwardly close to my mom and said, "That offer I gave your husband will put you into a beautiful new house here in Littleton. And I will even get you into a nice used car so you can get rid of that World War II-era station wagon you've got parked out there."

Ooh, that was the nail in the coffin... you don't ever insult my dad's pride and joy.

To my surprise, both Mom and Dad maintained their composure and turned away from Mr. Dalton, turning their attention and a smile to Mr. Fitzgibbons instead.

The door closed loudly behind Mr. Dalton, and I watched him stomp to the curb and try to climb awkwardly into the passenger seat of a brand-new gray pickup truck. The truck was too big for him, as he had a noticeably hard time getting up and into the passenger's seat. After a few attempts, the driver offered his hand to pull him up.

The truck had the words 'Dalton Mall' hand-painted on the side with a cheesy logo that looked like it was from the 80s.

Mr. Dalton's driver was a large, bearded man that wore sunglasses and looked like someone straight out of a Navy Seal action movie. He even wore khaki pants, black boots, and a brown shirt – although the sleeves had been cut off to expose the skull tattoo taking up a large part of his arm. It was odd seeing someone like that sitting next to someone who dressed like Colonel Sanders.

I could see the driver and Mr. Dalton sharing some conversation, and then they stared back at us at the same time. The truck revved its engine three times and then peeled away, leaving a black cloud of diesel smoke lingering in front of the law offices.

Mr. Fitzgibbon apologized to all of us. "I'm sorry folks, I asked Mr. Dalton to leave on numerous occasions, but he was adamant about handing you that letter in person. He seemed to know you would be meeting with me today. How about a nice cup of coffee and some comfortable seats for you three?"

We all followed Mr. Fitzgibbons back to a beautiful conference room that had glass cases surrounding the room. Inside the cases were various Native American artifacts – seemingly found all over the Littleton area – according to the few labels I could read as we walked by them.

In the center of the room was a beautiful river table with enough room to seat 12 people. The table had rough, raw bark edges, and down the center was a bright blue river of epoxy that looked like it was glowing. The whole table was covered in a clear glaze, which made the 'river' look as if it were moving. I swung around and stared at some of the objects in the cases.

"Many of those artifacts were found and gifted to me by your grandfather, Oliver!" Mr. Fitzgibbons said as he noticed me eyeing an axe head. He turned to my parents with a soft smile.

"Oren was a good friend of mine, and I will miss him dearly. He wanted to make sure I handled his estate and final wishes if he were to ever pass away. Have a seat... I will be back with some coffee and we can continue."

After five minutes, Mr. Fitzgibbons came back into the

room with three cups of coffee, a chocolate milk, and some shortbread cookies.

He left the room once more, returning with a 2' x 2' wooden crate from the back room. He carefully set it on the river table, making sure not to scratch the finish. I noticed a shiny, stamped metal nameplate on top of the crate. It read "Property of Oren Appleton."

Very carefully, he pried the top off with one of the arrowheads he grabbed from a bowl in the middle of the conference table.

The arrowhead did the job but cracked and fell apart as soon as he set it back onto the table. I must have made an audible gasp because Mr. Fitzgibbons said, "Oh, don't worry Oliver... that wasn't a real arrowhead. I buy a few fakes to keep on the conference table because people always seem to want to handle my real artifacts. If they touch and break those fakes, it's no skin off my back and they don't know any better."

I can see why Poppy liked Mr. Fitzgibbons – he's friendly and as smart as a fox.

"Oren had a few things he wanted me to give you in person upon his death. Firstly, here is the signed copy of his will, as well as the deed to the property on Oak Hill. I suggest you put both of these into his safety deposit box in the local bank TODAY. The deed is the only copy showing your ownership of that land. Mr. Dalton would surely love to get his hands on that!" Mr. Fitzgibbons said.

Mr. Fitzgibbons dug some packing material out of the top of the crate and pulled out an object wrapped in brown paper. He gently laid it on the table and told me to open it.

"What's this," I asked.

Mr. Fitzgibbons smiled and said, "Your grandfather thought you would take care of this unique artifact. He told me that it will have meaning to you one day."

I opened the brown paper very gently, making sure I didn't leave any scratches on the table. I could tell it was quite old because the paper smelled a bit musty as I unwrapped it.

Inside was a statue, about 8" in length. The body of the statue was made mostly of hard, gray stone and was shaped like a mushroom, but it had human characteristics – small eyes, a mouth, arms, and legs. The very top of the statue – the part that looked like a mushroom cap – was made of a semi-transparent black stone... worked down to a shiny, smooth surface and it looked like it may have been made from obsidian. I sat the statue on the table and it stood perfectly upright. I looked at my mom and dad, bewildered.

"Any idea what this is or why Poppy gave it to ME?"

My dad said, "You know your grandfather – he was always a bit eccentric. I am sure it has something to do with your love of nature or the adventures you shared in the woods."

"There's something inscribed there on the back," my mom said.

I turned the statue around, and on the back was a drawing etched in the stone. From what I could make out, it looked to portray a sun with rays emanating, then a line and a circle underneath. Inside the circle's outline was a simple mushroom shape with the infinity symbol scratched directly above it.

"Any idea what this is?" I asked Mr. Fitzgibbons.

"I have no idea, Oliver, but this statue was very important to your grandfather. He didn't want it to get into the wrong hands, and wanted to make sure you got it if anything ever happened to him," Mr. Fitzgibbons said as he patted my shoulder.

Mr. Fitzgibbons returned to the box and began handing my mom and dad some other paperwork as I re-wrapped the artifact as best I could.

I wonder what Poppy meant about this having meaning someday?

The rest of the meeting was pretty boring, as Mom and Dad and Mr. Fitzgibbons talked about the legality of Poppy's estate changing hands. As they signed a stack of papers, I circled the room two times making sure I didn't miss any of the artifacts displayed in the cases or the descriptions written underneath.

"Ready to go, son?" my dad said.

"Yes, thank God!"

"We have one more stop at the bank and then we can head up to the house on Oak Hill," Dad said, noticing my head drop. I was quickly losing interest in the tasks for the day and wanted to see the house on Oak Hill.

I grabbed the artifact off the table and placed it carefully into my backpack, surrounding it with some of the packing material from the open wooden crate. I realized my backpack was going to inherit the old, musty smell from the artifact – which kind of reminded me of Poppy – but in a good way.

Our next stop at the bank was much more boring, and I decided to just sit in the lobby while Mom and Dad went into a secure vault to look into Poppy's safety deposit box. It took them a while to clear the contents of the box, and replace them with the deed and the signed will.

As I sat there, I happened to notice the sheriff leaving the diner across the street.

I knew you were ditching us for a hamburger. I bet you'll still finish that wonderful sawdust sandwich when you get back to your office.

Just then, Mom and Dad came back into the lobby laughing and joking quietly with each other.

"What's so funny?" I asked

"We will tell you in the car, Olly. Let's get up to the property so we can move our stuff in while there is still some light left. We also need to figure out what all of those keys Poppy left us go to."

We walked back to the car, and I noticed Fizzy was up in the front seat now, standing up against the steering wheel – looking around with her head on a swivel. She seemed happy and a bit agitated at the same time when she saw us nearing the car. She wasn't happy when Mom forced her back into the rear seat with me... her favorite travel companion.

As Dad started the car, Mom turned to me and said, "Your grandfather left about $90,000 in savings to us... and it seems your grandfather liked to collect gold, Olly! From our estimation, there was over $40,000 in gold nuggets in his safety deposit box. We have no idea where he got the gold – because Littleton and the surrounding areas are not known for having gold deposits. But the money and the gold will help our finances to keep up the place on Oak Hill"

Poppy was full of surprises – first a botanist, and now part archaeologist and gold prospector.

8. A NEW HOME ON OAK HILL

I started to get excited about seeing the property on Oak Hill for the first time. As we got closer, I could tell my mom and dad were excited, too, as they started pointing at landmarks up on Oak Hill.

"There's Lookout Rock," my dad said, pointing to an outcropping high up on the hill. If you sit up there, you can see all of Littleton – all the way to my childhood home in Bumblebee Meadows."

We turned onto Harvard Drive and then took a right up Oak Hill Road. All three of us became very quiet as we all realized at the same time that we were coming to the spot on the road where Poppy was killed. We passed the spot, and I could tell my dad was holding back his emotions.

"There is no way they could not have seen Poppy walking on this stretch of road.... it had to be purposeful," Dad said.

Mom shook her head in agreement.

I tried to force Poppy's death out of my mind, so I

looked out into the woods and realized how beautiful and mature the old oak forest was. The oaks were huge – some of them looked to be almost four feet round. There were colorful wildflowers on both sides of the road, which made it seem like a very peaceful place – not the scene of a murder.

In the blotches of sunlight sifting through the trees, I saw a quick movement and a small animal running between two trees. I wouldn't have thought anything of it, except that the animal seemed to have something bright red on its back.

Just as I was second-guessing what I had seen, we topped the hill and the woods opened up to expose the big house on Oak Hill.

It was BEAUTIFUL, as if it were a gingerbread house straight out of a fairy tale.

It was big, painted in green and blue, and had a lot of character – from the decorative trim lining the roof, to the colorful stained-glass windows above all of the doors and windows. Everything was trimmed in white, and there was a large stone fireplace going straight up the three stories of the house. The porch was bright white, very big, and it wrapped almost around the entire house. I could see why Poppy and Grandma wanted to live here.

I could tell my mom loved it too, because she just kept asking Dad, "This is our new home?"

Dad seemed equally impressed with the amount of work Poppy had done to the outside of the house since the last time he saw it, too.

We pulled up as close as we could to the front door and hopped out of the car. All three of us rushed to the front door, not even realizing we had left the car doors open. Fizzy must not have noticed this because she just stared at us as she sprawled herself across the back seat. I ran back and picked her up so she could enter the house with the rest of us.

After trying ten different keys, Dad finally found the right one for the front door. We stepped inside and Dad told me my room would be the uppermost room – he thought I would like to have that one. I set my backpack down and ran up the stairs. Four flights of stairs later, I found the only room on the third floor. It was the room in the turret that sat at the highest point of the house. It had clerestory windows on each side of the room, looking out into the Oak Hill woods on one side, and over the conservatory and garden on the other.

I can see everything from here!

The room was empty, and Poppy and Grandma had never used it – I could only guess that they never wanted to climb the four flights of stairs to get to this room.

It had hardwood floors and enough room for a bed, desk, and dresser. It also had a walk-in closet which was a waste as far as I was concerned – because I only owned about five shirts, three pairs of pants, and two pairs of socks. I decided I would turn that closet into 'Olly's Plant Herbarium 2.0'.

The bedroom was much bigger and brighter than my room in Medina.

I ran back downstairs to the first floor and noticed Fizzy had already found a spot on the top of the couch, perched a perfect distance from the big window overlooking the woods. It was time for her fifth nap of the day.

The interior of the house was also beautiful - Poppy and grandma had decked the place out. There was hardwood everywhere, and the trim pieces outlining the ceiling were made of oak and had been stamped or embossed with small, intricately-carved leaves. The stone fireplace was made of large, round, multi-colored stones that looked to have been taken from the Oak Hill property.

It looked as though Poppy had just left the place – the mail had been collected and was sitting on the coffee table near the living room. I sifted through the bills and letters and underneath was a small box addressed to Oren Appleton, 25 Oak Hill Ridge, Littleton, Massachusetts. The sender was listed as A. Muscaria, PO Box 1245, Littleton, Colorado.

I took the mail and the box into the kitchen where I found Mom and Dad. Mom was fawning over her beautiful new kitchen. Dad just stood in the corner smiling and watching, realizing that Mom and I were going to be very happy here.

I set the mail and the box on the kitchen island.

"I found these in the living room."

Dad pushed the mail aside, which was mostly junk mail and a bill, and looked at the box.

"This is marked UPS Express Critical."

Mom and I didn't know what that meant.

"People usually ship things that are valuable or time-sensitive with Express Critical," Dad said as he started inspecting the box. "That's odd, it's sent from Littleton, Colorado. Let's open it."

Dad started tearing into the box. He pulled out packing bubbles wrapped around something. Unraveling the packing bubbles revealed a black velvet pouch about 5 inches by 8 inches in size. It was cinched shut with a black tie. Dad excitedly opened the tie and turned the bag upside down over the opened box.

All of us were silent and looked at each other with

amazement when quite a few large nuggets of gold rolled out into the box.

"This has to be a good 10 ounces of gold," Dad said with a huge smile on his face.

Mom picked up one of the nuggets and twirled it in her fingers under the light hanging over the kitchen island. "This looks like it was just plucked from the ground – it still has dirt on it."

Dad felt something inside the black velvet bag. He pulled out a small note that had dirt stains on it. He unfolded the note and read it aloud.

"Oren, thank you for the new harvest. All is well and they are acclimating to their new home. Enclosed please find a gift for your continued contributions and dedication to the community."

It was signed, "Your friend, Amanita." Under the signature was the same symbol I had seen on the back of the mushroom statue that Poppy had left me. It was a mushroom with the infinity symbol drawn directly above it.

All three of us were silent, trying to figure out what Poppy could have done to have received a note and payment like this.

"I guess the mushroom business is more lucrative than I thought," Dad said with a chuckle.

We didn't have much time to explore the rest of the house as we only had an hour of sunlight left to get the car unpacked. We still had to figure out how to untie Dad's puzzle of crisscrossed ropes holding our items to the top of his car.

Most of the items ended up in the living room until they could find their final resting place. Mom was smart and had ordered pizza right when we arrived at Oak Hill, so the knock at the door was a pleasant surprise and a much-needed break from moving things around the house.

I must have been really tired because after eating four slices of pizza, I sat on the couch with Fizzy, and the next thing I knew it was morning. Mom was in the kitchen moving around pots and pans loud enough to purposefully wake me and Dad.

"Good morning, Olly!" Mom said when she noticed I stirred on the couch. I grunted something indiscernible, and realized we hadn't gone grocery shopping so breakfast was probably not an option yet.

"We will stop in town to get breakfast and groceries once your father gets up and has his coffee," Mom said. "He's useless until he's had his coffee."

Dad was around the corner and I realized Mom had said this loudly and in earshot purposefully for Dad to hear, too.

"Very funny, darling. I am only half useless."

Then Mom remembered, "Oh, we need to get your school supplies today, too. School starts tomorrow and we don't have any school supplies for you yet. Too bad we don't have a mall here in Littleton!"

Dad and I looked at each other and quickly realized she was being sarcastic again and was trying to get us riled up.

"I'm joking!" Mom said. "I will never root for a mall in Littleton, let alone a mall built outside my beautiful new kitchen window here on Oak Hill."

In my language, "school supplies" instantly translated into a full day of unbearable shopping for clothes, pencils, paper, staples, and shoes.

While my dad finished his coffee, I decided to explore the first floor of the house. Just as I left the kitchen, I saw a plump tan and brown pile of fur run past me, almost tripping me. Fizzy had seen something and was on the hunt!

I decided to chase after her, and we ended up in the front hall. Fizzy was moving so fast, and the floors were so slick, she couldn't slow her momentum. She skidded across the waxed floor and ran head-first into a small table pushed against the wall supporting the stairs.

"Are you after a mouse, Fizzy?" I asked her.

Mom and Dad aren't going to enjoy hearing we have mice.

I got down on a knee to pet Fizzy and thank her for doing her one job. That's when I noticed a 2" hole in the baseboard, behind the hallway side table. The odd thing is that the hole didn't seem to be gnawed, made by a mouse. The hole seemed to have been man-made and had even been finished with trim.

Why would Poppy want to make such a nice hole in the wall for mice?

I moved the table and tried to look inside the hole, but it was too dark on the other side.

That's when I noticed it – about a foot to the left of the hole was what looked to be a keyhole, and a small symbol stamped in ink. The symbol was a semi-circle of leaves with a small mushroom etched in the center. It looked familiar.

I stepped back from the wall to get a better look at the hole. That's when I realized two slits were running the full height of the wall, about 3 feet apart, just to the right of where the table was.

It's a door!

A person walking by would probably never notice the door entrance, as the wall was paneled and the slits of the door lined up with the grooves in the paneling.

I heard my mom and dad coming from the kitchen, so I gave Fizzy a little nudge with my foot to get her attention away from the hole. Fizzy scolded me with a loud meow, turned her back to me, and sauntered away.

I decided I would investigate the door more when my parents weren't around.

Dad decided he would forego the school shopping, and instead head to Harry's Hardware to get a doughnut, have small talk with Harry, and order supplies for the house repairs.

Mom and I left for the office supply store in the next town over, then the grocery store in Littleton. She also made me stop at two clothing stores – which was hell for a boy my age.

My day of shopping with Mom resulted in enough supplies to fill TWO backpacks, two new shirts to add to my 'designer' clothes collection, new jeans, and a new pair of shoes.

Mom wanted to keep shopping, but I was simply done with it all. It was close to dinner time, and I felt I had the maximum of what I needed. I had no desire to spend the rest of my day running between any more stores.

We got home and Mom made my favorite for dinner — chicken paprikash with spaetzle and fresh homemade rolls. I ate so much, I had to loosen the string on my shorts before getting up from the table.

Dad helped me move my bed, mattress, and dresser up into my room on the third floor. It was not an easy feat to get the bed around the three landings on the stairs leading up to my room. The damage we caused would give Dad an excuse to make yet another stop at Harry's hardware store tomorrow morning, I am sure.

It was almost ten o'clock by the time I had all of my boxes of stuff moved into my room. I yelled a good night down to Mom and Dad, who were busy unpacking on the first floor, and quickly realized I would have to walk down the four flights of stairs for them to even hear me. This was an inconvenience, but also a blessing. They would have to walk up the same four flights of stairs to ask me to do any chores.

I walked downstairs and after exchanging goodnights, Mom said, "Ember's mom, Maisie, just called and introduced herself over the phone. She also said that Ember will be here at 8:00 in the morning to show you the way to school and get you situated. I thought that was a nice gesture."

My heart fluttered a little and I could feel my face starting to flush red. I turned and started up the stairs so my parents wouldn't notice my condition.

"Thanks, uhm... good night," I blurted out and rushed up the stairs quickly.

I could hear my mom and dad chuckling at me as I made my way upstairs to my room.

They are so embarrassing.

Although my room on the top floor was warm, opening the four clerestory windows gave me a cool cross-breeze that smelled of fresh oak and pine. I also realized that when laying on my bed, I could see the stars in almost all four corners of the sky.

I love my new room.

Before settling into bed for the night, I unpacked my bag that had all of my items, including the items Poppy had left me: the map, the key, and the stone statue from the crate at Mr. Fitzgibbons's office. I laid them all out on the bed and unrolled the map. Staring out the four windows, I was able to orient the map to be in the correct direction matching the Oak Hill property. I decided I would go exploring after school tomorrow when it was light out again.

After memorizing everything I could on the map, I began to pack it all back up. I picked up the key to put it back in the bag and that's when I noticed it... it had the same design as the stamp imprint next to the keyhole I found in the wall downstairs.

My heart raced a little. Poppy had specifically left this key and map to me for a reason. I fell asleep excited... knowing that all of these pieces had to be a clue to some new adventure. That was how Poppy liked to do things. Everything was a puzzle or a riddle, waiting to be solved.

I fell asleep trying to connect all of the dots in my head... the map, the statue, the key, and the matching symbol next to the hole in the wall, the hidden door, the gold nuggets.

9. LITTLETON HIGH

I woke up and realized I was sore from moving boxes and furniture the day before. I decided a warm shower might help. It was also the first day of school and a cute girl was coming to pick me up early.

I splashed some of my dad's cologne on my new shirt, which Mom had ironed and laid out on my chair for the first day of school. I think I may have overdone it with the cologne because Fizzy walked in, put her nose up in the air, sniffed a few times, and then scurried back down the stairs in a hurry.

I was up pretty early, but Mom was up even earlier. She had hot oatmeal and fresh fruit sitting on the table waiting for me. She had already packed my new backpack – which looked like a stuffed sausage casing. It was so full that one of the zippers wouldn't close. I assured her that, at most, I will probably only need a pencil and a notebook today.

"Better to be prepared," she said.

There would be no winning this argument, so I let it go.

"This will make it harder to run from the bullies, you know," I said and Mom smirked.

I was staring at the clock and realized I was getting excited to see Em. I started to get flush again and of course, that's when the doorbell rang.

Mom and I both rushed for the door. I stopped her.

"I've got this!"

Mom stood back as I opened the door.

I had forgotten how beautiful Em was. And she looked especially cute in the outfit she picked out for today. She wore blue jeans and a Littleton High t-shirt that she had balled into a knot in the front, which exposed just a little bit of her stomach. She had white converse shoes with laces to match the school colors. I told myself that she had dressed up for me, but in reality, I knew she was dressed for the first day of school like every other 9th-grade girl.

"Hi, Olly," Em said with a big smile.

"Hi, Em," I said with a bigger smile.

"Are you moving again? What's up with that big backpack?" she said.

I turned toward my mom and gave her an eye roll and a glare at the same time. Mom just smiled.

"I wasn't sure if I needed all of this," I said under my breath, making sure my mom would hear.

"Just a pencil and a notebook. You better not let that huge pack slow us down... I'm not going to wait for you if you fall behind." Em said while shaking her head.

"You'll be staring at the back of this huge pack the whole way, Em," I said.

"Let's see about that," she said as she leaped down from

79

the porch and jumped on her bike. "We have a 15-minute ride to get to school... saddle up! Bye, Mrs. Appleton!"

Mom waved at Em and then started moving closer, trying to kiss me goodbye. No way I would let Em see that. I gave Mom a quick wave and ran out the door and down the steps before my mom could get any closer.

My bike was already on the front lawn since I hadn't found a good place to store it yet. By the time I lifted my bike from the wet grass, Em had already started peddling down the driveway at breakneck speed.

"Hey, slow down, Em... I'm not even on my bike yet!"

Just down the driveway, Em slowed enough to let me catch up so we could talk on the way to school.

"So, what's your favorite class, Em?"

"Oh, definitely biology or any type of science class. If it has anything to do with nature or plants, I am in head-deep," she said.

I got excited. "Science was my favorite class at my old school. I had a teacher that collected plants from all over the world, and I helped him categorize and mount them on a special wall at the back of his class. I'd visit with him every chance I could, and I guess our friendship rubbed a few of the more popular kids the wrong way. I guess I brought some of the torment on myself in middle school."

Maybe I'm offering too much information.

Before I could change the topic of conversation to end further embarrassment, Em blurted out, "Why would anyone be mad that you were doing something you enjoyed? We have a few of those bullies here, too. You already met the worst ones in Buzz Dalton and Trent McNabb. Those two will find any reason to pick on a person."

I could tell Em was a kind person at heart.

"Today will be fairly boring... getting class syllabuses, books, and lockers. Good thing we won't need to bring any books home... that backpack of yours can't squeeze one more thing in it," Em said with a chuckle.

"I'll remember that when you ask to borrow something from my bag."

We made it to the high school in under 15 minutes and locked our bikes up at the bike rack outside the front door of the school. That took an extra five minutes because my bike lock just happened to be the deepest item in my over-stuffed backpack. Em laughed a little harder each time I pulled another item out of my backpack to get down to the lock.

I don't care what Mom says, I have to get rid of some of this crap before school tomorrow... I am going to get scoliosis carrying this thing.

Em and I shared homeroom with Mr. Eggerton – the 9th-grade algebra teacher. It was nothing like Mr. Harvey's herbarium-filled classroom... Mr. Eggerton kept decorations in his room pretty simple. Aside from freshly-cleaned blackboards covering every wall of the room, the only thing showing his personality was a poster behind his desk. It read, "MATH – The only subject that COUNTS".

I liked puns, but this was more of a dad joke. Em seemed to notice the poster at the same time I did because we both looked at each other with the same disgusted looks on our faces.

The day went pretty smoothly, and I was excited that Em and I shared almost every class. I was worried that I was being too assuming and clingy with Em, so I made sure I got to the cafeteria before her so I could sit at an empty table. That would give Em the chance to sit with someone else if I was getting on her nerves.

To my surprise, Em made a conscious effort to sit right next to me, which made me happy. She could have chosen to sit with her old friends if she was sick of being around me. To make things even better, some of her friends from middle school decided to join us, too.

Em introduced me to her friends.

"Olly, this is Kylie – my neighbor and friend since 1st grade."

Kylie smiled at me and gave me a quick wave. She had big brown eyes, and auburn hair and seemed like one of those quiet, smart, studious types.

"Oh, and that's Brielle... we joke that she always wears purple or pink – her favorite colors. She and I became friends at a summer camp back in fourth grade. And yes, she wore pink that entire summer, too."

Brielle laughed at Em's comments and nodded her head in agreement. She had blonde hair and blue eyes. She flashed a smile that exposed the biggest dimples I had ever seen.

As they were introducing themselves, a boy with blonde hair and blue eyes hovered in earshot of the table. He seemed afraid to get near the table. When everyone was quiet, he walked up to Em.

"Hello, Ember, it's nice to see you again. Which homeroom did you get?"

Ember smiled at him. "It's nice to see you, too, Ben. We have Mr. Eggerton, room 501. This is Oliver Appleton, he just moved to Littleton. His grandpa lived in the house up on Oak

Hill."

"Oh, I'm sorry about your grandpa, Oliver. What an awful way to go," Ben said. "Oak Hill is a pretty cool place. A little bit scary, too. When did you move in?"

What did he mean by 'scary'?

"We just got into town this past weekend. I haven't even had a chance to explore my house or the area yet."

I was just about to invite Ben to sit with us, when Em said, "I'll see you around, Ben! Nice seeing you again."

I could tell there was some history between Em and Ben.

Ben walked away looking a bit rejected.

Em turned to me and whispered, "Ben and I were going steady for about a month in 8th grade. I found out from a friend that he was kissing Becky Tisdale at one of the football games. I broke up with him the next day, and haven't spoken to him since."

"Why did he say Oak Hill was a bit scary?"

Em, Kylie and Brielle all started to chime in at the same time. But Em cut them off and decided it would be best if she filled me in on the rumors.

"There have always been plenty of stories about unexplained sightings and odd happenings up on Oak Hill. Ben was one of the more recent 'victims'. Seems he was trying to kill bullfrogs with rocks in Tophet Swamp, and he says he heard something creep up behind him. When he turned, there was nobody there – and everything had gone silent – no birds, no frogs, no leaves rustling. Just as he was about to turn around and continue throwing rocks at the bullfrogs, he was bombarded from behind with branches, acorns, and pine cones.

He turned to see who or what was attacking him, but there was nothing and no one... no squirrels or other animals in the trees from what he could see. He said the attack was steady and was coming from high up in the oak trees. I guess it spooked him enough that he ran off the hill, and hasn't returned since."

Kylie jumped in, "My dad does survey work, and he was up on Oak Hill doing work for Mr. Dalton's new mall. He said when he got up near the water tower, he walked through a strange dust cloud that seemed to shoot up from the ground. After laying on the ground and hallucinating for about 15 minutes, he was able to walk back down the hill and recover. When his partner went back up to check out the area, he couldn't find anything that would have caused the dust cloud. The doctors couldn't explain what caused the hallucinations and said it may have been a plant allergy. My dad has refused to go up there ever since that happened."

Brielle jumped in, "My brother was climbing up Tophet Chasm, and swore he saw a small creature – not anything like a squirrel or chipmunk – run into the rocks. When he went to explore the area where it disappeared, he thought he heard a faint voice whisper 'GET OOOOUUTTT'. After that, he sprinted home because he had to change his underwear."

Em, Brielle, and Kylie all started laughing out loud at the same time.

Em got serious again, "Littleton is filled with a lot of folklore and superstitions. There are rumors that there are creatures in the woods around Littleton. According to legend, they are called Nikommo, and although they can be menacing, they supposedly assist those who treat them with respect. The chasm Brielle was talking about, Tophet Chasm, comes from the word 'Tophet' which means 'fiery hell'. English settlers claim they would hear drums and shrieking coming from Tophet Swamp and feared for their lives when going into that area."

"Well, now I can't wait to get home and take a nice stroll through our lovely property," I said with a smile. Em, Brielle, and Kylie all laughed again.

"I'll go with you, so you don't have to be scared," Em said with a flirty smirk, putting her arm around me as if to comfort me.

Brielle and Kylie got up to get to their next class, leaving Em and me alone for a few minutes. I decided I had to tell Em about the items Poppy had left me.

She's smart and might be able to help me solve his riddles faster than working alone.

"So, Em, don't think I'm crazy, but I have something to tell you."

"I can assure you, Olly, that I will always be just a little crazier than you. Go for it!"

"Ok... so my grandpa loved riddles and puzzles. He was a little eccentric and some may even say crazy – but I know he was smart and had no dementia when he passed. I heard my parents talking and they said he claimed to have seen creatures up on Oak Hill. Creatures that nobody had ever seen before. It was one of the reasons he was fired from his teaching position at Harvard."

Em noticed I was embarrassed about the last statement. I hesitated a little and she urged me to continue.

"My grandpa left me some items when he passed, and I haven't figured out what they're for yet. There is a map with markings of some unusual features up on Oak Hill. There's also a small statue made of stone – shaped like a mushroom, but with human characteristics. The item that has me most excited is the key he left me, and a hidden door I discovered yesterday in our hallway. I think the design of the key matches the symbol etched next to a keyhole near that door."

"Did you try the key?" Em asked.

"My parents were home when I discovered the door yesterday, and I just have this feeling that my grandpa wanted me to discover the meaning of these items without their involvement – one last adventure he could share with me, I guess. I haven't had a chance to try the key yet, but my parents won't be home until late tonight. Do you want to try it with me after school?"

Em looked overly excited... enough so that she was bouncing slightly in her chair.

"YES! Of course... I love a good adventure. I'll call my mom and let her know I'll be a little late."

The bell rang and we had to get to our next class. Em's excitement lasted through the rest of the day. When the clock hit 3:15 and the last bell rang, Em grabbed my hand, practically pulled me out of my desk, and led me out of the classroom. She pulled me down the hall and out to our bikes. She didn't even stop to talk with her friends.

She was excited, and I hoped I hadn't oversold the things that I had found. For all I knew, the key just opened a storage closet filled with garbage – being chewed on by the mouse that Fizzy has been hunting. At least Fizzy would be happy if we found the mouse's hiding place if that were the case.

It seemed like the bike ride back to Oak Hill went twice as fast as the morning trip to school. Em and I threw our bikes down in the grass on the front lawn and ran up the front porch. My parents left the only key to the house under the front doormat because they still hadn't made an extra house key for me yet.

I opened the door and let Em go in first. Em stepped in and held her mouth open in awe as she stared at all of the stained glass and hardwood details.

"This is so beautiful... I had no idea how nice this house was. In all my years walking around on Oak Hill, I have to honestly say I've never really paid much attention to it," Em said.

Fizzy popped out from behind the couch – looking a little bothered by all of the commotion. She looked disheveled from her fifth nap. Fizzy sauntered over to Em and instantly started rubbing up against her leg. I could tell Fizzy liked Em as much as I did, and Em seemed to love Fizzy, too. She bent down and started rubbing Fizzy's cheeks. Fizzy fell over, exposing her stomach for belly rubs.

"I'll let you two lovebirds get to know each other while I go get the key!"

I ran up the four flights of stairs – skipping every other step to make the trip faster. I went into my bag and grabbed the key. I figured I would show Em the map and statue some other time. It would be an excuse to spend more time with her.

I flew down the stairs with even more speed. Em was at the base of the steps still rubbing Fizzy's stomach and I could swear she had lulled the cat into another nap.

I motioned to the hallway leading around and behind the stairs. "The door's back here, Em."

Em helped me move the small side table away from the wall, and we both kneeled to look at the keyhole. I held the key up and Em instantly recognized the matching design.

"The key has the same design as the symbol above the

keyhole!" Em said with excitement.

I put the key in and slowly turned it.

"Here goes nothing..."

Behind the wall, it sounded as if a weight slowly settled to the floor, just next to the keyhole, followed by a loud CLICK.

The hidden door abruptly popped out from the wall – just enough to get a finger in the opening. Em stood behind me as I started to pull open the door, but I stopped just before opening it fully.

"Em, you have to promise me that you won't be disappointed if this is nothing more than a cleaning closet or garbage storage... promise me."

"I promise, Olly... just open it!"

When I pulled the door fully open, a waft of cool, damp air came out. It smelled of wet sawdust and cardboard. It was dark in there, but I could already tell it wasn't just a closet – so I was a bit relieved.

Inside the door was a wall switch and I flipped it on. An overhead string of lights buzzed with electricity, flickered, and gradually brightened to full strength.

As the lights shined brighter, it exposed a set of ten stone stairs leading down to a stone pad landing. The stairs and walls looked like they had been there for a long time, and they had visible marks as if someone hand-chiseled the passage and stairs right out of the rock foundation that the house seemed to be sitting on.

I could see what looked to be sawdust spread on the tops of the steps – I wasn't sure if it was put there purposefully, or if it had just been spilled there by mistake.

I went in first and Em held my arm as we walked down slowly. The walls were cold and damp and the stairs were a bit slippery. The sawdust seemed to help with the traction – which made me believe it was put there just for that reason.

We reached the landing, which led to another small set of steps going off to the right, leading into another room... it was more like a cave.

The 8' x 8' room had a rounded ceiling making it seem fairly open. I could see the chisel marks on the floors, walls, and ceilings in here, too... as if someone had also carved this room right out of the rock.

The same string lights were anchored with eye hooks along the top of the stone walls, all around the circumference of the room. It was surprisingly bright.

Em was quiet, and I wasn't sure if that meant she was scared or disappointed that it was just a room, so I turned to check on her.

Her eyes were wide open, and a huge smile let me know she wasn't at all disappointed.

"This is AWESOME! This will make a great secret hangout," she said.

Against one side of the cave was a wooden workbench with shelves built up almost to the ceiling. On the other side, opposite the workbench, hung a floor-to-ceiling framed map of the United States which looked to be permanently attached to a large 4' x 6' wooden panel.

Em and I walked over to the workbench and started sifting through the boxes on the shelves to see what purpose this room had. All we could find were rolls of packing tape, cardboard shipping boxes, scissors, mailing labels, and red markers. One side of the table had a tall stack of brown fiber egg cartons.

Two large plastic bags sat on the other end of the workbench, with the tops cinched open on both. I stuck my hand into the closest one and pulled out a handful of sawdust – the same light-colored sawdust we had seen on the stairs. It smelled like pine and also had a musty smell as if it had been soaking up the humidity that had seeped into the stone room.

Em had reached into the other bag at almost the same time and came out with what looked to be dark, chunky, moist soil.

"I think this is manure," Em said as she quickly dropped the dirt back into the bag with a disgusted look and then started to wipe her hands off.

"Looks like you got the crappy end of that deal," I said with a smile.

Before I could react, Em swiped her finger across my upper lip, making sure she left a dark mustache of manure.

"Definitely manure," I said as I wiped the manure off my lip and spit out the small bit that had fallen into my mouth. We both laughed.

"Any ideas what this place was used for?" Em asked.

"I heard my grandfather was growing and selling mushrooms. But I don't see any mushrooms growing down here. It would be odd to grow the mushrooms somewhere else, carry them down those stairs, package them up here and walk them back upstairs. He has a greenhouse out back where he could do all of that work anyway."

"He was shipping SOMETHING from down here", Em

said with a quizzical look on her face.

Em turned around and looked at the large map on the other wall.

"Look... there are pins on that map."

She moved closer and started reading some of the city names where the pins were located.

"Littleton, Colorado... Smallville, Mississippi... Littleton, Utah... Littleton, Idaho... Your grandpa was shipping to some pretty odd places if you ask me. And I think he had a fascination with towns containing a 'little' theme in the names."

Maybe Poppy was going mad after all.

"Let's agree not to tell anyone about this place – especially our parents. I wouldn't mind keeping this our little secret."

"Agreed!" Em said as she proceeded to spit in her hand and hold it out – so we could shake on it. I did the same and we made our pact.

"We better get back upstairs before my parents get home. Our secret won't last long if they find the hidden door."

We walked back upstairs quickly, careful not to slip on the stone steps. Em went out first and I turned around to turn off the lights.

Just as I switched the lights off, I heard a noise at the bottom of the stone stairs – it sounded like the pitter-patter of footsteps in a puddle. I flipped the light back on, and there was nothing there.

Em had heard it, too, and it was evident that it freaked both of us out. We stood in silence for a second hoping to hear the noise again. We didn't have the nerve, or the time, to go back down the stairs to see what might have made the noise.

"Maybe that was just the mouse that Fizzy was hunting," I reassured Em.

When I closed the door behind me, I heard the familiar CLICK! and what sounded like the weight falling behind the wall again. The door snapped shut so tightly again that you could hardly see the lines in the paneling. It was quite an ingenious design, and it made me proud to think Poppy might have designed and built it – but why?

We agreed we would come back to our secret hideaway again after school tomorrow.

10. INTO THE "FIERY HELL"

The second day of school was much like the first. Em had decided to make a habit of showing me the way to school. We rode our bikes to school and made it through the day without much excitement... until, that was, we had gym class during the last period of the day.

It seemed the school's pod groupings didn't apply to gym class. Many of the pods came together on the last period of the day to compete in gym class together. Me, Em, Kylie, and Brielle walked out onto the football field behind the school, where we assumed we would be told about all of the different sports we would learn and play during the school year.

I was sure we would also be told that taking showers was mandatory, even though gym class was the last period of the day.

Why take a shower just to head home? These schools will find any way they can to embarrass us.

As we walked to the edge of the football field, we noticed a group of students circling out near the center of the 50-yard line. The boys were laughing and the girls seemed to be yelling at them.

The four of us walked over to see what was happening.

As I stepped up to the outer ring of people, I noticed there was a small, brown rabbit cowering in the middle of the circle. And sure enough, Buzz and his friend Trent were on either side of the rabbit, trying to trap it with their feet. At one point, Buzz stepped on its paw, and the rabbit let out a scream – which made the circling crowd yell in anger.

"Leave it alone, Buzz," screamed one girl.

"You hurt it, you idiot," screamed another.

The other boys that had been watching and egging on Buzz and Trent stopped their encouragement when they saw Buzz go too far, hurting the rabbit.

I could feel my blood starting to boil.

I pushed my way past the crowd in front of me, and before Buzz and Trent realized what I was doing, I picked up the rabbit which was trapped and cowering between Buzz and Trent. Without slowing, I ran to the other side of the group and pushed through. Once outside the crowd, I set the rabbit down and urged it to run... which it did at a lightning-fast pace.

When it got about 40 feet away, it stopped and turned, sitting up on its hind legs. It stared at me for a few seconds and then continued into the woods at the side of the football field.

I think I just made a furry friend and embarrassed my two enemies at the same time.

I realized, once again, that I would need to be punished for interfering in Buzz and Trent's business.

When I turned around, I realized the crowd had opened up the circle so that I was now in the 'ring' with Buzz and Trent.

I could hear the other boys in the circle commenting about how much of a beating I was in for. The girls just stood in fear, knowing they couldn't do or say anything to stop Buzz and Trent from beating me down.

I noticed Em push through the crowd, planting herself between me, Buzz, and Trent. She stared them down and tried to remain between us as they tried to advance toward me.

She is one brave girl.

Just then, the gym teacher yelled over to the crowd and demanded we all come back to the sideline to start gym class. Trent and Buzz gave me a glare that could kill and watched me in anger as I walked toward the gym teacher with Em.

Thank God... saved again.

I realized that I wasn't going to be able to avoid Buzz and Trent forever, and I would eventually have to face off with them. Right now, luckily, was not that time. Although, it may have been better to have this happen with a large group of people there to keep the fight fair.

As Em and I walked toward the teacher, Buzz and Trent followed closely behind.

"We'll see you after class, nature boy," Buzz whispered as he pushed past me, jabbing his elbow into my rib, just out of the teacher's view.

Em looked at me and rolled her eyes at their neanderthal ways – she knew I was in for trouble, and we didn't have much time for a plan as the school would be letting out soon.

The next 45 minutes of gym class flew by, and I didn't catch a word of what the gym teacher said. I was too busy trying to think through which limbs I could do without, or ways to escape.

Maybe they will break my left arm so I can still write. If I roll up into a ball, like a potato bug, how much damage can they do? Maybe I can outrun them...

Em must have noticed my brain spinning because she nudged me out of my trance.

"Don't worry, Olly. I have a plan to get us out of here safely... at least for today."

Em slowly moved over toward a blonde boy standing a few feet away, trying to not make it obvious to Buzz and Trent what she was doing. I noticed they were too busy talking about how they were going to beat me silly anyhow. They made sure I overheard them.

She leaned in toward the boy, who was rather large and built like a linebacker. After whispering for a minute, the boy shook his head and smiled, and Em slowly stepped back toward me with as little movement as possible.

Em leaned in toward me. "That's Chase... he's what we like to call a bully to the bullies in Littleton. He's known for standing up for the little guys. He doesn't like Buzz and Trent at all, and said he will help us buy some time to get a head start out of here."

Em ended her plan with a wink as if to tell me she had my back.

The end of class was growing near... I could tell because my palms were sweating even more profusely. I was hoping Em wouldn't grab my hand when we made a run for it, because her hands would probably just slip right off.

I noticed that Chase and his even larger friend, Andrew, started walking toward Buzz and Trent, strategically positioning themselves behind the pair. Not a minute later, the gym teacher announced class was over and that we should go back to our homerooms to gather our things before leaving for the day.

With that announcement, Buzz and Trent turned to look at me and quickly realized they had two large obstacles in their way. Chase and Andrew put their arms around Buzz and Trent's shoulders as if they were old pals. As much as Buzz and Trent fought to break free, Chase and Andrew seemed to tighten their grip.

"Time to go," Em said, grabbing my sweaty hand and leading me to the nearest door to the school.

"We need to get our stuff and get on our bikes right away... I don't know how long Chase and Andrew can keep those two ogres busy. Every minute counts."

We ran into our homeroom to grab our bags and pushed through everyone jamming up the halls to get to our bikes outside the main door.

Em had her bike unlocked quickly, but I struggled to get my combination to work.... it didn't help that I couldn't hold the lock with my sweaty hands.

Em grabbed the lock from me, "What's the combination, Olly?"

"Uhm... Poppy. P-O-P-P-."

Em had the lock off before I could finish spelling it out.

She turned me around forcefully, so she could stuff the lock into my backpack. There wasn't much room for it, so it just hung out of the bag.

"Promise me you'll ditch some of this stuff before tomorrow... alright? We have to go, Olly!"

I jumped on my bike and we started peddling as fast as we could down the sidewalk. Just then, we heard Buzz and Trent burst out of the main doors of the school. They saw us peddling away, shouted something at us, and then started unlocking their bikes in a rush.

"I think he said something about adding me to some rabbit stew, Em."

That got a small laugh out of Em, but I could tell she also knew we were in some serious trouble.

I followed Em, knowing she could find the fastest route home. We cut through the senior class parking lot and a field behind Indian Hill Music. We landed on the main road and jumped onto King Street. It was busy this time of day, but somehow we managed to cross the street right when the crosswalk sign turned.

I looked back and saw that Buzz and Trent were peddling hard through the field where we were just a few minutes ago.

"THEY'RE GAINING ON US, EM!"

"Just keep peddling, Olly... we're going to try and lose them in Tophet's Chasm."

My lungs were burning and I didn't want to tell Em that I was having a hard time keeping up with her.

We turned right onto Harvard Road, which was even

busier than King Street.

"Not much further, Olly."

Without much notice, Em shot left, crossing the busy street and ending up at a small trailhead in the woods.

She's crazy! I don't think she even looked to see if any cars were coming.

I had to look to make sure no cars were coming before I crossed, and when I turned my head left to look, I saw Buzz and Trent about 100 yards back, peddling as hard as they were before, and still screaming at me.

Luckily, my heart was pounding so hard in my ears, it masked whatever threats were thrown at me.

I flew across the street and entered the woods where Em was waiting for me. She was off her bike, and held it as if she was about to sprint up the hill with it.

"Ready for a little fast hiking uphill?" Em asked.

I didn't realize I was in for a triathlon today.

I lied and nodded my head yes, then jumped off my bike and tried to keep up with her.

"This is the bottom of Tophet Chasm... an old, dried-up waterfall. There are a lot of brushy areas up here we can hide in. I'm hoping Buzz and Trent will tire out before they can find us."

I realized after starting up the hill that there was no way we could make it to the top of Oak Hill quickly, so Em's suggestion of hiding was more realistic.

"Isn't this where you said the townspeople used to hear screams, Em?"

"Hopefully not today, Olly! Get your butt moving."

A little way back, Buzz and Trent had entered the trail into the woods.

"This new kid's going to be the death of me," Buzz said with a winded breath.

"There's no way they will make it to the top, they're going to have to stop and we'll be able to catch up with them," Trent said with an evil grin on his face.

Buzz yelled up ahead into the woods, "YOU'RE NOT GOING TO GET AWAY! YOU MIGHT AS WELL STOP AND TAKE YOUR PUNISHMENT … MAKE IT EASY ON ALL OF US."

Buzz and Trent peddled harder, staying on their bikes as they rode up the hill. They both had top-of-the-line mountain bikes, provided by none other than Buzz's daddy dearest. This made it much easier to ride uphill in low gear, unlike our old 3-speed bikes.

Em and I both heard Buzz yelling, and realized we weren't as far ahead as we had hoped.

"We're going to have to stay on the flat, rocky part up to the waterfall area, then try to find a place to hide. We may need to ditch our bikes," Em said.

"I know a new mall where we'll be able to buy some new bikes," I said with what little air I had left in my lungs.

This made Em laugh, hard enough that it forced her to stop to catch her breath.

I was relieved to get a break – even if it was for just a second.

I guess I should savor these last few minutes of my life.

Just then, I thought I heard Em say something.

"What did you say, Em?"

"I didn't say anything... did you?" Em replied.

We both heard it again, this time a little more clearly.

"Come in here... you'll be safe in here," a little voice whispered.

We both looked around but saw nobody.

I stared at Em, a little bit scared and worried we were both hearing things. I could tell she was also wondering where the voice was coming from.

The voice spoke again, slightly louder this time. "Look to your right... hurry, before it's too late."

I set my bike down and walked to my right a few feet. There was nothing but a rock face with overgrown ivy and moss in spots.

"Look... for... the... door...," the voice said.

It was then that I noticed it. There was a symbol, barely visible, etched into the side of the rock wall, along with a keyhole. It was the same symbol that was near the keyhole by the secret door at my house. It was the mushroom encircled in ivy.

Em had just noticed it, too, and she stared at it, and then at me, with a look of amazement on her face.

I touched the etched symbol on the rock, and when I did, the rock face moved just slightly.

"I think it's a door, Em!"

I pushed again on the spot where the etching was, this time a little harder. There was a click, and the rock face popped open a few inches, revealing a camouflaged door that had been hidden within the rock face. The outline of the door followed the natural cracks in the rock, and you would never know it was there if the door wasn't open.

That's when I heard Buzz and Trent talking – they were getting closer.

"Grab your bike, Em, we're going inside!"

Without hesitation, Em grabbed her bike and pushed it through the opening. I quickly followed with my bike. Even with the door open, I could only see a little way into the opening. Neither of us could see the person that had invited us in.

When we were both fully inside, I noticed a handle cut into the inside of the door, allowing me to pull the door shut with a quiet click.

It wasn't a moment too soon, as Buzz and Trent peddled past the door only 30 seconds after the door had closed.

Em and I stood perfectly still and listened. I felt like my heart was pounding so loudly, that Buzz and Trent would surely hear it through the door.

It was almost completely dark, except for a stream of light entering through a small peephole penetrating the door just at eye level.

The sounds outside seemed to be amplified inside the space. So much so that it sounded like Buzz and Trent were standing just outside the door when they spoke.

I carefully peeked through the hole in the door and could see that they were only ten feet away from the door, looking around in the bushes.

"They couldn't have gotten far, Buzz... they were pushing their bikes," Trent said with a sense of frustration in his voice.

Buzz, obviously angry that they had lost their prey, picked up a large log and threw it down the side of the hill, muttering, "They have to be hiding somewhere around here... there's no other way out."

After five minutes of searching, Buzz and Trent continued further up the hill and well out of sight.

Em decided it was safe to start a quiet conversation with the person that had invited us in. She couldn't see him in the darkness but knew he was there because we could both hear him moving around a little further back in the tunnel.

"Thank you for saving us!"

"You are most welcome. It is the least I can do since you two saved my friend from a terrible predicament back at the high school," the voice said in a whisper.

We weren't sure what he had meant.

"Who is your friend?" I asked

"My friend Clover, the brown rabbit you freed from those nasty boys. She's been my friend since I found her orphaned in these woods 4 years ago."

"Who are you?" I asked.

"My name is Cremini and I was a good friend of your grandfather's, Oliver! Your grandfather helped my family and we owe him a great deal of gratitude. I was with him on the day that he was killed, and we have been mourning his death ever since. The only thing that has brightened our days recently is watching you and your family move into the Oak Hill property."

There was a long pause while I digested what this stranger was saying. I realized I had just started feeling a little bit angered by his last statement.

"If you were there when my grandfather was killed, why didn't you report it to the police, or identify the killer?"

"Well, Olly, that's a little bit tricky to answer with words..." Cremini said with a little disappointment in his voice.

"Well try," I said, still upset.

"I guess I'll have to trust my secret will be kept by you two. I hope I am a good judge of character because I will need you both to not tell a living soul about what happens from this point forward. Olly, your grandfather already told me you would be someone that I could trust. Ember – I know all about your mom's work with the environment, and also your passion for keeping Littleton populated with forests rather than malls – so I am going to take a chance on you. Olly... would you kindly flip the switch on the wall to your right?"

I stretched out my hand in the darkness and found the wall – which was slightly damp and slippery.

Feeling around, I came across something that felt like a light switch. I flipped the switch and a string of lights clicked on, flickering overhead, exposing the full length of a chiseled tunnel leading away from the door.

It took a minute for my eyes to adjust to the bright lights. Once focused, I looked straight ahead and didn't see anyone. I turned to Em and noticed she looked just as confused.

"Down here!" said the soft voice.

We both looked down at the same time and stared in disbelief. Em and I looked at each other to make sure we weren't crazy, then looked back at the creature.

About 6 feet in front of us was a small being that resembled a mushroom, but with arms and legs, that moved as if it were human. It wore a dark red cap that made it look even more like a mushroom. He had two black shiny specks for eyes and a thin sliver of a mouth. His eyes and mouth had an almost child-like character to them. At this moment, he seemed to be smiling and holding his hand out in anticipation of shaking our hands.

Em moved forward and fell to her knee, reaching out her hand.

"It's a pleasure to meet you, Cremini. Your secrets are safe with me," Em said with a big grin on her face.

Cremini moved forward and grabbed Em's pinky finger with a tiny hand that looked more like a glove.

Em looked up at me, as I was still staring at what was in front of me, trying to get over the shock of what I was seeing.

"Olly, don't be rude," Em said, patting the ground next to her to let me know I should come down to meet our new friend.

I knelt carefully and stretched out my hand.

"I'm sorry, Cremini. I've just never met a... talking mushroom before."

His hand touched mine and I noticed his skin even felt like a mushroom – spongy and a bit moist.

"We call ourselves Spores, but it is not an offense to call us mushrooms. It's such a pleasure to finally meet the grandson of Oren Appleton, and his friend," Cremini said with a smile as he bowed to me and Em.

"You're so cute, I could just squeeze you," Em blurted out uncontrollably.

I was instantly embarrassed that Em would say such a thing – we had just met this new creature.

"Looks like you might have some competition, Oliver!" Cremini said as he winked at me and then smiled at Em. "Come on, let's get you two out of this damp tunnel and back home. I'm sure you are both thinking you are crazy right now. I'll explain as much as I can on the way out."

Cremini spun on his feet and started to walk further into the tunnel. Em and I followed behind with our bikes, finding it hard to keep pace with Cremini, even at his small size.

11. THE GRAND PLAN

Cremini led us through the long tunnel. Em and I were both checking him out, in awe at how such a small creature could move so fast.

Cremini talked while we walked the tunnel, "Oliver, your grandfather and I met when he moved into the property on Oak Hill – just before your grandma had passed. It was actually an accident. I was stupid enough to get my leg stuck in the door of his fridge when I was trying to 'borrow' some cream. When he opened the fridge in the morning... there I was, stuck hanging from the door. Before he could grab me, I dropped out and was able to run (or rather hobble) to freedom."

Cremini stopped abruptly and swung around to face us, "Your grandfather's first instinct as a professor at Harvard was to tell the world about me – I was going to be his big discovery. It wasn't until I purposefully introduced myself again that he got to know me and my family better."

Cremini then continued his walk through the tunnel, "I explained to him the importance of the Oak Hill property and the devastation it would cause my community if anyone had found out about us. That's when he stopped talking about us to his peers and decided to protect us and help our community flourish."

"There are more of you?" I asked.

"Oh yes, many more... and not just here in Littleton... although Littleton, Massachusetts is where our ancestors originated," replied Cremini.

"I couldn't tell you how far back our kind goes, but I do know my ancestors were friends with the local Nipmuc people hundreds of years ago. We lived in harmony and worked together to protect nature and each other. When the Nipmuc people left Littleton and the settlers moved in, we went into hiding and only trusted a small handful of people. We have been living and growing our community under Oak Hill for a very long time, and many a superstition has been created to explain away any accidental interactions with my kind."

"Wait, are your people also known as the 'Nikommo'?" Em asked.

"Ah, yes, the Nipmuc came up with that one. They also called us 'puckwudgies' when necessary."

"Puckwudgies? I've never heard of them," Ember said.

"Nikommo were known to be friendly, but Puckwudgies supposedly caused death and destruction. But, in all actuality, we Spores are a very peaceful society. The Puckwudgies name was one of those superstitions purposefully created to keep people away from our home and our secret. We also use to go out into Tophet Swamp at night and scream as loud as we could – blood-curdling screams – to make it seem like there were evil spirits around here. The settlers didn't like that story and it kept them away for quite a while."

Em and I looked at each other and laughed at how even we were scared by this superstition earlier in the day.

Cremini paused and spun around to face us again. "We call ourselves Spores, and our goal is to protect and live peacefully with nature. You will find all of the forest animals are our friends, and we all work together to make this a happy little place." Cremini said with a proud smile.

"So, I have to ask... when we arrived at Oak Hill, my mom and dad and I were driving up toward the house, and I could swear I saw a rabbit or an animal running in the forest with something red on its back. I thought I was hallucinating at the time. Was that you?" I asked.

"Oh yeah, it was pretty silly of me to be seen... I am usually much more careful than that. I had been up there thinking about your grandfather and his death when your family's car came around the corner. I was just lucky you didn't catch me out in the middle of the road. I would have been cream of mushroom soup had your dad not been driving so slowly in that awful beast of a car."

That made me laugh. I liked that Cremini considered our car a beast, just as I did.

As we walked, I noticed some tunnels shooting off in different directions from the one we were in.

"Where do those tunnels go, Cremini?" I asked.

"I'll eventually take you and Em through all of those tunnels – but that's the least of what I want to show you... but there is not enough time today. We're almost back to your house, and I would like to have you two meet my family and the

Spore community under better circumstances – when Buzz and Trent aren't traipsing around so close to the neighborhood."

Just as Cremini said that we came to a plywood panel at a slight turn in the tunnel.

"You should be able to find your way from here!" Cremini said. "It's been such a pleasure meeting both of you."

"It's been wonderful to meet you, too!" Em said with the biggest smile I have seen on her face yet.

I reinforced her sentiment with a smile and a slight head bow toward Cremini.

"We are in luck... It will be a full moon and we are doing our summer feast on Friday. I would love for you to both come as my guest. I will be able to introduce you to my family and community and explain more about the work your grandpa was doing here. Would you two be available Friday night?" Cremini asked.

Without hesitation, Em and I both blurted out at the same time, "YES!"

"Then I tip my cap to you and will plan to meet you here at 7 pm sharp on Friday. And remember – please don't tell anyone about what you've seen today. If our secret gets out, that will be the end of our community's hundreds of years of living peacefully here on Oak Hill."

Em and I both nodded reassuringly to Cremini.

With that, Cremini gave another quick bow, spun on his little feet, and pitter-pattered away. We could hear him whistling a show tune as he traveled further back into the tunnel.

It was then that I realized that Em had been holding my hand the entire time we were walking through the tunnel. She must have just realized it, too, as she got a little embarrassed and let go. We both smiled with a little bit of embarrassment.

I quickly turned toward the plywood panel and gave it a push. It swung open easily and revealed a well-lit room... the secret room that Em and I had just discovered yesterday. Walking into the room, we realized the plywood panel was the back of the large map that hung on the wall.

Em and I walked into our secret room and proceeded to walk up the stone steps toward the hidden door in the wall. We hadn't noticed it the first time we came down these steps, but there was a rope hanging to the right of the door, and I was about to pull it when Em stopped me.

"What if your parents are home? What if they see the door open?"

I was glad Em stopped me... opening the door could have given away our secret just as quickly as we had learned it. I took a step down and peered through the small opening that I had originally thought was a mouse hole. I looked out and listened carefully for any sign that anyone was home. I could only see Fizzy asleep on top of the couch in the living room.

"The coast is clear, Em." I said as I walked back up the stairs and pulled on the rope. With the now familiar 'CLUNK' sound, the hidden door in front of us opened slightly. I turned off the light switch and pushed the door open just a little more, listening once more to make doubly-sure nobody was around.

Now confident that we were alone, I opened the door fully and Em and I walked our bikes out, making certain I closed the secret door tightly behind us.

We walked our bikes out the front door and set them against a wall on the front porch.

"Holy crap, Olly!"

I hadn't been paying much attention, but Em's stare directed me to look out across the lawn. There were Buzz and Trent, sitting on their bikes, just staring at us from the edge of the woods. They were completely still... probably trying to figure out how we happened to escape their claws and get home safely before them. After what seemed like five minutes, Buzz gave us the middle finger, and then he and Trent peddled out of the woods, across our lawn, and down the driveway leading off Oak Hill.

"Not sure how many more times we are going to be able to avoid them, Em."

"I agree... we're going to have to recruit some more help from Chase and some other big friends, I think."

Em sat down on the wicker sofa on the porch, keeping an eye on the driveway to make sure Buzz and Trent didn't come back.

"I'll be right back, Em... you going to be okay here?"

"Yes, I can always come back in if they come back around, right?"

"Of course! I'm just going to run up to my room and get some things for you to see."

I ran up to my room to grab my backpack with the map, key, and statue in it, sprinting back down the stairs to make sure Em hadn't gone missing in the time I was gone. I poked my head out the front door and found Em right where I had left her.

"Come into the living room, Em."

I went into the living room and unpacked the items for

Em to see. I set them out on the small coffee table in front of the couch.

Fizzy popped up from the top of the couch cushion, walked over to Em on the couch, and started nudging her elbow with a wet nose. Em scratched Fizzy's ears and then pushed her forehead against Fizzy's furry forehead. I guess that was enough attention for Fizzy, as she returned to her perch for another nap.

I unfurled the map... "Here is the map my grandfather left for me!"

It was then that it occurred to me that the X located just over the top of the Oak Hill house must have indicated the door to the hidden room Em and I had found.

Em picked up on this, too.

"Look, Olly, the X marks where we just came out of the tunnel, under the house. If we follow the line from that X to Tophet's Swamp, it shows another X. That must be the hidden door we entered in the rock face. There are six other X marks around Oak Hill."

"That must mean there are six more doors and tunnels," I said.

Looking at the other landmarks on the map, Em ran her fingers to the area behind the house. "I wonder what 'The Community' and the 'Sporing Oaks' are?" Em asked.

"No idea... but I have a feeling we'll find out on Friday night!"

I pulled the small statue out of the bag and unwrapped it from the brown paper wrapping. It still smelled musty as if it had been sitting on a shelf in an antique store.

I set it on the coffee table, facing Em.

"Wow... That looks like a statue of Cremini," Em noticed. "But it looks really old."

Em picked up the statue carefully, turning it very slowly, feeling the smooth top and rough body. When she got to the back, she noticed the drawing etched into the stone.

"I wonder what this drawing means, Olly?"

"I haven't figured that puzzle out yet. We also received a package in the mail containing gold nuggets and a note that had the same drawing on it. We'll have to ask Cremini what it all means the next time we see him."

Just then, I heard a car pull up on the gravel outside. I jumped up, looked out the window, and saw that my mom and dad were returning.

"My mom and dad are home, let's put that stuff back in my bag."

Em helped me pack everything up quickly and I set it next to the couch, out of sight.

We finished in time to meet them just as they opened the front door.

"Hello Ember, what a pleasant surprise!" Mom said with a big grin on her face. Dad wasn't far behind and he also greeted Em with a smile.

"How was the second day of school, you two? I noticed that Dalton boy and his friend heading down our driveway. Were they bothering you again?" Dad asked.

"Long story... but let's just say I made several friends and two enemies today," I said with a smirk. Dad shook his head knowing that couldn't be good.

"Buzz and Trent will always be picking on someone, but we have a plan to deal with them," Em said.

"Let me know if I need to go and talk to Mr. Dalton... not sure it will do much good, but I can at least try," Dad said showing concern. "As long as he is trying to buy my property, I can probably get him to do anything I ask."

I turned to Em and then back to my dad, "We'll be able to handle them together."

"Would you and your mom like to join us for dinner, Em?" Mom asked. "I'm making lasagna. I would love to meet some people in the neighborhood. I'll be starting up my hair salon soon and could use a few friends and clients."

"I'm sure my mom would love to, but let me call her. What time?" Em asked.

"I should be able to have dinner ready by 6 o'clock if that works!"

"Perfect, I'll ask her," Em said and walked out onto the porch to make the call.

My mom gave me another big smirk, winked at me, and turned into the kitchen to start making dinner.

"You can thank me later, Oliver!" she said under her breath as she walked away.

Dad had moved to the kitchen counter where he was opening mail and just shook his head during the whole interaction, knowing full well what Mom had up her sleeve.

I noticed his expression change when he started reading one of the letters he received. At the same time, Em walked into the kitchen.

"My mom said she would love to come for dinner. She said she will bring dessert!" Em said happily.

"She doesn't need to do that, but Mr. Appleton here will never turn down a good dessert!" Mom replied. Dad didn't seem to hear the comment, as he was head-deep into the letter in his hand.

"I can't believe this..." Dad grumbled. "It seems as if the city has already decided to take our property and give it to Dalton. There's a hearing to discuss any issues or opposition to the eminent domain claim. The council will then vote at that meeting.

"They can't do that... we just moved here, and it's our family's property. We have to be able to do something," Mom said angrily.

Em interjected, "They are talking about taking five acres of our land for the parking lot. That land has been in our family for over a century. My favorite flower gardens are on that property. My mom and I have been fighting them for a while, but it seems some people on the council have already made up their minds... or had their minds made up for them. Mr. Dalton likes to get what he wants – no matter what it takes."

Em continued to tell us about all of the struggles she and her mom had with the mall development, and especially with the Daltons. I could tell that, to Em, her concern with giving up the land wasn't about the money, but rather the fact that some of the land would go from a beautiful prairie into a concrete parking lot.

Time had gone by quickly as Em told us all of her stories about the Daltons, their land grab, and the ever-increasing pressure Dalton was putting on her mom. Just as she had finished her last story, the doorbell rang.

"That must be my mom!" Em said excitedly.

All four of us proceeded to the front door. My mom opened the door and pulled Em's mom into the foyer with a big Ohio hug.

Ugh, how embarrassing!

I could instantly see where Em got her looks. Em was a smaller version of her mother. They even dressed alike and had the same red hair, big blue eyes, and dimples. Mrs. Fein didn't wear a lot of makeup and didn't need it.

"Welcome to our home, Mrs. Fein," Mom said

"Oh, please call me Maisie... My mom is Mrs. Fein, and I don't feel THAT old yet."

"Very nice to meet you, Maisie," Dad said.

Before I had a chance to introduce myself, Mrs. Fein turned to me and said, "You must be Olly. It's great to finally meet the other half of the dynamic duo. Ember told me you two have already shared many great adventures. And I hope that Dalton boy and his friend get bored and decide to leave you two alone."

I gave Mrs. Fein a handshake and a smile.

"I think we can handle them, Mrs. Fein."

I turned to Em, "Anyway, Em always seems to pull a rabbit out of her hat and finds a way to deal with them."

"Well, I am pretty well known here in Littleton and can make it very uncomfortable for those two, if it comes to that," Mrs. Fein said. "I've lived here long enough to have helped some pretty influential people."

"Hopefully it won't come to that," Mom added. "Well, let's get to the dining room before the lasagna starts to burn. I am known for making extra crispy meals."

Dad and I both gave a slight cough at the same time and tried not to laugh.

"Okay you two, I've never had any complaints from either of you, and there never seems to be any leftovers," Mom retaliated with a laugh and a glare.

We sat at the dining room table, and for a minute I felt a little uncomfortable at how easily we were taking over Poppy and Grandma's house. It was as if we had hijacked their home and called it our own. I didn't feel like we had been there long enough to call this place 'our home' just yet.

As we passed the slightly burnt lasagna, overly-browned garlic bread, and salad around the table, Dad started right into questioning Mrs. Fein about the proposed mall. He was still upset about the letter from the city.

"So, Em told us you are having the same issue with this eminent domain ordeal. Do you have any ideas about how to fight this thing?"

"Not yet... I have been in the battle for over six months now. I've met with a lawyer, and gone to the council meetings to plead our case to keep our family's land intact, but three of the five council members seem to be on Dalton's side. I've asked around to see if anyone knows why those council members won't budge from a yes vote, but everyone seems to be pretty tight-lipped. The two dissenting council members won't even give me the inside scoop. Short of proving the eminent domain won't be for the financial good of the town or barring some environmental barrier, it seems we are facing a monumental challenge."

"What do you mean by an environmental barrier?" Mom asked.

"In a nutshell, unless there is something historically unique to the land or some near-extinct species would be harmed by the city taking over the land, we don't have a leg to stand on. Unfortunately, where the development is slated – here on Oak Hill, and toward the front of my property – there is no proof of either."

Em and I looked at each other. I could tell we were both thinking the same thing.

If only they knew what was actually under Oak Hill...

We both shook our heads, knowing full well that neither of us would go back on our promise to keep Cremini's secret.

Mrs. Fein continued, "I'm an environmental scientist, and I performed environmental impact assessments on my land and yours. A couple of weeks before you arrived in town, Oren asked me to check if any of the land on that part of Oak Hill met either criterion. Unfortunately, I couldn't find any type of impact that would stop the development. I was just about to let him know when I learned that he had passed. I am so sorry about your father's death... I knew your father only through a few chance meetings when we ran into each other in town, and the few times I saw him walking to and from Oak Hill. You would think, with our properties being so close, we would have known each other a little better."

"Don't feel bad, my dad became a little bit of a hermit over the past few years, from what I have heard," Dad said. "Consider yourself lucky to have talked with him. Not many can say they've ever had a conversation with him."

"Well, he was very pleasant and quite memorable, the few times I did get to talk with him!" Mrs. Fein said.

Mom decided she had enough talk about this depressing topic because she made sure to change the topic of the conversation.

"Olly, I think we would all love to hear about the adventures you and Em have had. Why don't you tell us what's been happening?"

"Well, I have learned that Em is a much better storyteller than I am... I will let her tell the stories," I said.

Em smiled, and I could tell she took that as a compliment.

She shared the story of our first time meeting out in front of Sawyer's Hardware store. I found it funny that the story had already become more legendary than it was. Em made it sound like I lifted Buzz above my head and threw him ten feet. This made me chuckle.

She also made it sound like I was the one who got Chase and his friends to block Buzz and Trent so we could escape. I couldn't claim the credit for that one, so I quickly corrected that part of her story and gave her credit.

I shared the details about how Em and I shared a love of nature and exploring, and how science was our favorite subject in school.

My parents and Em's mom both laughed as we told the stories, but also seemed concerned about our return to school. They realized that Buzz and Trent might become a bigger problem over time.

I could sense that Em noticed their worry. She quickly tried to calm them.

"Buzz and Trent have been picking on people all of their lives. I have a few friends that dislike them, and will watch our backs and set them straight when I ask them to."

This made our parents seem to calm down a little. I was not equally calm, as I knew we had to be careful when we were outside of school.

Before we knew it, the grandfather clock in the other room chimed nine times, letting us know it was already 9 o'clock.

Mrs. Fein followed the last chime, "Well, we should get going... it's a school night, and Olly and Em have to be alert and on their feet at school tomorrow. Rebecca and Ron, I am so glad you invited us to dinner. It was a pleasure to meet all of you, and I hope I can get to know you all better since we are now neighbors!"

My mom and dad got up and hugged Mrs. Fein.

"Likewise, Maisie! Let's get a coffee sometime soon. I am not sure if Em told you, but I will be opening a hair salon in town soon and I would love to have you as my first customer. I'll even give you the first cut for free, in exchange for a good reference around town," Mom said.

"Enough of the sales pitch, hon, it's obvious she has a hair person already," Dad chimed in.

"Everyone knows you always have to have a side hairdresser, dear!" Mom quickly replied.

Mrs. Fein jumped in, "I would LOVE to try your new salon. My current hairdresser's place is far outside of town, and her business hours seem to shrink every time I go there. It's so bad, I almost asked Em to cut my hair just a week ago."

"And I would have made her hair into a topiary sculpture," Em said laughing.

"And there you go... when can I make an appointment, Rebecca?" Mrs. Fein said while shaking her head.

I said goodbye to Em's mom and snuck in a hug with Em as she walked out the front door.

"See you tomorrow, Em."

"Bye, Olly. I'll swing by and ride to school with you again tomorrow morning."

I didn't realize just how tired I was after the long day. I sat on the couch next to Fizzy and fell asleep while petting her. Mom woke me with a little nudge.

"Wake up, Olly... why don't you get up to bed? Dad and I are almost done cleaning the kitchen and plan on going to bed right after."

"Goodnight, Mom and Dad! Thanks for having Em and her mom over for dinner," I said as I walked out of the living room and toward the stairs half-asleep.

"No problem, Olly! It was nice to make some new friends already," Mom said and Dad nodded in agreement. "That Ember is a cute one... you two are made for each other. I'm so happy for you."

I smiled and made my way up the four flights of stairs, which seemed never-ending.

12. A LITTLE PINCH SHOULD DO IT

TAP-TAP-TAP... TAP-TAP-TAP...

I opened my eyes and looked around the room to see where the noise was coming from. It was morning and the sun had cast a beautiful orange glow all around my room. I heard the noise again, this time a little louder.

TAP-TAP-TAP...

I noticed the door to my room was slightly ajar, and it moved just a little with the last round of taps.

"Hey, is that you, Fizzy?" I whispered.

"Good morning, Olly. It's just me, Truffle... I'm Cremini's son. I hope I didn't startle you."

The door opened just a little more, and I could see a mushroom cap peaking around the bottom of the door. The cap tilted up and underneath was a Spore which looked very similar to Cremini, just slightly smaller, and with a mischievous grin on his face.

"Oh, nice to meet you, Truffle! No, you didn't startle me..." I laughed a little, straightening up in my bed. "I'm just still trying to figure out my new room. I've heard quite a few weird noises in the short amount of time I've been here – mostly old house noises – creaks and wind, you know... all of those sounds that come with an old place like this."

"This house sure does make some odd noises! My dad asked the mice and raccoons to try and stay out of the house, but they must like how warm it is in here. It's a never-ending struggle convincing them to stay out of the walls," Truffle replied.

"I'm glad to meet another Spore," I said. "I started to think I had dreamed everything that happened yesterday, so I am glad you stopped by."

"Is it okay if I come in, Olly?"

"Of course, please do!"

Truffle moved over to the front of the bed to where I couldn't see him anymore. After a few small grunts, I saw his mushroom cap pop up over the bed rail. Truffle seemed to be very agile as it only took him a few seconds to climb to the top of my bed.

To make the feat even more impressive, Truffle was also dragging a small leather bag behind him.

"My dad told me about you and Em, and the bullies at the school. I have something for you two... something I hope will get you out of any trouble you might run into with those two bullies," Truffle said as he un-cinched the leather bag.

He pulled out a small brown spherical object, slightly larger than a marble, but smaller than a ping pong ball. Its outer shell was brown and wrinkled like old parchment, and it had a small hole at the top. It wasn't man-made and looked like it had been picked right from nature. Truffle motioned for me to stick out my hand. He was very careful as he placed one of the objects in my hand.

"This is a puffball, Olly. There are eight of them in that bag. I want you to give four to Em, and you hold onto the other four," Truffle said very seriously.

"You need to listen carefully and repeat these instructions to Em when you give them to her."

"These puffballs, when squeezed, will expel a special mold that will look like brown dust. The mold causes humans and animals to hallucinate, almost instantly. And aside from the initial effects, they are fairly harmless, so don't worry about hurting anyone with them."

Truffle's face turned to a smile, "We like to say these will help in a pinch, pardon the pun."

I rolled the puffball around in my palm, noticing how light and fragile it was.

"You simply aim the hole toward your enemy and squeeze quickly. Oh, and before you do that, make sure to take a deep breath... you don't want to breathe in the mold yourself. Give the mold a few seconds to work, then you can start your getaway. The hallucinations will wear off after five minutes," Truffle said.

"What kind of hallucinations do they create, Truffle?" I

asked out of curiosity.

"Well, it's different for each person... but it usually appears as something that you are afraid of. It might be spiders, attacking dogs, I even heard someone say they saw a charging rhinoceros once. That's why you need to be careful when handling them, Olly. We don't want you to be screaming in front of Em, right?" Truffle said with a giggle.

I told Truffle I would be extra careful with them, and warn Em, too.

"You and Em are still coming for the feast tomorrow night, right Olly? The rest of my family is very excited to meet you and Em," Truffle said.

"Yes, of course! Em and I can't wait!"

With that, Truffle got excited, gave a quick bow, and then turned around and hopped off the bed onto the floor with hardly a sound. He turned and waved once he got to the door of my room, and started down the hall.

Just as he went out of sight, I saw Fizzy running past the door and down the hall after him.

I jumped to my feet and ran to the door.

"No, Fizzy, stop!"

As I looked out the door, I was sure I would find Fizzy laying on top of Truffle, eating him. Fizzy was rather fast for her size. Instead, I noticed Fizzy cowering in a brown dust cloud at the end of the hall. She was growling and rolling on the ground, with an occasional hiss aimed at whatever she thought was tormenting her. It occurred to me that Truffle must have used a puffball on Fizzy, and she was hallucinating.

"Truffle, are you okay?" I whispered down the hall.

Truffle poked his head around the corner of the wall by the stairs at the end of the hall, and he was smiling. "Oh yes, Olly. I think I am going to have to get Fizzy here to realize I'm not a toy or a tasty snack. She hasn't yet learned that it's not a good idea to chase after me! She'll be fine in a few minutes. See you tomorrow!"

I decided I would get ready for school and check on Fizzy in a few minutes.

Sure enough, after getting ready and dressed for school, Fizzy was sitting at the end of the hall, licking herself clean, as if nothing had happened. I startled her a bit as I passed her on the way downstairs – obviously, the hallucinogen hadn't completely worn off yet.

Mom and Dad were up and waiting for me at the breakfast table. I was glad we had gone grocery shopping as today's breakfast consisted of eggs, bacon, sausage, and fresh crescent rolls.

Before I could scarf down a second helping, the doorbell rang.

"Em's here. I have to go... love you both!"

"Have a good day at school and stay out of trouble's way, Olly," Dad warned me with a troubled look on his face.

"I'll be just fine."

Little did Dad know we now had a secret weapon.

I grabbed my backpack, from which I had already removed about 90% of the items from the first day, and ran to open the door.

Em was dressed just as cutely as she was the day before.

"Morning, Em!

"Morning, Olly! Ready for battle?" Em replied with a smile.

"More than you know," I said with a wink.

I decided I would tell Em about the puffballs once fully out of sight of my parents – just to be safe. We made it halfway down the curved drive on our bikes when I told Em to stop. Em's bike slid to a halt and I pulled up next to her.

"Em, I have something I want to give you. It's a gift from Truffle."

"Who the heck is Truffle?"

"Truffle is Cremini's son. He stopped by my room this morning. He was worried about us running into trouble with Buzz and Trent. He gave me these, and wanted you to have half of them."

I handed a bag of four puffballs to Em. Em opened the bag and pulled out one of the puffballs, holding it close to her face.

"Whoa, careful there! Those things are nasty little suckers," I warned Em.

"What is it?"

"Truffle called it a puffball. When you squeeze it, it will release a cloud of mold that will cause a hallucinogenic attack. He used one on Fizzy, and it knocked her onto her butt. Don't worry, she deserved it and was fine a few minutes later!"

"Also – I almost forgot… you need to make sure you hold your breath and do not breathe any of the mold when you squeeze it. If someone breathes it in, they will see scary things.

Truffle said it doesn't have any long-term harmful effects and usually only lasts five minutes. He thought they might come in handy. I've got mine in my sweatshirt pocket, just in case."

Em smiled with an evil grin, "I can't wait to see these suckers work!"

Em put the puffball back in the small bag, and carefully put the bag into the top of her backpack, so it would be easily accessible.

We made it to school in record time. Em and I were getting our routine down, and found a few shortcuts to get to school quicker, while also being careful to avoid Trent and Buzz on the way.

The day went pretty well, and Chase and his friends were doing a great job keeping their eyes on Buzz and Trent for me and Em. That was... until we neared the end of lunch.

I had too much lemonade at lunch, and I had to go to the bathroom something fierce. I looked around a few times and Buzz and Trent were nowhere to be seen. Em agreed that they must have gone out to the courtyard and wouldn't pose a problem. Chase and his friends also seemed to be watching as I began to leave the cafeteria area, so I felt pretty safe.

I walked the long way around the cafeteria, just to make sure the two weren't hiding in a corner somewhere. Worst case, if they did pop up, I could make my way back into the center of the cafeteria to the protection of Em's big friends.

I turned into the hall toward the bathroom, and it was very empty. When I was about ten feet from the bathroom door, I saw Trent turn the corner at the far end of the hall. I stopped in my tracks.

This isn't good.

I turned to head back to the cafeteria, and that's when I saw one of the classroom doors between me and the cafeteria abruptly open. Buzz pushed the door open hard enough that it made a loud "BANG" - which shook the floor and almost broke the glass in the door.

I'm in trouble.

I didn't have time to plan a getaway as Trent and Buzz started running toward me. The only place to go was into the bathroom.

They weren't far behind, so I ran into a stall and locked the door behind me, hoping to buy some time, and hoping someone would come in and stop them before too much harm came to me.

I turned and put all of my weight against the door, pushing my feet against the bottom of the toilet for added bracing. I was hoping it would be enough to prevent both of them from pushing their way in. I also wanted to make sure they couldn't grab my legs from outside the stall.

It had crossed my mind that they could easily climb under or over the walls to get to me, but for some reason, I didn't think they were smart enough to figure that out.

I heard them whispering to each other when they came into the bathroom – discussing what they were going to do to me once they got me out of the stall. I knew I was cornered and it wouldn't be long before they worked out how to get the door open.

It went silent for a moment… and then "WHAM."

I felt a solid shove against the door, and it was forceful enough to break the stall door's metal locking mechanism – which fell to the floor in two pieces with a clanking sound. I could tell it was Buzz slamming into the door because he was much bigger than Trent, and each hit launched me off my feet a little bit.

Just then, I remembered I had the puffballs in my pocket. I was hoping the fragile balls weren't already crushed from me pressing my full body against the door.

"Open the door, brave Oliver Appleton," Buzz grunted.

BAM... Buzz slammed into the door again, this time so hard it caused my footing to slip off the bottom of the toilet. I almost fell to my knees but happened to grab the toilet paper dispenser and pull myself back up.

I re-adjusted my feet, firming them up against the toilet again, not sure how long I could hold the door closed.

I reached into the pocket of my sweatshirt and carefully grabbed two puffballs out of the bag. I wasn't going to risk using just one puffball on the two of them. I put one in each hand, making sure the opening of each puffball was facing away from my face.

With my back pressed firmly against the door, I quickly reached both arms up above my head, making sure both puffballs were now facing out and over the top of the door.

I took a deep breath and that's right when Buzz hit the door again... this time I could tell Trent was joining in.

The pressure of the door hitting my back made me clench every part of my body. I realized it had also made me squeeze the puffballs.

My back was sore and I was seeing stars from the last hit to the door. I wasn't sure if I had accidentally breathed in some of the puffball smoke and that's what was causing the stars.

"Hold your breath, Olly," I remembered Truffle's words.

On the other side of the door, I could hear heavy breathing – and then some wheezing and coughing.

"What the heck is happ..en..ing..." I could hear Buzz say. Trent was coughing so hard he couldn't get any words out. It went oddly silent for about 5 seconds, and then it started...

Screaming... the type of screaming that you hear in horror movies. Blood-curdling screams coming from both Buzz and Trent. Surely, people in the cafeteria had to hear their screams – that's how loud they were. I had to hold my ears they were so loud.

I realized I had been holding my breath for a while and didn't have much time left before I had to suck in some air.

I have to get out of here.

I pulled open the door, crouching down in case any fists were coming at me.

Instead, Buzz was screaming and trying for dear life to hold onto Trent – hallucinating that Trent could somehow save him. And Trent was screaming and trying to push Buzz off, acting as if Buzz was some scary monster. I couldn't help but laugh (without breathing) as I ran past them and out into the hall.

Once out in the hall, I bent over and took a big gasp of air.

Just as I stood up straight, I turned and noticed a crowd had just turned the corner, running from the cafeteria, wondering what all of the screaming was. At the front of the pack were Em and Chase.

Just then, the bathroom door behind me flung open, and

Trent and Buzz rolled out, still screaming as they fought with each other on the floor.

Chase asked me what was happening and I just shrugged and then looked at Em with a slight smile. Em gave me a big smile back. She knew I had used the puffballs. The crowd got larger as the screams continued.

By this time, the commotion and screaming had drawn four teachers out from the teacher's lounge and into the center of the pack of students that had gathered.

After a minute of trying to figure out what was going on, it took all four of the teachers to separate Buzz and Trent.

Mr. Moore tried to pull Trent away from Buzz, but Trent clawed at Mr. Moore's face and neck – leaving a rather large, bloody scratch mark.

The students started laughing when Buzz stopped hanging onto Trent and began clawing his way up Mrs. Flanigan's legs and waist – finally resting his head on her shoulder while whimpering like a toddler.

Three teachers worked together to drag both students into the nurse's office while Mr. Moore urged the crowd to disperse and go to their next classrooms.

Em walked up to me, leaned in, and quietly asked, "puffball?"

"Two!" I replied with a grin.

"Dang, those ARE powerful. I almost feel bad for them."

"Don't, I'll explain later," I replied while shaking my head, and we went to our next class together.

Once in class, I was able to quietly explain to Em how Truffle had saved my butt by giving me those puffballs, "I would have two black eyes and a few missing teeth, otherwise."

A half-hour passed, and we heard two ambulances pulling up to the school, sirens blaring. This worried me and made me start to think that maybe I had caused them injury. Em assured me that the EMS had to be called to check them out – just to cover the school's butt.

By the time the sixth period rolled around, the PA system clicked on, interrupting class and signaling an announcement from the principal.

"Your attention, please. Many of you witnessed a sad event at lunchtime today. Two of our students decided to experiment with some type of hallucinogenic drug, not only harming each other but also injuring two teachers. Both students are now at the hospital recovering. Our school has zero tolerance for any type of drug use, and these students will be punished according to the rules as outlined in our student handbook – which you all signed at the beginning of the year. Remember, kids... say no to drugs!"

Before the loudspeaker crackled off, the principal mumbled something like "Darn stupid kids...," not realizing the microphone had not yet been fully turned off. This made everyone in our class, including the teacher, chuckle out loud.

"I guess we don't have to worry about Buzz and Trent harassing us at school for a while," Em whispered across the aisle.

The rest of the day consisted of people telling their versions of what they had seen and what they thought had happened to Buzz and Trent. The stories grew more and more exaggerated by the time the last bell rang. I think I even heard a freshman saying something about Buzz and Trent being part of an alien abduction. I just kept my mouth shut, trying to make sure nobody remembered I was near the bathroom when it all began.

Em and I laughed the entire ride back home, wishing we could be there when the school told Buzz and Trent's parents about today's events. We also took bets on what their punishment would be. Em and I finally agreed that it had to at least be a two-week suspension.

Just before heading separate ways on our bikes, we came up with a good excuse to meet at my house tomorrow around 6:30 p.m. so we could make it into the tunnels to meet Cremini on time. We would tell our parents we were going to the football game, and then out for pizza at Salvatore's Pizza Parlor afterward. I knew my parents were going out tomorrow night, so we would be able to get into the hidden room under the stairs without having to enter through another tunnel.

I got home, and right when I walked through the front door, Mom and Dad were sitting on the couch waiting to grill me with questions about what had happened today.

I guess word does travel fast in Littleton.

"So, what happened to Trent and Buzz at school today, Olly? We want to hear everything!" Mom asked.

"It was actually kind of funny, Mom. Well, not funny that they were doing drugs, but that they were acting so crazy. They were rolling on the floor screaming. Trent was doing everything to get Buzz off him, and all Buzz wanted to do was hug Trent. Then Buzz hugged Mrs. Flanigan and cried on her shoulder. Trent lashed out at a teacher and scratched his face."

"I guess living with someone like Henry Dalton as your father takes its toll," Dad said.

135

"Well, all I know is that Em and I don't need to worry about them bothering us at school for a while. Speaking of Em, she and I are going to the football game together tomorrow, and then we will probably grab some pizza at Sal's with some friends – Em said it's the best pizza in Littleton."

"That sounds like fun, Olly. There's money in the cabinet above the sink in the kitchen – make sure you treat Em to pizza tomorrow," Mom said.

"Thanks! I have a lot of homework already so I am going up to my room to get some of it done before dinner."

I didn't have much homework, but I wanted to spend some time studying the map and statue Poppy had given me before we met with Cremini tomorrow.

13. THE GRAND CAVERN

I woke up early and noticed the map still spread out at the bottom of my bed. The statue sat safely on my side table, and it was almost as if it was staring at me.

I folded the map, grabbed the statue, and carefully put them away in my closet.

It's finally Friday.

I was sure Em was just as excited as I was, and she probably woke up just as early - in anticipation of the day to come.

I took my time getting ready for school, then went downstairs to watch the morning news to see if there was any mention of the event with Trent and Buzz at the high school. Sure enough, Buzz's dad was being interviewed by the local news, and he claimed his "poor son" must have been given some bad food. You could tell he was already starting to lay the groundwork for a lawsuit against the high school cafeteria, or at least some cover story to prevent his son from looking like a drug addict.

Buzz and Trent better not get off that easy.

I was so focused on the news coverage, I had forgotten to eat the breakfast Mom had set in front of me, and it was just about time for Em to swing by. I scarfed down the eggs and took a few bites of the bagel, and grabbed my backpack.

"Bye, Mom and Dad! Don't forget... I am going to the game and then for pizza with Em tonight!"

"Love you, Olly! Dad and I probably won't see you until late tonight... we're doing a date night near Harvard University, and will be leaving just before you get home from school," Mom said.

I shut the door behind me, and sure enough, Em was waiting for me outside.

"Three weeks it is, Olly!" Em said.

"Three weeks for what?" I replied.

"Buzz and Trent – they got two weeks of suspension out of school, then detention in Mr. Moore's room after school for another week. That gives us three weeks of not having to worry about them. Plus, they are already on thin ice with the school, so they won't do anything to us while on school grounds after that."

I didn't realize how relaxed that would make me feel.

"That's amazing! Remind me to thank Truffle again when we see him tonight."

"I can't wait," Em said with an ear-to-ear smile.

We tried to beat our record time to school... we wanted to hear everyone talking about the day before and what Buzz and Trent's punishment was going to be.

Pulling into the school, we happened across Chase at the front door.

"Guess I get a break and you won't be needing my services for a few weeks?" Chase laughed.

"I can always find something for you to do," Em replied with a smirk and her hands on her hips.

I told Chase I appreciated him and his friends watching out for us. He smiled and patted me on the shoulder.

"It's been a pleasure for us, Olly! We're looking forward to picking up where we left off in a few weeks. I haven't had this much fun terrorizing Buzz and Trent in a long time," Chase assured me.

The rest of the day flew by, mostly because we didn't do any schoolwork. Most of the teachers spent their class time talking about what had happened – trying to get all of the different accounts of the story.

Our health teacher, Mr. Spencer, was the only one who tried to teach us something – albeit teaching us about the dangers of experimenting with drugs. I laughed to myself as I envisioned a poster showing up on his wall – one of Buzz and Trent hugging, along with the slogan "This is your brain on drugs" underneath their photo.

At the end of the day, Em and I rode together most of the way back to my house. Em split off just before we got to the bottom of Oak Hill. She had to go home first to get dressed into something nice for the feast with Cremini and his family. It also would help sell the story to her mom that we were going to the game and for pizza afterward.

I hadn't thought about dressing up, so I was glad she pointed out that this feast might be more than just a meal at a kitchen table. I realized I should put on a nice pair of pants and one of my three new shirts for the special night.

I got home and noticed Dad's car was gone - my parents had already left for the night. I pulled my bike into the woods at the edge of the property, just in case they came home early. If my bike was at the house, they would have wondered how I had gotten to the football game.

I took a shower and put on my new khaki pants – which were just a little too long. I decided to go with the new green polo shirt – which my mom said 'went perfectly with my beautiful hazel eyes.'

I put the special key to the hidden door into my pocket and stared into the mirror.

Not too shabby!

In the reflection, I noticed the hat that Poppy had been wearing when he was killed. I had hung it on a shelf by the closet. It was the one made of bark from a white birch tree. It still looked in fairly good condition, although the pine needles would probably need replacing soon.

I decided that I would bring the hat to the feast, in honor of Poppy.

Just as I grabbed the hat off the hook, I heard the doorbell downstairs ringing. I sprinted down the four flights of stairs and could see Em's outline through the stained glass window on the side of the front door. I wasn't sure if my heart was beating from the sprint, or from seeing Em through the window. I gave myself a second to catch my breath and check my hair one more time in the hall mirror.

"Coming!"

I opened the door and instantly felt warm inside. Em looked stunning.

She was wearing a sundress – off-white and covered in small pink flowers. A blue denim jacket and tan cowboy boots topped off the outfit. She had straightened the curls out of her red hair, aside from one braid that she had pulled across the front of her hairline. It almost looked like a tiara. In the braid, she had randomly placed small clover flowers.

I guess I was staring for longer than I had thought because she laughed at me.

"Do I look okay? Are you going to invite me in?" Em asked.

"I'm sorry, Em. You just look... I mean..." I stammered. "I haven't seen you this dressed up before."

"I clean up pretty well, I know. You look handsome as well. What's with the hat?"

"Oh, this was Poppy's hat. He used to wear it into town and was wearing it the day he died. I thought I would bring it to the feast in memory of him."

"That's a great idea, Olly. You should wear it – I am sure Cremini would love to see you in your grandfather's hat."

"Yeah, maybe I will... but first, let's get that bike put away."

I stepped past her and pushed her bike out to the edge of the tree line where I had hidden my bike. I came back and realized it was already starting to turn to dusk, which meant it was almost 7 p.m.

"You ready for this, Em?"

"I've been looking forward to this all week. Let's go!"

We walked into the hallway and I knelt and placed the key in the hole. The hidden door clicked open. I pulled the door open wide and stepped inside first so I could turn on the lights.

The lights blinked on and off, then flickered on again with a slight buzzing sound. Em walked past me and we had to hug slightly to reposition ourselves on the top step.

I reached past Em and pulled the door shut, making sure I heard the click telling me it was locked and hidden again. As I reached past, I could tell she had put some perfume on for the occasion.

I smiled, and then started walking down the stairs in front of Em... just in case she slipped in her boots, which might not have been the best wardrobe selection considering the slightly damp stairs.

The smell in the room at the bottom of the stairs was different this time. Em noticed it, too.

"It smells like someone is baking, Olly," Em said.

"I smell it, too... and it's making me hungry."

We got to the big map on the wall, and I pulled at the wooden frame on the edge of the map. The map on the wall creaked open, we looked in and there stood Cremini, smiling. Em and I both smiled back at him.

Em noticed something before I had noticed it... "You look very nice tonight, Cremini! And I like your new cap."

"Well, thank you, Ember! You two look stunning as

well," Cremini said with a small bow.

I had just noticed that Cremini was wearing what looked to be a jacket with small black pearl buttons down the front. His hat was no longer the red cap, but rather a dark brown cap with white spots, slightly smaller than his red one. The tone of his body looked whiter, although it might just have been that he was wearing darker clothes, or maybe he had cleaned himself up for the feast.

"Are you two ready for the big night?" he asked.

I turned to Em and back to Cremini and answered for both of us, "Yes, we've been excited to meet the rest of your family."

"Then, please follow me!" Cremini said as he swiveled on one foot and started walking to the right, down a part of the tunnel we had not yet visited.

As we walked, I remembered that I wanted to thank Cremini, and his son, for saving me twice now.

"Thank you for saving Em and me out at Tophet's Swamp the other day. And I can't wait to thank Truffle for the puffballs. They came in handy yesterday. I might have been bruised and missing some teeth tonight if it weren't for you two."

"Oh yeah, Truffle told me he had given them to you just in time… I heard they worked wonders on Buzz and his friend! Those things have come in quite handy for me and Truffle on several occasions. Oh, by the way, I assume Fizzy has also gotten back to her normal self?"

"Yes, unfortunately. She has been napping a little more than usual, but she seems just fine."

As we walked through the tunnel, the smell of baking

food became even stronger.

"Smells like someone has been cooking up a storm," Em mentioned.

"You have no idea... my wife, Bella, uses the feast as an excuse to show off her cooking skills to the whole community. You will get to try many of her specialties tonight. I hope you are both hungry!" Cremini said, rubbing his stomach as he talked about the food.

Cremini abruptly stopped and turned around.

"We're here!"

Em and I both looked at each other. We seemed to have stopped halfway down the tunnel, but there wasn't anything to see, even with the lights illuminating the tunnel.

"Do you have your key, Olly?" Cremini asked, pointing to a small keyhole in the wall just above the floor of the tunnel. Next to the keyhole was a small opening, just large enough for Cremini to fit through.

Looking closer, I could see the faint outline of the mushroom and half-circle of ivy symbol – exactly like the one near our hidden door in the hallway at the house.

"You do the honors this time, Em!" I said with a smile, handing Em the key.

Em got very excited, grabbed the key from my hand, and bent down to push the key into the hole. With a turn, we heard the familiar click, and the door in the wall of the tunnel separated slightly.

I reached into the crack and pulled the door away from the wall. I could tell the door was very heavy, but it slid open easily as it seemed perfectly balanced on the hinges holding it to the wall. A simple pull and the door swung out to reveal another tunnel – but this one did not have string lights hanging from the ceiling – it seemed to be illuminated by a bluish glow coming from around the bend ahead.

A rush of fresh air and a slightly earthy scent mixed with baked food came pouring out of the entrance. Cremini had already started walking ahead – obviously excited by the thought of his wife's cooking.

Em stepped through the door and I followed, pulling the door closed behind us. Em grabbed my hand, and I decided to put Poppy's hat on, so I would have a free hand to touch the walls.

"That looks cute on you!" Em said with a wink. I smiled back, a little embarrassed about how big it was on my head.

I reached out to touch the wall and it was dry and slightly warm to the touch... which was surprising to me. I fully expected it to be damp and cold, like some of the other tunnels we had traveled during Cremini's previous tour.

This tunnel was smaller than the one we had just left but still big enough for me and Em to walk side-by-side, standing straight up. Cremini had walked so fast, he was already making his way around the turn of the tunnel ahead of us, which was illuminated in the blue light. Em and I sped up our steps to keep up.

We turned the bend and the tunnel grew bigger and glowed an even brighter blue. Em and I stepped through some strange moss hanging from the ceiling. It was unlike anything I had ever seen – the moss was glowing blue. We both reached out to touch it, and when we did, it pulsed a brighter blue, as if it was reacting to our touch. We passed underneath the blue moss and both stopped at the same time, staring in awe.

We were at the entrance of a grand cavern. It was immense and surprisingly bright for being completely underground. I had no idea how a cavern this large could fit under Oak Hill.

We both looked up to the ceiling of the cavern, to see where the blue light was coming from. The same strange blue moss-like substance hung from the cavern ceiling, much like stalactites, in patches that spanned the entire length of the cavern. It glowed and reminded me of thousands of lightning bugs hanging from the ceiling and the walls – glowing blue instead of yellow. Some of it clung to the cavern walls, too, almost like sconces, illuminating the lower portions of the cavern.

The blue moss pulsed every so often and illuminated the entire place with a color that made me feel warm inside. It made the whole place feel alive.

In-between the blue moss clumps on the ceiling were inter-twined roots, which almost looked as though they had been grown purposefully. The roots looked to have been shaped to form wooden rafters crisscrossing the cavern's ceiling. The pattern appeared to make a structure that added strength to the cavern's ceiling, but it was beautiful and artistic at the same time.

Dug out of the walls of the cavern were small circular doors, spaced a few feet apart from each other, in evenly-spaced rows. Each door had a colorful, translucent curtain that obscured the interior, but I could make out from the shadows cast against the curtains that many had chairs and tables inside.

Those must be their homes.

There was also a root system that clung to the walls, connecting each of the homes to an intricate system of walkways. The walkways made their way from the doors of the homes, down to the ground level. In the larger roots, I could make out carvings. Carvings of Spores dancing, working, laughing, and caring for animals. Some of the carvings were large, and others were smaller and hardly noticeable. But they were everywhere and looked like they had been carved over a long period of time, as some seemed to have stretched as the roots grew.

I was so excited about the blue moss and root system, that my eyes hadn't noticed all of the activity happening around the cavern. Spore families, looking very much like Cremini, were making their way down the root walkways, heading toward the lower level of the cavern. They were accompanied by a variety of animals – rabbits, squirrels and I even spotted a skunk.

All of the Spores looked to have mushroom caps on – albeit in all different colors, patterns, and sizes. Certain groups stuck together closely and shared similar hats.

The colored hats must represent a family unit in some way.

Through the center of the cavern was a winding creek that curled its way through a large, bright-green moss carpet wrapping both sides of the creek. There were small hills that obscured the view of the rest of the cavern further down.

The sound of the creek was calming as it gurgled its way past us, and out through an intricately-carved gateway to our right. Above the gateway was the now-familiar design – the mushroom with the half-circle arch of leaves above it. I could only guess from that symbol the waterway must have been another entrance or exit that made its way outside the cavern.

About 50 feet down the creek was a stone bridge, and it looked well-built and sturdy – as if it would handle the weight of at least one, if not two adult humans. The Spore families seemed to be hurriedly crossing over the bridge, across the green moss, and over the hill. They seemed to be making their way toward an area further down in the cavern, away from where we stood.

I don't think any had noticed us entering the cavern just yet, as they seemed to talk and laugh amongst themselves as they hurried along. The flurry of small voices and laughter echoed through the cave, and I could tell by the way Em was squeezing my hand, that we both felt the excitement in the air.

A small group of three Spores broke away from a larger group and walked toward us, followed by a brown rabbit.

"Ah.... let me introduce you to my whole family," Cremini said.

Cremini's family lined up in front of us. Not sure if it was intentional, but they had lined up in order of height. The rabbit lay down in front of them.

"This is my wife and also the fabulous chef of today's feast, Bella."

Bella was shorter, and rounder, than the other Spores in Cremini's family. She had slightly pudgy cheeks which had a pink tinge to them, and she was wearing a cooking apron. Her cap, like the rest of Cremini's family, was dark brown with white spots and seemed slightly too large for the size of her head.

Bella curtsied, and then spoke with a very high-pitched voice, "It's such a pleasure to finally meet both of you! Oliver – I knew your grandfather very, very well, and he was such a friend to our family and the community. He used to talk about you and your adventures together all the time. He was so very proud of you."

"Thank you, he was a great grandpa and I am going to miss our adventures," I replied.

Bella continued, "Now, don't worry if certain foods

don't meet your taste today... there should be plenty of things to try, and you won't offend me by turning anything down. Oh, and Ember – everything is vegetarian, too... so there won't be any weird surprises like slugs or frog legs on the menu."

Em laughed and said sarcastically, "I kind of like slugs."

"I'll remember that when I am cooking for our next meal together," Bella replied with a smile.

We all laughed, and Truffle stepped forward.

"Hello again, Olly! Very nice to meet you, Ember!"

"Hello, Truffle!" I replied. "Those puffballs were a lifesaver, I owe you one for saving me from a beating ... or two, really."

"No problem at all, Olly. We try to protect our friends. And, it's fun to hear that those bullies screamed like little girls," Truffle said.

"Truffle, we have ladies present," Cremini said sternly.

"Oh, my... I am so sorry. I meant no offense, Ember. But, from what I have heard, you do not scream like a little girl either," Truffle said.

Cremini and Bella dropped their heads in embarrassment, as Em and I both started laughing out loud with Truffle.

"It takes a lot more than that to offend me, Truffle. And thank you for having our backs. I, too, owe you one for protecting Olly when I couldn't," Em said.

Cremini seemed slightly relieved and motioned toward his other child, Magpie.

"This is Magpie, Truffle's sister. She doesn't talk much,

but she is the smart one in the family."

Magpie seemed slightly younger than Truffle. She was almost a half-inch shorter than him and was too shy to look up at us. She did attempt a curtsy. She was thin and wore small overalls – a much hipper style of clothing than her mother and brother were wearing. Her overalls looked kind of like the overalls Em was wearing when I first met her…but Magpie's were a muted pink color, and almost looked like they were made from flower petals. She wore a black leather sash across her chest that had a pocket where a small set of eyeglasses were poking out. She was also carrying a small book with a black leather binding.

"Nice to meet you, Magpie," Em said.

"Hi Magpie," I said as I bowed to her.

"You've met my furry friend, Clover," Cremini said as he stepped up to the brown rabbit and scratched her ear. I could swear the rabbit bowed to both Em and me. "You saved Clover from Buzz and his mean friend on the football field. She wants to thank you."

Just as Cremini finished his sentence, Clover hopped up and proceeded to dart between my feet and then Em's, rubbing against our legs as she passed. Clover sat back down in front of Cremini's family.

"We Spores have a special bond with all animals, but we seem to bond with certain ones… Clover is like a third child of mine," said Cremini. "She's been a friend for a long time."

"Okay, enough with the introductions," Cremini said. He must have been really hungry because he cut off any further talk to remind us we had a meal to get to.

"Come on, kids… the food's going to get cold."

14. THE FEAST & THE HARVEST

We followed behind Cremini very closely, walking down and across the bridge and onto the green, mossy floor. The moss had the texture of carpet but squished more like a sponge when we walked on it. It was almost too hard to walk on because it was so spongy. Em had to stop to take off her boots for fear she might fall over and embarrass herself on our first visit.

I saw movement in the creek to my left and noticed one of the Spores floating down the river on the back of a small turtle. He steered the turtle to the shore, jumped off, and was on his way across the mossy lawn. The turtle kept swimming past us and under the bridge we had just crossed.

The few Spore families that were late making their way to the feast had just noticed us - waving and smiling at us as they scurried past us, giggling.

"They're adorable," Em whispered to me.

Cremini turned and shouted slightly, so we could hear him over the ever-growing crowd making their way down a path, "I will introduce you two when we get to the feast. I've asked them to place chairs for you, and you will be seated with my family at the head of the table."

We crested a slight hill on the mossy lawn, and as we stepped over, a large crowd of Spores hushed almost to complete silence. I noticed a few of the Spores were whispering to each other and pointing at me, specifically at the hat which I had almost forgotten I was wearing.

Cremini stopped us and then stepped a few feet in front of us, raising his arms.

"Fellow Spores, I would like to introduce our two guests of honor tonight, and I know you will all be excited to talk with them. I just ask that you let them eat first, and then you can make full introductions before the Sporing Ceremony happens. You may have noticed the beautiful young lady to my left. Meet Ember Fein – she has been canvassing the neighborhoods trying to stop the Daltons from building the mall on Oak Hill. She doesn't know it fully yet, but she has become an ally and a friend to our community through her activism."

Anyone not already standing in the crowd stood up and joined in a large celebration of claps and hoots. I looked over at Em, and she was fully blushed with all of the attention. I squeezed her hand and gave her a big smile.

After some time, Cremini calmed them all down by raising his arms once again.

"You might already recognize the young man to my right, wearing the hat Poppy used to wear during his many feasts with us. Poppy used to tell us all about his grandson, Oliver... he and his family just moved here to Oak Hill and I have a feeling he will be just as gracious as his grandfather was to our community."

Instead of a round of claps and hoots, every one of the Spores fell to a knee, removed their caps, and bowed in silence for a moment, to honor Poppy. I could instantly tell that Poppy had made as big an impression on them as he did on me.

I am not sure what prompted me, but I took off Poppy's hat, held it to my waist, and bowed in mutual respect to all of them. I just knew in my heart that Poppy had a great reason to protect their secret, and I vowed to myself that I would continue with his mission.

When I bowed to them, they got back up to standing and let out a large cheer, welcoming us to the feast. The cheering was so loud, I feared their cheers would be heard outside the cavern and by anyone walking out on Oak Hill. Cremini didn't seem worried and he added a few hoots himself.

It was when I straightened up that I noticed a long table extending a good 40 feet down the mossy cavern floor. On each side were hundreds of small chairs intended for the Spores. The table was made from a long, hewn piece of timber, flattened on one side and set on the ground. The chairs looked like human chairs, just much smaller.

At the head of the table, a taller section of table had been added to accommodate larger chairs for me and Em. Our chairs were beautifully crafted and almost looked as though they were thrones. They were made of beautiful red oak, stained and polished. Long, straight pine branches made up the back supports. At the top of one of the chairs, they had affixed clumps of colorful pink clovers. I assumed this was Em's chair, and it went perfectly with her outfit. Flumes of pine needles topped my chair, and I realized that my hat wasn't going to look so out of place after all.

Cremini motioned to our chairs and asked us to take a seat.

It wasn't until we sat in the chairs, with all of the Spores joining us, that the full beauty of the place got to me.

"I feel like I am in a dream," I whispered to Em.

153

"Pinch me," she replied.

I saw a bird fly from one root to another in the ceiling overhead, and it looked rather small – making me realize just how high the cavern ceiling was. And there had to be at least 300 homes carved into the walls of the cavern, which I could fully see end-to-end now.

Cremini stood again and hushed everyone.

"It's time once again for all of us to participate in another Autumn Feast, a tradition we celebrate before welcoming in our newest Spore community members. We pray tonight's Sporing celebration will once again bless us with another great harvest... as it has in years past. With this wonderful meal made by my beautiful wife, Bella, we want to remember the friend we had in Poppy, and the new friends we have in Ember and Oliver. Let's raise our glasses."

Em and I both noticed a wooden mug that had been set in front of our place settings, filled with something dark and slightly red.

"Don't worry, we just filled yours with our version of fruit punch," Bella whispered to us with a wink.

Em and I both lifted our glasses.

"To a great Sporing!" Cremini yelled out loud, then took a big sip from his cup.

"Harvest bless us," the crowd yelled in a thunderous reply, then took a long drink from their mugs.

I took a small sip and it tasted wonderful. It was sweet and tart and tasted like concord grape juice combined with cherries and some strange spice I had never tasted before.

Em had already downed hers and turned to me with a

smile, letting me know she liked it, too. I noticed her teeth were dyed a slight purple color from the juice, and I laughed at her.

"What?" Em asked.

"Oh, nothing, I just like to see you so happy," I said as I took another larger gulp and smiled back with the same purple teeth.

Trays of food started being passed around the long table in a clockwise pattern. When they reached our end of the table, I picked it up from the lower table, took a sampling, and handed it across to Em. Em took her share and then set it down on the lower table next to her, where the food continued its way around the rest of the table.

With each tray, Bella explained what she had cooked up.

"That one is summer squash with sweet butter and acorn shavings."

"Ooh, this is one of my all-time favorites – wild baby carrot souffle with leeks and parsley. And coming up is Cremini's favorite… fresh-made corn cake with strawberry rhubarb jam on top."

Em and I took small portions of each, and with each taste, we wished we had taken more than just a sample. We were surprised at how much food there was, even when considering how many Spore families sat around the table.

As we ate, Cremini taught us about the Spore community.

"You'll notice that each family wears similar mushroom caps – it's an easy way to tell who is related to who. The cap colors will be similar among family groups… and the spots on the caps tell you the number of generations they have lived here in the community."

Cremini continued, "Your grandfather played a huge part in growing our community… after a harvest, we would take some of the new Sporlings and pair them with a foster family that was willing to move to a new community. Your grandfather would help package up and ship some of the new foster families for their journey to our other Spore communities. It is our way of safeguarding our community by creating new communities outside of Littleton, Massachusetts. With Henry Dalton's new mall looking more like a reality, we may need to eventually move our entire community elsewhere."

"Wait, did Poppy use boxes with dirt and sawdust to ship the foster families out? Did the boxes have holes in them?" I asked.

"Yes, he would prepare the boxes with comfortable sleeping compartments made of cardboard, dirt, sawdust, and moss… the holes allowed our Spores to breathe on the two- to three-day trip. The journey could be rough due to the clumsiness of some of our friends at the postal service. I had almost convinced your grandfather to stop writing "FRAGILE" on the boxes because that just seemed to encourage the postal workers to throw them around a bit more. One of the families we shipped out wrote back and said their box was assaulted by a few of the younger mail couriers. Seems they were working on the back dock of the postal facility and started an impromptu game of hockey, with our shipping box being their puck. Luckily, they weren't very good hockey players and no one was injured too badly. Your grandpa started beefing up the packing materials after that incident."

"Em, that's what our hidden room was for… Poppy would assemble the boxes there and walk them into town to ship them off," I said.

"Yes, he and I were coming back from one of those shipments when we were hit by the truck, Olly," Cremini said sadly.

"We still haven't heard any more news about who did that," I added.

"I can pretty much bet it was Henry Dalton's goon. He drives a large truck, and Henry had a reason to get rid of your grandfather. Henry had repeatedly propositioned your grandfather to purchase half of Oak hill… the half that our community is sitting on. Your grandfather did everything he could to deter Henry and went as far as deeding the property to your parents so there would be no issues upon his death. We even believe Henry Dalton has paid off a couple of the council members to vote for eminent domain – basically giving Henry the property for the supposed benefit of the community," Cremini said.

"I didn't get a good feeling when I met Mr. Dalton, and I know my father dislikes him, too. He hasn't liked him since they were students together at Littleton High School. Mr. Dalton even proposed to buy our property when we first got into Littleton. He offended my mom in the process. My dad said he would think about it – but that was just so my dad could buy time to find ways to legally block him," I said.

"Olly, we are trying to figure out our options, but haven't had any good ideas to date. Things are getting dire. I hear the council meeting is coming up quickly, and the vote to give Oak Hill to Henry Dalton will quickly follow. It's not like we can expose our community, and without your grandfather fighting for us, we are left with few options. We may need you and Ember to help ship us all away from Oak Hill to another community – if the development plans go through. It will be sad to lose hundreds of years of history here on Oak Hill – the worst part is that townsfolk have no idea what they would be losing. We have been protecting the land and the animals in these parts for a long time."

"We will figure something out, Cremini, we promise…" Em said, looking at me with a mix of fear and anger in her eyes. "We will take on the fight and still make sure we keep your secrets."

"I agree, Cremini. If Poppy was behind you, I am too!" I said.

"So, Cremini, out of curiosity… when we first got to the Oak Hill house, we received a package from someone named Amanita from Littleton, Colorado. It had gold nuggets in it. What was that for?" I asked.

"Amanita, like your grandfather, is a community ambassador. She helps one of our newest communities just outside Littleton, Colorado, set in the front range of the Rockies. They established their community in an abandoned 1800s gold mine that has since been hidden from the public. As they dig into the tunnel to make their new homes, they send back gold nuggets to help pay for the supplies and shipping costs needed to ship out new foster families. Gold has little use to them, so it is just their way they could thank Amanita and your grandpa – it more than covers the costs of keeping our operation going. Your grandpa would use the gold to fund the shipping of our Spore families, and for buying supplies for us down at the hardware store and around town," Cremini said.

"Em and I can continue helping with that. We will have to get creative and get the gold shipments before my parents do. We'll also have to hide our shopping trips so they don't ask questions."

"Thank you both, you can't believe how much stress it takes off me and the community knowing you two are willing to take over the work that your grandpa used to do."

A few members of the Spore community began walking up to introduce themselves and made sure that I knew how much my grandpa helped them. It was nice to hear stories about Poppy, and how he affected others. It took a good hour to talk with all of them.

Cremini stood again, raised his arms, and clapped three times. Everyone turned to Cremini, and silence took over the entire cavern.

"The moon is almost overhead, and it is time to proceed to the harvest room."

The Spores all jumped from their seats and excitedly headed off into a side tunnel that I hadn't noticed before… probably because the tunnel entrance was covered by the hanging blue moss. With the excitement I noticed the blue moss in the cavern started pulsating a bit quicker than before.

Em and I looked at each other, not knowing what was happening.

"It's time to show you how our community flourishes. It's a magical experience and it will show you both how our community has grown through the generations. Follow me," Cremini said as he started walking toward the tunnel.

We walked behind a large group of Spores as they traveled through a short tunnel and into another large room. This room was circular, and there were rows of seats carved out of the stone walls around the room – it reminded me of an amphitheater, but built for smaller visitors. The seats were too small for us, so Em and I just sat on some moss near the entrance of the room. In the center of the room was the trunk of a large oak tree, about eight feet in diameter, on a small island that was encircled by two creeks. The creeks split apart on one side of the trunk and then rejoined again on the other side before leaving the room through another marked gateway. In the center of the island, mixed amongst the roots of the oak's trunk, was the blue moss, pulsating in waves of light.

I turned to Em and grabbed her hand.

The room went quiet, and I heard a rustling toward the ceiling where the tree trunk touched the ceiling. Roots were entangling each other at the top of the trunk near the ceiling, and they started to move and appeared to unravel themselves. As they did, some dirt and dead leaves fell from the ceiling to the floor, and I could see the sky and stars start to appear from above.

It's a huge skylight.

The roots unraveled faster, exposing the full moon, and the rest of the oak tree as it extended almost 100 feet out of the cavern and into the sky. When the roots stopped moving, Cremini stood and the entire room fell silent again.

"We come to the Sporing Oaks twice a year to ask for a plentiful harvest," said Cremini, loud enough so the entire room could hear him. "We should be thankful for any Sporlings as they are all a blessing from our maker."

He began walking toward a small wooden bridge that crossed one of the creeks. It was then that I noticed something very familiar at the foot of the bridge. There stood a small stone mushroom statue, almost identical to the one I had been given by Mr. Fitzgibbons in his law offices.

Cremini carefully picked up the stone statue and walked across the wooden bridge. Near the base of the oak tree, there was a spot illuminated by a moonbeam from above. Cremini carefully set the stone statue dead-center of the moonlit spot.

The moon's light shone down and refracted through the clear glass cap sitting atop the mushroom statue.

It was beautiful... the only way I could describe it is like the lights of a Christmas tree reflecting through a glass ornament. The rays were a bluish color and sprayed across different parts of the moss around the base of the oak tree.

Cremini quickly stepped back across the bridge and turned to watch along with all of the other Spores, who sat quietly in anticipation.

At first, nothing happened. Em and I shrugged at each other wondering if the Spores were seeing something that we weren't. But then, one by one, small white objects started popping up in some of the spots where the moon rays touched the blue, pulsing moss. It started slowly, and then the objects sprouted faster. I counted nine of the small white stems randomly spaced across the moss. They were miniature Spores, without caps, and they wriggled slightly where they stood. As each one moved, you could hear some of the Spores in the audience gasp in excitement.

I turned to Em and whispered, "They're baby Spores. What did Cremini call them… Sporlings?"

Em shook her head in agreement, and I noticed her eyes were tearing up.

As the moon moved across the sky, the reflections through the statue changed and started to dim. Eventually, the moon moved over the leaf canopy of the large oak tree and was no longer casting light down into the room.

Six groups of Spore families came down and crossed the bridge, standing near the new Sporlings that were still wriggling in the moss. They carefully picked up their Sporlings and wrapped them in what looked to be the leaves from a water cabbage. Some of the families picked up only one Sporling, and others picked up two. I assumed there was some planning in advance to determine which families would take on more Sporlings than others.

As the Spore families coddled their new Sporlings, the rest of the Spores in the audience began cheering.

When the Sporlings had all been swaddled, the roots in the ceiling began to wrap around each other and pull together, closing the opening around the large oak tree like a big drawstring. The skylight was closing as if on cue.

Cremini walked back up to where we were and gave his wife a big hug.

"It was a great harvest, Bella," said Cremini with what looked to be a tear in his eye.

Bella was already in tears, and she wiped her face in her apron. "The makers outdid themselves this harvest."

Cremini turned to me and Em.

"You two must be good luck. We have never had more than six Sporlings at any harvest. We've been given nine this season," said Cremini.

Em and I got caught up in the excitement and hugged each other. I looked down and noticed Truffle and Magpie were both hugging Em's ankle. This had been the best night ever.

I turned to Cremini. "Cremini, that stone statue… I was given one just like it by Poppy's lawyer."

"Yes, your grandpa and I felt it would be a good idea to store the second statue separately from the one we have here in our community, just to be safe. We will eventually ship your statue to the community in Colorado so they can have their harvests. For now, would you mind keeping it safe? Without them, we can't have a harvest… and they are very hard to come by as you can imagine. We can make a new one, but it takes quite a few years to get them just right," said Cremini.

"Of course. I'm glad I asked… I was about to put it in the garden outside our front door as a decoration," I said with a sarcastic smile.

Cremini and Em both looked at me in faked disgust and shook their heads.

"I know you are kidding, else I would deliver you right to Buzz Dalton's front step so he can continue to torture you," said Cremini.

"I'd help carry you over there," said Em.

"Tough crowd!" I said chuckling.

It was then that I realized quite a bit of time had passed, and it was getting close to when my parents would be getting home.

"Oh no, my parents will be home soon and will wonder where we are, so we need to get going."

"Of course! You and Em are always welcome to use the tunnels to visit us anytime you would like. I will need some help shipping off these new Sporlings and their new foster families in the coming week. I can have Truffle let you know when it's time," Cremini said.

"Of course!" Em and I both shook our heads emphatically.

With that, Cremini let out a sigh of relief and continued, "I assume you have seen enough of the tunnels to be able to make your way home? It's my job to welcome in the new Sporlings, so it would be rude of me to leave now." Cremini said.

"I can take Olly and Ember back through the tunnels!" Truffle interjected.

With that, Magpie scooted over and grabbed Truffle's hand. "I guess now it is WE can take them," said Truffle.

Cremini agreed. Em, Truffle, Magpie, and I left the room and made our way through the grand cavern and out into the tunnels.

As the four of us entered the tunnels, where it was much quieter, I thought it would be a good time to talk about the upcoming deadline for the mall development.

"So, Truffle and Magpie, do you have any ideas about how to stop the mall development?" I asked.

"We've been trying to figure that out, but aside from doing harmful things to the Daltons (which would go against our morals) we haven't come up with anything," said Truffle. "If you two come up with any ideas, I am all ears… I don't really have ears, but you get the point."

Em and I both wanted to laugh at Truffle, but the thought of everything we saw tonight being destroyed put a damper on our humor.

"Let us see what we can come up with, Truffle," Em said with a serious look.

With that, Truffle and Magpie both bowed and said their goodbyes, then turned back to return to the Sporing ceremony.

Em and I were both quiet on the walk back to the hidden room. I knew we were both deep in thought.

"It's the weekend, let's get together to explore the rest of Oak Hill and see if there is anything that would give us ideas about stopping the Daltons," I said.

"Sounds great! I'll come over around 10 in the morning."

We made our way back upstairs through the hidden room and luckily arrived before my parents returned. I walked Em out to her bike at the edge of the woods. I was just about to say goodbye when Em quickly turned, grabbed me by my shoulders, and landed a kiss on my lips. I honestly wasn't expecting it, and I wasn't sure how to kiss a girl, so I could only imagine that it was a pretty awkward experience for Em.

"I'm sorry… I wasn't expecting that," I said as my face turned red.

"That's the best kind of kiss, Olly. See you tomorrow, bright and early."

With that, she jumped on her bike and peddled off.

It was difficult to get to sleep that night. It was probably due to a combination of everything Em and I got to see, my first kiss with Em, and also because my parents would be harassing me for details about my "date" with Em. Luckily, I had already come up with a solid story about what we were supposedly doing that night. I made up some details about sitting with our friends Kylie, Chase, and Brielle at the football game, followed by a stop at the pizza place. My mom would make sure to ask if I had paid for Em's dinner, and of course, I would say yes.

As I expected, Mom and Dad got home only 10 minutes after Em had left. I had to stay up another 30 minutes because they both wanted to hear every detail of my night. I told my mom about the kiss with Em, and that seemed to get her mind off of all of the other details of the night. My dad just replied with a grin on his face and a wink behind Mom's back.

15. THE OAK HILL MAP

As I had anticipated, my parents left the house early Saturday morning to go and pick up some things from town.

I was up at 8 a.m. and had already put together a backpack containing the key to the tunnels, the map of Oak Hill along with a bagged lunch and water bottles for me and Em. I figured we could end up at Lookout Rock and share a lunch overlooking Littleton. I looked forward to walking around the whole property since I hadn't had a chance to see it all yet.

Em promptly rang the doorbell at 10 a.m.

"Good morning, sunshine!" Em said when I opened the door.

"Right back at you! Sounds like you're ready for this!"

"YES! I hardly slept a wink last night. It was tough not to tell my mom any of the magical things we saw, but I would never."

"Same here. I had a fun night explaining everything we 'supposedly' did at the football game and the pizza place… my mom wouldn't let me go to bed until she had every detail. We may need to sync up the details of our stories today, just in case she starts asking you questions the next time she sees you."

"Probably a good idea. So, where do we want to start our tour of Oak Hill?"

"Let's start in the garden and greenhouse, then go out above the Sporing Oaks to see where that big oak tree is that we saw last night during the harvest. I thought we could do lunch on Lookout Rock and then jump into one of the tunnels to check out the other entrances we haven't yet seen. It would be good to know where they all are in case we ever need to make another quick escape."

"Sounds like a good plan, especially the part about lunch on Lookout Rock."

At the foot of the front steps was a cobblestone pathway that led to the driveway, but also broke off around the side of the house toward the backyard. Em and I followed the pathway around the house until it ended at a stone archway. The archway was made of yellow sandstone and had an iron gate for a door. It opened to the small garden courtyard behind the house. The sandstone archway and tall arbor vitae shrubs created a natural wall that seemed to protect the whole garden area. The iron gate was intricately designed and at the top was the now-familiar design – a mushroom surrounded by a semi-circle of ivy. This gate didn't have a lock on it, though. It opened easily with a slight push, exposing a beautiful cobblestoned courtyard with a stone fountain in the middle. The fountain had not been running for some time as it had green water festering in it. It reminded me that my grandma probably wasn't able to tend to the garden after she got sick. The flower beds that lined the outside of the courtyard were overgrown but still looked beautiful with a mix of multi-colored perennial wildflowers popping through the weeds. At the other end of the courtyard was a small greenhouse that also looked unkempt. The glass was so dirty you could hardly see inside.

We opened the door to the greenhouse and peeked inside. If the glass was clean and the sun was allowed in, it would have been a beautiful place to grow things. There were vibrant, hand-painted pots on the shelves lining the perimeter of the greenhouse, but many of the plants within the pots seemed to have withered a slow death or showed no sign of life at all.

Another casualty of Grandma's sickness.

Out of the corner of my eye, I saw some dirt fall out of one of the pots on an upper shelf at the far end of the greenhouse.

I nudged Em's arm and pointed to the corner, motioning to let her know something was moving back there. We quietly walked toward the back corner.

Just before we got to the pot, a small, red mushroom cap sprang up from the dirt. Just as it pushed through, the pot started to tip and fall off the shelf where it had been precariously set.

I leaped forward just as the pot started to tumble, catching it mid-air, but also spilling its contents to the ground.

There in the pile of dirt on the ground sat Truffle and Magpie, trying to shake off the fall and wipe the dirt from their clothes. They were embarrassed as their cheeks had a tinge of pink to them.

"You poor things, are you okay?" Em asked as she picked each up separately and brushed the remaining dirt from their clothes and caps.

"Oh yes, sorry about that. That was a bit embarrassing!" Truffle said. Magpie just looked down as if she was going to be scolded.

"What are you two doing in that pot, Truffle?" I asked.

"I guess we wanted to follow along with you two as you explored the hill, but that plan went to pot," Truffle said, laughing at his pun. "I didn't want to intrude and be a third wheel, and then Magpie demanded I bring her along."

Em and I both looked at each other and laughed.

"We would love to have you two tag along with us," Em said with a smile, and she placed Truffle and Magpie on her shoulders. "Are you two able to hang on up here okay?"

"Oh yes, this is much easier than holding onto my rabbit," Truffle said. Magpie nodded with a smile.

"It looks like we're now the four musketeers!" I said, turning to leave the greenhouse.

Imagining us as the four musketeers made me miss Poppy. I realized Poppy's sense of adventure and imagination still lived within me. That made me smile.

I extended my arm out as if I was holding an imaginary saber in my hand. "All for one and one for all, united we stand divided we fall!" I yelled.

If Em, Truffle, and Magpie don't already think I'm weird, they probably do now.

Em interrupted that thought, yelling "Besides we are men (and WOMEN), and after all, it is our business to risk our lives."

I was dumbstruck, and Em noticed it.

"I have been in drama club for the last three years, Olly. I know the story of the three musketeers like the back of my musketeer-gloved hand. I can quote almost every important line from Alexandre Dumas' book."

"I must say, I am overly impressed and a tad bit intimidated," I responded.

We both realized Truffle and Magpie had no idea what we were talking about, because they were just staring at each other, looking confused.

"Sorry you two, we will read the three musketeers to you sometime and this will ALL make sense," Em said. "I'm sure Olly and I can put on our best musketeer costumes and make quite an event of it."

We left through the greenhouse and exited through the iron gate. We followed the map as best we could in the general direction of the Sporing Oaks – the place where the harvest festival took place the night before. Truffle was a big help and was able to point us in the exact direction, too. He and Magpie had grown up on Oak Hill and this was their playground.

The forests on Oak Hill were majestic. There were groves of tall, bright green pines as far as my eyes could see, and those groves opened up into large patches of tall oak trees.

We came upon an area where the ground became wet and almost marshy, and it was difficult to walk through. Em almost lost her shoes in the mud a couple of times. I noticed when we entered the area, it got eerily quiet. The birds chirping and squirrels rustling in the trees above seemed to go silent. Em seemed to have noticed it, too, as she was looking around in the tree canopy for any sign of life.

Several old trees had fallen through the years, blocking off a direct route further into the oak forest, so we had to climb over or walk around many of them to continue. After climbing a few of the larger ones, I noticed one tall Oak that stood above the others.

"That must be the Sporing Oak!" I said.

Em, Truffle and Magpie agreed and we worked our way closer to the tree. As we got closer, the ground dried up as if the tree was on a raised island within the marsh. There were no other oaks within a 50-foot radius. The base of the oak was covered in large 6-inch diameter vines that almost looked like grapevines – brown and tangled with stringy bark. There were many of them and they wound their way around the base of the tree, and then entered the ground at different places. They almost seemed to have purposefully weaved themselves into a protective blanket around the base of the tree, as if they were holding the oak to the ground.

"It even looks magical when the ground is closed," Em said.

"But, I can see why people would never happen across this tree accidentally, it's almost impossible to get to."

Truffle spoke up. "We also have a nice family of wolves that have guarded it for many generations. I saw them watching us on our way in. Luckily Magpie and I are with you, or you would have been nipped at and run off even before we entered the marsh!"

"I felt like we were being watched," I said.

"That must be why it got so quiet when we entered this area," Em said.

"Now that they have seen us together, you shouldn't

ever have any issues with them. And I'll also make sure I let them know who you two are the next chance I get," Truffle said.

"Our butts appreciate that!" Em said with a smile.

"So, the area just downhill and over from here is where the Daltons are planning to build the mall. If they build it, you can be sure this oak and our community will be exposed to surveyors, developers and curious hikers," Truffle said. "We were almost exposed when the city built the water tower just uphill from here. It took a team effort to keep the city workers to stay in the area they were working. We scared most of them from coming down here by using those puffballs, and your grandfather also added a little scare with some old Nipmuc ghost stories. Luckily, the water pipes don't go far below the ground, so they never threatened our tunnels or community. And once they finished the water tower, they hardly ever come back up here."

"Let's check out the water tower," Em said.

"It doesn't look to be too far from here, and we can get out of this wet mess and back on solid ground," I replied.

It took us a good 10 minutes to make our way uphill and out of the marshland. As we crested the top of the hill, we could see the large olive-green water tank. It was about 60 feet in diameter and about 30 feet tall and had a series of pipes leading into and out of the tank. All of the pipes seemed to disappear underground. As we got closer, we could hear flowing water, so either water was being pulled out of the tower, or it was being filled back up by a pump somewhere further down the hill. I noticed a hose reel and a few other short pipes that extended out of the tank, but they were closed off with round valves that looked like small steering wheels. They were locked in place with a chain and padlock. I could only imagine the valves and hose were put there to clean out the water tank if there was ever any need. There was a maintenance trail just large enough for a single truck, which made its way down the side of Oak Hill and toward the main road below. It had been overgrown with weeds, making it obvious nobody had been up here in quite some time.

The tower wasn't as interesting as we thought it would be, so we didn't spend much time exploring it. We decided it was time to get to Lookout Rock and eat some lunch.

We hiked along the top of Oak Hill until we found a small foot trail with an old wooden sign marked "Lookout Rock" nailed to one of the larger oaks. Within five minutes we poked through a pine barren and were standing on top of Lookout Rock. It was a series of large boulders that sat almost at the peak of Oak Hill.

"I've always loved this view. You can see to Bumblebee Meadows from here," Em said.

"That's where my grandpa, grandma, and dad had a house. My dad told me stories about him and his friend Harry and how they gathered rabbits out there in Bumblebee Meadows," I said.

"That would explain why so many of my rabbit friends live out that way," said Truffle. "I guess there are quite a few farms filled with fresh vegetables for them to eat, too."

"It's sad to think that entire side of Oak Hill might someday be a mall," I said.

"And that prairie across the road will no longer be my front yard, but rather a beautiful asphalt parking lot shining under one hundred flickering, bright overhead lights," Em replied.

"And we will no longer be able to live in the only home I

have ever known," Truffle said.

We all sat silently for a minute, staring out over the woods and as far as our eyes could see.

"I don't know about you three, but I'm starting to get hungry," I said, trying to break the sad spell.

The three of us found a flat place to set out lunch and Em took Truffle and Magpie off her shoulder so they could sit with us. I unpacked the lunch I had made, and set it out on a paper towel I had brought specifically for this purpose.

"I hope you like peanut butter and strawberry jam, Truffle and Magpie, because otherwise, you'll have to settle for some Cheetos or an apple. That's all I brought. I wasn't expecting two other mouths to feed," I said.

"We usually eat acorn butter and rhubarb spread, but I am sure peanut butter and jelly will be similar," Truffle continued with a big smile, "I guess you can't be picky... when you're in a jam."

His pun wasn't lost on Em as she started to chuckle and gave Truffle a little nudge in appreciation of his humor. I just shook my head and smiled at him. Magpie gave him a customary little sister eye roll.

I split the two sandwiches into halves and gave them to Em, Truffle, and Magpie. Truffle downed his piece so quickly I didn't even realize he was done until I went to bite into my sandwich and noticed him staring up at me.

"Wow, I guess you like peanut butter and jelly, then!" I said.

Truffle shook his head emphatically and I split off another piece of my sandwich to give him. This time I watched as he ate the piece of the sandwich in what seemed like three quick bites.

Em laughed and said, "Little guy has quite an appetite."

Magpie seemed to like the peanut butter as well, although she didn't beg for seconds. Em still gave her another helping from her sandwich.

As we were eating, I noticed a large owl swoop down through the trees in front of us, landing in a meadow further down the hill.

"I love owls… I wonder what kind that was?" I asked.

"Looked like a barn owl to me," Em replied.

"I wish it was a Short-eared Owl, I haven't seen one of them in a long time," Truffle said. "They're endangered now. Ever since people started walking dogs around Oak Hill, they seemed to have fled this area and moved out further into the countryside. They're known to build their nests in grassy areas, and I guess it is not such a safe place to have a nest when everything from Yorkies to Labradoodles are roaming nearby."

Em stood up quickly, held her hands to her head, and said loudly, "That's it! That's how we save Oak Hill! You're a genius, Truffle!"

Truffle, Magpie, and I all looked at each other, not sure what Em was talking about.

"The Short-Eared Owl!" Em said.

Once again, we all shrugged at Em, not knowing why the Short-eared Owl was getting her so riled up.

"They're ENDANGERED. If they are endangered, it is illegal to invade their nesting areas," Em said.

I had already started to put the plot together in my head,

but Em interrupted to explain the idea.

"What if we could get one or two Short-eared Owls to nest on the hillside where the Dalton Mall is supposed to be built?" Em asked.

"Then the Dalton's wouldn't be allowed to build there… ever!" I added.

"Right! And guess who we could get to do the environmental study?"

"Your mom!" I replied.

Truffle chimed in, "You're a genius, Em!"

Magpie ran over to Em and hugged her ankle. Em started to blush.

"So, the trick is… how can we get a Short-eared Owl to nest here, especially if they are endangered and difficult to find. And aside from that, how do we force one to nest exactly where we need them to in the coming week?"

"Magpie!" Truffle yelled.

"What are you talking about, Truffle?" I asked.

"Magpie is a friend to all of the birds in the area. She is the one who cares for all of their injuries. I am sure she could get some of her bird friends to fly out in search of a Short-eared Owl, and explain why we need their help. I am sure they could convince at least one owl to help us out – even just for a short period… long enough for the council to dash Dalton's hopes of building on Oak Hill," Truffle said.

Magpie gave two thumbs (or rather stubs) up.

"That's brilliant, Truffle," Em said.

It was Truffle's turn to blush.

"We don't have much time to waste. The council is meeting next week, and we won't have much time to convince them… and we will need some good evidence showing an endangered species lives here on Oak Hill," I said.

We all stood up at the same time. Everyone threw the rest of their uneaten lunches in my bag, Truffle and Magpie jumped on Em's shoulder and we started running back up the hill. Truffle pointed us through some almost indiscernible trails, which eventually led to another one of the secret entrances. This one was at the base of a huge Oak tree stump, surrounded by old grape vines and thorn bushes. The stump's circumference was at least six feet, and there was a spot on the side of the stump where the bark had completely fallen off. Truffle pointed to the small keyhole at the base of the bald spot in the tree's bark.

Em kept a lookout to make sure nobody was around to see us entering the hidden door. I took my key out of my bag and inserted it into the keyhole near the bottom of the door. The face of the stump popped up, much like an old tilt-up garage door. A ladder, made of thick grape ivy, made its way down inside the stump. I motioned to Em to go through and followed. I quickly swung the door down behind us.

Em and I hadn't been through this tunnel yet, but it was very similar to the ones we had already been in. Truffle and Magpie were familiar with all of the tunnels and shortcuts to get to them… seeing as this is how they got around Oak Hill most of the time.

The tunnel was well-lit and wide enough for all of us to travel together, side-by-side. Truffle directed us until we came to the entrance of the grand cavern.

We all walked into the cavern and headed for Truffle and

Magpie's home. Em and I hadn't been in the cavern during the daytime, and I was surprised by the flurry of activity happening around the community. I noticed a gathering of rabbits, of all different sizes and colors, sitting on their haunches on one side of the cavern. They encircled a female Spore who seemed to be training them with small pieces of carrot. She would hold up a carrot piece and try to get all of the rabbits to sit up, which worked for about a second until a bird would fly by and grab their attention away from the teacher.

Other Spores were busy doing various jobs. Some of the younger ones didn't look all too happy about cleaning out the overgrown weeds in the creek, while the older, more daring Spores were hoisted up to the cavern ceiling where they were pruning the blue moss. I noticed that when they clipped a piece of the blue moss, it lost its luminescence as it fell to the floor. As the pieces hit the floor, some of the rabbits in training class would break away and nibble on the fresh blue moss clippings. I could tell the teacher was getting impatient, both with the rabbits' attention spans and the moss clippers doing their job almost directly above her classroom.

Truffle and Magpie's home was about halfway down the cavern, and about four feet off the ground. Truffle and Magpie ran up the root system to get to their door, which ended up being about eye level with where Em and I were standing on the moss floor.

They threw open the curtain, and Magpie tied it off to the side of the cavern wall so we could see inside. The homes were much larger than I had imagined they would be. Just inside the opening was what looked to be a spacious family room with small couches and chairs – but instead of cushions, they were covered in layers of straw and moss. They looked quite comfortable, if you were the size of a Spore.

On a little table in the center of the room there looked

to be a board game made out of lined birch bark and painted pebbles, as well as a chess board. I noticed that the chess pieces were hand-carved out of wood, with characters of all different sizes. The king and queen pieces were shaped as Spores wearing crowns. The bishops were made to look like small oak trees. The knights were shaped like rabbits and the rooks were made to look like owls.

The walls of the living room were patterned with splotches of bright yellow color as if they had been rubbed with dandelion flowers. The paint pattern reminded me of the walls of a Tuscan home but in much brighter colors.

Along the longest wall hung a collection of mushroom caps – in all different sizes and colors, all with four white spots on each.

Four generations, four spots!

Some caps weren't so colorful and didn't have the spots. I guessed these brownish-green caps were for working outside when they didn't want to draw attention to themselves with bright colors.

Just beyond the living room was a large kitchen where Bella was once again cooking a meal. In the corner was a hearth made of multicolored stones that were intricately placed and cemented in place. In the center of the hearth was a large fire, and surrounding the fire were several holes carved into the hearth where Bella was placing different dishes to be cooked.

The smell brought back fond memories of Friday's dinner. Em and I startled her when we both said hello at the same time and she saw our big faces smiling through the door.

"Oh, my! Hello, Olly and Ember! What brings you back so soon? Did you smell my cooking?" Bella said with a giggle.

Before we could answer, Magpie ran up to Bella and whispered in her ear. Bella's face turned from a curious look to a big smile.

"That plan is BRILLIANT!" Bella exclaimed. "Go tell your father right away – he will be so relieved that we might have a plan. He was dreading telling the community that all might be lost."

Magpie ran off into one of the side rooms that was out of our site, in search of Cremini.

I could see doors to four additional rooms which I could only guess were the bedrooms and a bathroom. I wasn't sure if Em was thinking it, but the thought did cross my mind...

How do the Spores go to the bathroom? Is it much different than us?

I decided I would keep that question to myself and ask it at a later date.

Cremini came running out of a bedroom with Magpie in tow. He had a big smile on his face. He hugged Magpie and grabbed Truffle to include him in the hug.

"Ember, you have no idea how this could change everything for us," Cremini said.

Em stood up straight and gave him a proud smile. "It was a group effort. If we weren't all eating lunch out on Lookout Rock, and watching the owls hunt, I never would have had the idea."

"There isn't much time to get this idea in motion. The council meeting is next week," said Cremini. "Magpie... you'll need to go out to Bumblebee Meadows and find an owl willing to move back and help us out. And, we will need to coordinate getting a nest built for her to move into. Ember, I assume you can get your mom to do her study after all of that is in place?"

"Oh, this is the type of work she LOVES to do, and if she has any chance of stopping Hank Dalton's mall, she will jump at the opportunity," Em replied. "If Magpie can help get the owl out there and in a nest, I can take a picture and show it to my mom. That will surely get her on board. She'll be able to force an environmental study that should be more than enough to list Oak Hill as a protected wildlife area."

"Sounds like we have a plan. It's all up to our bird whisperer now, right Magpie?" I said.

Magpie grinned, walked over, and gave me a high five to show she had it under control.

"Magpie – I know it means eating dinner later, but can you go find Clover and ask her if she can plan to run you out to that field where the owls have moved? You will need to get out there as quickly as you can, and before it gets dark," asked Cremini.

Without hesitation, Magpie ran out the door and down the root system to find Clover.

"Would you two like to stay for dinner?" Bella asked.

"I won't speak for Em, but since I didn't see my parents last night, I am sure they are planning to see me at dinner tonight," I responded.

"Can I get a raincheck, too? It smells amazing, but I haven't seen my mom either, and I want to start feeding her ideas and rumors of owls to get her thinking about doing the environmental study," Em replied.

"Well, that just means more leftover corncake with strawberry rhubarb jelly for me!" Cremini laughed.

"Oh, I almost forgot... could Truffle teach you two how to set up the first shipment of the new Spore families tomorrow, so they can get shipped out this week?"

"Of course! I have all day tomorrow" I said.

"I'd like to help, too!" Em said.

"Great, Truffle can show you both what we learned from your grandfather... he had a system of designing boxes that were comfortable for the families to travel in, but strong enough to withstand the abuse of our friendly neighborhood mail workers," Cremini said. "He can meet you in the packing room under your house tomorrow morning!"

Em and I both nodded in agreement.

"I'll give you the cash to cover the shipping expenses," Cremini said. "We don't have much use for money around here... so nobody sees much value in human currency here. I saw my inventive neighbor using a $10 bill as a tablecloth the other day. It looked like it had made it through quite a few meals. Turns out those bills do clean up quite well. I even saw another Spore using a $100 bill as a nice picnic blanket just over there in that mossy greenspace."

I must have been daydreaming about all of that money just lying around in different places because it took a good nudge from Em to get me back into the conversation.

"Give me a minute!" Cremini said as he rushed back into the furthest room. After some rustling, he came running back into the living room with a crisp $50 bill.

"This should be more than enough to cover the mailing costs," Cremini said. "Whatever is left feel free to use at the pizza place or the ice cream parlor. Our treat to both of you for helping us out!"

We thanked Cremini, said our goodbyes to Bella and Truffle, then headed back out into the tunnels. It was already late afternoon and we needed to get back home. Rather than risk getting caught sneaking out of our secret room under the stairs, we decided to explore a tunnel we had never taken before.

Surprisingly, the tunnel was short and ended in a ladder ascending to a hatch.

I climbed the ladder and gently pushed the hatch open to take a quick peek, making sure that nobody was around. After making sure the coast was clear, I pushed the hatch fully up and crawled out from under the floor just below one of the wooden planter shelves in our greenhouse. Once Em climbed out and closed the hatch behind her, we both realized the top of the hatch was disguised as a large flagstone, which fit perfectly like a puzzle piece into the rest of the floor. We both also noticed the small mushroom symbol etched into the stone, signifying another tunnel entry, although this one didn't seem to have a keyhole, but rather a small finger hole we could use to lift the stone door.

We walked back to the side of the house where both of our bikes had been hidden in the bushes. I asked Em if she wanted me to ride with her back to her house, in case Buzz and Trent happened to be around the area.

"Oh, I'm not worried about them… they would have to deal with Chase and my mom if they ever did anything, and they know better than that. Plus, you can't keep up anyway, slowpoke!"

With that, she jumped on her bike and pedaled off, leaving me insulted and laughing at the same time.

"See you tomorrow, speedy!" I yelled.

I walked back around the front of the house and noticed the sheriff's car was sitting in the driveway.

This can't be good.

I walked in the front door to find Mom and Dad sitting on the couch, with the sheriff sitting across from them in the large rocking chair. They were deep in discussion when they noticed me standing there.

"Well, hello there, Olly!" Sheriff McGough said.

"Hello, sheriff."

"I just came by to fill in your parents on the investigation, and to return this," the sheriff said.

He held out a light tan leather satchel that had a long strap. The satchel had holes punched around the perimeter and looked weathered and a bit beat up.

"This is the satchel your grandfather was carrying when he was killed. We've looked over it with a fine-toothed comb to find any additional clues about your grandfather's death and we don't need it any longer," the sheriff said.

This was the first time I felt the sheriff cared about my grandfather and our family.

"Thank you, sir," I said as I took the satchel and looked at it quietly for a minute.

"Your dad and I thought you might like to have that, Olly," Mom said, slightly shaken up. "It's the bag he used to take on your adventures in the woods. I know he would have wanted you to have it."

"Yes, this is where we used to store all of the treasures that we found in the woods… thank you!"

The sheriff gave me a sincere smile and continued with the conversation they were having when I entered the room.

"We know for certain Oren was struck by a large truck, whether intentionally or by mistake. By comparing the spacing of the wheelbase, the tire width, and the depths of the tire tracks in the gravel, we can pretty accurately say it was a Ford truck, most likely a heavier truck like an F-350," said the sheriff.

"Hey, that's the same truck Mr. Dalton's goon drives," I blurted out loudly.

I guess I said it a little too loudly as all three of them jerked in their seats when I said it.

"Great eye for detail, Olly, we might make you a detective yet! The goon, as you call him, is Stanley Blackwell. We ran background checks on him, and he has quite a rap sheet of misdemeanors, public nuisance, and assault incidents, but has no warrants that would allow us to take him off the street. We've called around and learned that he also has a history with a well-known gang in California. And, we know Mr. Blackwell drives a Ford F-350. Deputy Ostran has already questioned him and thoroughly inspected his vehicle for any matching damage to the bumpers. His truck didn't show any signs to indicate that he had hit anyone. The truck seemed very new and the bumpers and the entire vehicle were as clean as a whistle. It looked like it just left Mr. Dalton's dealership."

This made me even more convinced it was him and Mr. Dalton. I could guarantee that they simply switched out vehicles, or replaced the bumper after the murder of my grandfather.

"The deputy also collected and spent hours watching any available security video footage leading into and around the roads going to Oak Hill. Unfortunately, although we can pick out the shape of a few pickup trucks, the footage was pretty grainy and of no use at all. It seems Littleton is still using

185

security cameras bought from Radio Shack back in the 80s."

My dad interjected, "We all know the only person with a motive to kill my dad is Henry Dalton. He has been after this Oak Hill property since my mom and dad acquired it. I have numerous offer letters sitting in the credenza over there to prove it, and they're all addressed from Mr. Dalton's office. Each one is more forceful than the previous one. It would have been in Dalton's interest to have my dad out of the picture so that the property would go back up for sale. He has been badgering me and my wife since the first day we got to Littleton."

"Trust me, Mr. Appleton, I know that Henry Dalton can be pretty aggressive. But he is a businessman, and after years of dealing with him, I've come to realize that he goes head-first like a Pitbull after whatever he wants. He can go to the edge of being too aggressive sometimes, but he has never gone to the point where he breaks any laws. And although I would love to have him sitting in my jail for personal reasons, I can't just arrest him over a few forceful real estate offers he made to you or your family."

Sheriff McGough continued, "Just so you know, Deputy Ostran has some concerns about Mr. Dalton, too. Seems Mr. Dalton doesn't like that we hired a woman onto the Littleton police force. He has made it very clear that he doesn't like being questioned or being told what to do by her. Mr. Dalton has kept the chair in my office warm from the number of times he has come in to complain about her, but I know she is just doing her job. We get quite a few complaints from the local college kids telling us Henry Dalton has swindled them out of their money for cars that turned out to be lemons. And Deputy Ostran has a duty to investigate each allegation, much to Mr. Dalton's disdain. Everyone at the department lovingly tells Deputy Ostran to 'spank Hank' every time we send her out to talk with him. I think she has come to enjoy the responsibility."

"So, what are the next steps, sheriff?" Dad asked, looking a little let down.

"We continue to put pressure on Mr. Dalton and Mr. Blackwell and hope they slip up somehow. Aside from that, we continue to ask around to find additional data to bolster the case that Mr. Dalton took it too far with your father. That's about all we can do at this point. I have asked Deputy Ostran to pay a little extra attention to watching the dealership and Mr. Blackwell's activities."

Mom stood up and walked toward the sheriff to hug him.

"We appreciate everything you and your deputies are doing for us. We've already begun to feel like we have been welcomed into the community, but the attention your office is putting on the case makes us understand why my in-laws decided to call Littleton their home," Mom said.

The sheriff seemed surprised and delighted by the hug. He gave my mom a warm smile, nodded to my dad, then picked his hat off the side table and brushed it off as he headed for the door.

"We will figure this out, I promise!" he said as he put on his hat and left.

It was nice to sit down over dinner and talk about how Littleton was becoming our new home. I had made new friends with Em, Chase, Kylie, and Brielle. My mom mentioned already having a few new clients in town and she seemed excited about looking for places to open up shop. Dad was already offered a job helping Harry Sawyer around the hardware store. He would be helping Harry organize the store, and be a local woodworking expert able to help customers with whatever projects they needed to get done around their homes.

I found it difficult to not add to that excitement by divulging our new secret plan to save Oak Hill from Henry Dalton.

16. AN EGG-CELLENT PLAN

I woke Sunday morning to the sound of Fizzy running up and down the hall outside my room, sliding and bumping into the walls at each end of the hall. She wasn't playing with a toy from what I could tell. I heard a small voice talking to her, telling her to slow down and turn this way or that. It wasn't until Fizzy slid to a stop in my doorway that I realized where the voice was coming from.

Truffle and Magpie were mounted atop Fizzy, holding onto the fur on the nape of her neck. Somehow, they got Fizzy to allow them to ride on her, but Truffle was having a hard time getting Fizzy to follow his instructions. When they looked up and saw me poking my head out of the covers, he and Magpie waved, dismounted Fizzy, and took turns giving her a quick scratch under the chin. Fizzy rolled onto her back and seemed

189

happy to have Truffle and Magpie as new friends.

I guess Fizzy learned her lesson from the last time she tried to eat Truffle and got a face full of puffball dust.

"What are you doing?" I asked them, somewhat agitated that they woke me so early.

"We got tired of waiting for you to wake up, and we want to show you how to put together a travel box for the new Spore families that need to ship out tomorrow," Truffle said.

I turned to my clock and noticed it was only 8:45 am… much earlier than my normal Sunday morning wakeup time.

"Ugh, you are killing me! I usually sleep in until at least 10 o'clock," I said as I pulled the blanket back over my head. I could feel Truffle climbing up the side of my bed. He tugged at the blanket a few times, right near my face.

"Come on sleepy head! We have much to do today," Truffle implored.

With a loud grunt, I swung my legs out of bed. I pulled on the sweatpants and t-shirt I had bunched up and thrown next to the bed the night before.

I didn't even think about the fact that I just got out of bed wearing only underpants. It hit me when I noticed Magpie turned a pink hue and turned around quickly to avoid looking.

"I'm sorry, Magpie!" I said a bit embarrassed. "It's safe to turn around now."

Magpie stayed facing away from me for a few more minutes, probably waiting for the pink to leave her cheeks.

"So, what's the plan for today, early birds?" I asked.

"I have a sample travel box down in the packing room

under the stairs. It was one that your grandpa made, but we never used it because it didn't have enough padding and protection built into it. I watched your grandpa put together some of the newer models, so I should be able to walk you through building a better one. We have enough materials down there to build a few boxes, enough for this shipment and the next, at least," said Truffle.

"Great! Let me call Em. I know she wanted to be a part of all of this. I'll meet you down there in about 30 minutes," I said.

With that, Truffle jumped down off the bed, pulled Magpie out of her embarrassed state, and stepped toward Fizzy. Fizzy rolled back over onto her stomach – which she had been cleaning fervently - and bent down slightly to make it easier for Truffle and Magpie to mount her neck again.

Look at that… I can't even get her to come to me on command.

"We'll head down and get things set up! See you soon," Truffle said as he lightly patted Fizzy on the head and whispered something in her ear. Fizzy took off just as Truffle and Magpie waved to me. She took off so fast, Truffle and Magpie almost lost their hold. Before I could wave back, Fizzy had dashed out of the doorway and down the hall with her new friends hanging off her neck precariously.

I called Em right away, who also seemed a bit groggy and unhappy that I woke her at such an early hour.

"This better be something good, Appleton," Em said in a raspy voice.

She must be mad if she's calling me by my last name.

"It is! I was just woken up by our friends, Truffle and Magpie, and they want to show us how to build a travel box for the shipment we are supposed to make tomorrow. I know you wanted to be there to build it with us. I can meet you at the tunnel entrance by Tophet Swamp."

Before I could get another word out, Em simply said, "I'll be there in ten," and the phone clicked and went silent.

I sprayed too much Axe body spray on my chest, quickly brushed my teeth, and decided I would put on some nicer clothes. I grabbed the satchel that Sheriff McGough returned last night and slung it over my shoulder.

As I made it down the third flight of stairs, I could hear Mom and Dad toiling away in the kitchen. They heard me land in the hall at the bottom of the stairs.

"Good morning, Olly! You're up early," Mom said.

"Yeah, Em and I plan to do some more exploring today. I wanted to wait until after lunch, but she's such an early bird!"

"We planned to go into town again if you two want to join us," Dad said.

"We've only explored half of the hill, and want to finish exploring it together today," I replied.

"Well at least grab some breakfast before you head out," Mom said.

I grabbed a bagel, smothered it in some plain cream cheese and raspberry jam, then blew a kiss to both Mom and Dad. "See you later!"

"Give a kiss to Ember for us!"

"Will do!" I said as I rushed out the front door, not even realizing what they had said until it was too late. I could hear them giggling as I slammed the door behind me.

I jumped on my bike and pedaled as fast as I could to get to the Tophet Swamp tunnel entrance, hoping to make it there before Em.

It seemed I didn't pedal fast enough as Em was leaning against the entrance when I skidded around the corner.

"Still a snail on that bike, aren't you, Olly?"

I just smiled and let her get the dig in this one time.

We looked around and made sure there was nobody following us, or anyone just hiking nearby in the woods. When we felt we were in the clear, Em grabbed the key out of my hand and pushed it into the keyhole at the base of the door. It clicked open and we hurried inside with our bikes, closing it quickly behind us.

We walked pretty fast with our bikes at our sides and realized we could navigate the tunnels much better having been in them a few times over the past week. The string lights that Poppy had put along the tunnels helped but just weren't bright enough to expose the big roots popping out randomly along the tunnel floors. Em and I both had missteps a few times because of this and made fun of each other when it happened.

We got to the wooden panel and pushed it open, only to find Truffle and Magpie wrapping each other in brown shipping paper on top of the workbench. They fumbled a bit when they saw us, and Magpie fell over, not realizing Truffle had wrapped her lower half tightly in the paper.

Em helped her up and unwrapped her. Magpie gave a slight curtsy to thank her.

Truffle pulled a box out from one of the shelves stretching across the length of the workbench.

"So… this is the early prototype your grandfather built,"

Truffle said as he pulled open the box.

It was about the size of a dress shirt box, but slightly taller. Inside were six compartments, made of intersecting cardboard walls. Each wall had holes punched through, I assumed so the Spores could breathe and speak with each other on their multi-day journey. Inside each compartment was a layer of Spanish moss to offer them a comfortable place to sleep.

Em and I can handle building this!

Truffle interrupted my thought, "The trick is that this setup gets rather beat up when those young mail carriers throw the box around or use it as a hockey puck."

He pulled a bag of white feathers from one of the lower shelves of the workbench.

Our duck friends donated some of their down feathers to help us give them a little more padding. He pulled a roll of brown shipping tape off the shelf and laid four 8-inch pieces on the workbench, sticky side up.

"We create padded walls by sticking the feathers onto the tape, like this," Truffle said as he and Magpie pulled feathers out of the bag and neatly placed them all over the sticky tape. Once they had covered the entire length of the pieces of tape, Truffle folded each of them in half, leaving the feathers exposed on both sides. He climbed over the lip of the box.

"Hand me one of those, would you, Olly?"

I handed him a feathered tape piece, careful not to lose any feathers or mess up their tidy work.

Em and I watched as he pushed the feathered piece onto one of the walls of a compartment. After placing three more, he then put Spanish moss on the floor, enough to hold the feathered walls in place. He pushed a pencil through the tape every few inches to make a small opening into the adjacent compartment.

"Can't forget these holes, they are the most important part!" Truffle said, making sure we were paying close attention. "They'll be dead ducks if you forget this part," Truffle said as he giggled, pointing at the feathers. We all shook our heads at his awful play on words.

Em and I took turns laying out some pieces of tape, and Truffle helped me place feathers while Magpie helped Em.

It took about 30 minutes, but in the end, all of the compartments had comfortable and safe living quarters.

"The only thing left to do is to cover the inside of the lid with Spanish moss," Truffle said.

Truffle did this by taping the Spanish moss, similar to the duck feathers, onto longer pieces of tape. He stuck those moss-covered pieces into the lid so the Spanish moss was facing the lid, and the tape was exposed to the compartments.

"These are just in case the mail carriers ignore the '*This side up*' and '*Fragile*' warnings we will write on the outside of boxes."

Once completely covered in the Spanish moss, Truffle and Magpie got on opposite ends of the lid and flipped it over. It was pretty impressive to see Truffle write the warnings in a thick red marker.

"Fra... geeel...ayyyyy," Truffle laughed as he sounded it out. Magpie had heard this joke many times before... instead of laughing, she just shook her head.

I noticed his handwriting was rather stylish, not that it would impress the young mail carriers, and they would probably ignore it altogether.

They put the lid onto the box and proceeded to poke holes into the sides of the box, two in each compartment, for airflow I presumed.

"So tomorrow, all we need to do is let the Spore families choose their compartments and seal the box with some packing tape. Remember to NOT cover their breathing holes with packing tape," Truffle said with his hands on his waist as if scolding us for something we hadn't even done yet.

"Got it... no air holes and their goose will be cooked," Em said with a smirk.

Magpie and I both laughed, but Truffle just rolled his eyes, jealous that he hadn't thought of that one.

"Oh... speaking of cooked goose, one other important thing to remember," Truffle said as he pulled another bag off the shelf. This bag contained what looked to be rabbit food in pellet shapes.

"These are protein pucks. They are not at all bad tasting and will give the Spore families something to eat until they get to Colorado. You need to put about six per Spore in each compartment before you send them off."

"That reminds me, we won't be able to go to the post office until after school. Em and I will need to keep the travel box with the families in it inside my locker until we get out of classes. The locker has vents, probably to prevent that funky teenager smell from collecting in there, so they will be able to breathe. Then we can head straight to the post office. Is that a problem?" I asked Truffle.

"They should be fine. I'll warn them. I'll have them here at 7 o'clock so we can load them up and get you two on your way to school," Truffle said.

"Well… we have one more thing we need to do today. Magpie, are we all set to transport some owl eggs from Bumblebee Meadows to Oak Hill?" I asked.

Magpie shook her head emphatically. She leaned into Truffle's ear and whispered something.

Truffle repeated what she said so we could hear. "Magpie said Clover hopped her out there yesterday and she was able to speak with one very helpful owl mom who is more than happy to help us out. I guess the owl said she owes us for protecting her and her nest from a fox just last year. Seems someone from our Spore community was visiting some rabbits in the meadow last year and noticed a Fox creeping up on her nest. Just before the fox could attack, they hit it with a puffball. The hallucinations spooked the fox so badly, it left the meadow and was never seen again," said Truffle. "We just need to make sure we reassure her that we will take care of her three eggs on the way back to Oak Hill. She'll fly over us on the way back, just to keep an eye out for trouble."

"Then we should make a box to transport the egg. Em, hand me that box on the shelf and some more of that Spanish moss," I said.

This box was smaller than the ones we just made but large enough to hold three owl eggs comfortably. We added extra Spanish moss in the box, just to protect them from any rough roads or roots we might hit on the way back. I took my fist and pressed it into the moss to make little pockets, and filled the pockets with some feathers to add extra padding.

"That should do it. Now for you two… we are going to be passing through town, and it would probably be a good idea to have you two safely concealed, just in case. I brought the satchel Poppy used when traveling with your dad – the sheriff dropped it off last night. If you two would like, you can ride in here," I said, not knowing if they would be offended or open to the idea.

"That would be perfect… but can we put some Spanish moss and feathers in there to make our ride a little more enjoyable?" asked Truffle.

"Of course," said Em as she grabbed the satchel from me and started filling it with moss and feathers. When done, she pushed the feathers down and laid the satchel on the workbench.

"After you," Truffle said as he held the satchel open for Magpie. Reluctantly, Magpie stepped in, and Truffle followed. "It's not at all bad in here, actually," he said.

"I'll take them on this trip," Em said as she grabbed the satchel and carefully pulled the strap over her head so the satchel lay across her body. "It will less conspicuous if I am holding the bag."

She didn't give me a choice, but it worked out since I had to carry the egg box anyway.

We exited the tunnels and got on our bikes to start the 20-minute ride out to Bumblebee Meadows. Em was in the lead and I could tell that at each turn she was careful to think through the route she was taking. She stuck to the main streets, which offered the least bumps for our tiny passengers. Every once in a while, Truffle and Magpie would give us a whistle and a little thumbs up from one of the holes in the satchel… just to let us know they were doing okay.

The trip out to Bumblebee Meadows was uneventful, albeit a bit stressful, as we were trying not to make Truffle and Magpie sick. We mostly stuck to Harwood Avenue and went under Route 495. Once near Bumblebee Meadow, Truffle stuck his head out of the satchel.

"Take a right onto Bumble Bee Lane, and park the bikes," he said. "We'll go in on foot from there."

We entered the meadow off Bumble Bee Lane and left our bikes leaning against a row of bushes, so they couldn't easily be seen from the road.

Once we entered the thicker brush of the meadow, Truffle and Magpie poked their heads out of the opening of the satchel and Truffle gave us directions to the owl, with guidance from Magpie who was whispering in his ear the whole time.

"Go straight for that bright orange tree. She is nested near a path a few feet away," Truffle said.

The meadow had a few migration trails left by animals, but for the most part, we were trudging through tall wildflower patches to get to our destination. I understood why they called it Bumblebee Meadows now. It seemed every flower had either a bumblebee or butterfly munching on its pollen. Truffle and Magpie ducked into the satchel when the brush started hitting them in their faces. They were still able to peer out of the holes to make sure we were headed in the right direction.

We reached a path that ran directly toward the bright orange tree and walked it until we heard the tell-tale sign.

HOOT, HOOT, HOOT… HOOT, HOOT, HOOT, HOOT

She was calling out to us. It grew louder as we neared the tree. Truffle told us when to stop.

Off the trail, about five feet away, was a collection of gray sticks piled up haphazardly, and atop sat a beautiful gray Short-eared Owl. She popped her head up from the pile when she saw us.

Magpie jumped out of the satchel and ran to her. She

whispered something into the owl's ear and the owl slowly climbed off her perch of sticks and peered down inside.

We were all careful not to make any sudden movements but slowly walked over to where her nest was. The branches were covered in a layer of pine needles, and in the center were three small, white eggs.

"We need to take a photo so we can rebuild this nest back on Oak Hill," I said.

Em pulled out her phone and took a few pictures from a few feet away and into the nest.

Magpie whispered in the owl's ear again, and the owl stepped further away from the nest.

"It looks like she's ready for you to take them," Truffle said.

I set the traveling box down next to the nest, and one by one gently grabbed the eggs and placed them into the little pockets of feathers in the box. The owl mother looked a little nervous but still seemed willing to let this all happen. Magpie stroked the owl's neck feathers to let her know everything was going to be okay.

I closed the box and stood up, carefully placed the egg box into my backpack, and secured it. Truffle and Magpie thanked the owl, and Em and I also gave her a slight bow. The owl flapped her wings and took off into the air, landing on the branch of the bright orange tree only a few yards away. Her head was already on a swivel, looking for any sign of danger.

Truffle and Magpie jumped back into the satchel, and we set off to follow our trail back across the meadow. Every few minutes the owl would fly over to check on us and survey the surrounding area.

We were nearing the edge of the meadow when we all stopped at the same time. For some reason, there was an odd silence, all except for the owl sitting up in a tree ahead of us. She was screeching and looking down and we couldn't figure out why.

Truffle and Magpie popped their heads out of the satchel and looked around.

"Something's got momma nervous," Truffle said quietly.

That's when I saw Magpie do something I have never seen her do before. She pivoted so she was facing the meadow and whistled loudly – it sounded like a really short song, just a few notes long. It was the first time Em and I had ever heard a peep come out of Magpie so we both looked at each other in amazement. The whistle was so loud that I thought there was no way it could have come from something as small as Magpie.

Truffle and Magpie slipped back down into the satchel and we cautiously continued to where we had stowed our bikes. We reached the edge of the meadow and that's when we realized why the owl was so nervous. It was Buzz and Trent, leaning against our bikes, both with grimaces on their faces. We hadn't realized it, but they must have followed us from the center of town to Bumblebee Meadow.

We have to be more careful in the future.

"What do you two want?" asked Em.

"Just a little payback is all. It doesn't involve you, Ember… we just want to talk to the new kid," Buzz said as he started walking toward us.

Ember bravely stepped between me and Buzz. He stopped for a second, not sure how to react, and then pushed Em so hard she flew off the trail and into some thorny bushes.

Luckily she was able to avoid falling on top of the satchel with Truffle and Magpie in it. The satchel sat across her stomach safely.

Trent laughed at Em trying to get unstuck from the thorns, then stepped up next to Buzz and they both started to walk toward me. My fists were already clenched after seeing them hurt Em. I was just about to lunge at them when I heard the owl screeching above... which reminded me that I had her eggs in my backpack. I slowly took the backpack off, and gently set it down on some soft grass to my right.

I could feel my blood boiling, and they must have realized how mad I was because they both stopped and just stared at me. Only they weren't exactly staring at me, but rather past me, which I thought was weird. They started to back up slowly.

I can't be that scary.

That's when I heard a low growl behind me.

I slowly turned my head to find two large coyotes, about five feet behind me, baring their teeth and in an attack stance. I looked over at Em, who also had a scared look on her face.

I looked down to find Magpie just barely poking her head out of the satchel, and holding a thumbs up toward me. For some reason, that made me feel like I was going to be okay.

With each step Buzz and Trent took backward, the coyotes growled and took a step forward, until they were on either side of me. I gave Buzz and Trent a slight smile, and yelled at them...

"RUN!"

With that, Buzz and Trent fell over each other trying to be the first to turn around and start running. The coyotes followed them, making a good act of being ready to eat them alive if they were caught. It had been a while since I heard Buzz and Trent screaming, and it brought back fond memories.

I helped Em up and picked a few thorny branches off her back, then asked if she, Truffle, and Magpie were okay. All three smiled.

"Was that your doing, Magpie?" I asked.

Magpie gave me another thumbs up.

"You're brilliant, little Maggie," said Truffle as he hugged her.

Magpie whispered in Truffle's ear.

"She had asked those coyotes to watch out for us, just in case we got into trouble. All she had to do was call them. But we don't have much time... the coyotes won't chase them far, because they don't want to be seen by anyone else... something about not wanting rabid coyote rumors spreading around town," Truffle said.

"I think momma owl would be happy if we got a move on, too. Let's go!" Em said.

I am not sure if it was the adrenaline, or just replaying the looks on Buzz and Trent's faces as I pedaled, but it felt like we got back in half the time it took us to get out to Bumblebee Meadows.

"Let's take the service road, I have the perfect nesting spot picked out for momma," Em said.

I suggested we walk our bikes up the service road because it was much too bumpy for Truffle and Magpie to ride in the satchel.

"Thanks, Olly! We already feel like cream of mushroom soup after that experience," joked Truffle.

About three-quarters of the way up the road, Em stopped. We parked our bikes behind some large oaks and walked perpendicular to the road until we hit a clearing. The open area was surrounded by dead, fallen trees. The fallen trees overlapped each other, creating a natural fence around the clearing. They would make it very hard for anyone to get into this area.

One large tree, still alive, sat in the middle of the clearing. Em walked over and pointed to a bare spot in the ground under the tree.

"Right here. This is where momma's nest is going to be," Em said proudly.

Just as she said that the momma owl flew overhead and landed in the live tree overlooking the new nest area. She bounced her head up and down in approval, or at least that's what I could only guess she was doing.

"Olly, can you please gather some small branches and twigs? Truffle and Magpie, can you grab as many pine needles as you can and put them in the satchel?" asked Em.

"I'll leave this with you," I told Em as I pulled the egg box out of the backpack and handed it to her.

It didn't take long for us to gather all of the nest materials. I used my backpack to hold all of the twigs and branches I had collected. As I came back to the nest area, I could see Truffle and Magpie pulling the satchel behind them, overstuffed with pine needles.

They are surprisingly strong!

"Wow! Looks like we have some overachievers in our

group," said Em when she saw Truffle and Magpie with their pine needle bounty.

"Go big or go home is what they say, right?" Truffle replied.

Magpie tried to act like she was flexing her little arms, but they weren't long enough to achieve the desired effect, so she put them down and turned slightly pink.

We watched as Em recreated the nest, looking back to her phone every once in a while to make sure she had the nest looking close to the original. When she was done, she turned to me and held out the box with the eggs.

"Want to do the honors?"

I took the box and kneeled, arranging the three eggs gently in the center of the nest. Em took a photo of the new nest and the owl perched up in the tree above us. We all stood there for a minute in silence, proud of the work we had done.

"Odd to think this pile of twigs and pine needles might just save all of our homes," I said.

Just as I said that the momma owl swooped down in front of us and landed next to the nest. She inspected it for a minute, and then waddled on top and sat on the eggs. She seemed very content with our work.

Magpie walked over to her and whispered in her ear. The owl looked like it nodded in approval, and Magpie turned to us with a thumbs up.

"I guess that means it's up to her standards," said Em. "Let's go show the photos to my mom. I'd like to get her thinking about her environmental study and make sure she has enough time to finish it before the council meeting."

"Magpie and I will stick around here for a little bit to make sure everything is okay, and then head back home. We've had enough excitement for today," said Truffle.

The ride to Em's house was much less stressful since Em and I weren't worried about eggs in a backpack, or Spores in a satchel. I hadn't yet been to Em's house, and I was excited to see where she lived.

Her house was much closer than I had imagined. It was right at the bottom of Oak Hill and across the street, near the bend on Oak Hill Road. A short winding drive through some tall pines led up to her house.

No wonder she was able to beat me to Tophet Swamp!

"So, this is the new Dalton Mall parking lot," I joked.

"Funny, Olly," said Em as she sneered at me and got off her bike.

Her house wasn't big but was very cute. I could tell her mom had a green thumb, as there were beautiful gardens scattered around the property – some with wildflowers, others with hostas and ferns. The house was sided in yellow and had a cottage feel to it. She pointed at the two dormers on the roofline.

"That's my room up there. Be warned, I can see everything you do up there on Oak Hill from my window, Olly," she said with a mischievous smile.

"And that's why I have to get blinds," I joked back.

Walking through the front door, I could tell her mom had similar interests as me. She had pressed plant leaves mounted and framed as artwork on the walls – I had to admit that her presentation was much nicer than my pin-ups in Olly's Herbarium.

"Mommmmm, Olly and I are here!"

Mrs. Fein peeked around the corner from the kitchen.

"Hello, Olly! You two are just in time for oatmeal cookies, have a seat."

Em and I looked at each other with wide eyes.

"Day keeps getting better," I said.

Mrs. Fein delivered the warm cookies with a nice glass of cold milk and sat down to join us.

"So, what adventures did you two have today?" she asked.

Em looked at me, and then back at her mom. I could tell she could hardly contain her excitement.

"Mom, do you remember when we were talking about the only ways we could put a stop to the mall on Oak Hill?"

"Yes, of course," she replied.

Em pulled her phone out of her pocket, swiped at it a few times, and held it close to her chest.

"What would you say if we found this on Oak Hill?" she said as she turned the phone around.

Mrs. Fein took a look, got a huge grin, then put on her glasses and leaned way up close to the screen. She grabbed the phone and put her hand to her mouth.

"Is that an owl nest?" Mrs. Fein asked.

"Not just ANY owl nest... a Short-eared Owl. Better known as an endangered species in Massachusetts. Only 20 to 25 breeding pairs left in the state," Em beamed.

"Wait, how do you know it's a Short-eared Owl for sure?"

Em swiped at the screen in her mom's hand.

Mrs. Fein's eyes went as big as they could. She turned to me.

"Do you know what this means, Olly?"

I replied, "Yes, I do. It means someone is going to do an environmental study on Oak Hill before the next council meeting and save all of our homes from being Foot Locker stores and asphalt for as far as the eye can see!"

Mrs. Fein stood up and hugged Em, and then me.

"Okay, there's a process I have to go through to get this study done legitimately. I am going to start right away. Ember, you are going to have to take me to where this nest is in the next few days. And, please forward those pictures to me."

Em turned to me and winked. Our plan was working.

Mrs. Fein didn't sit back down and never even touched her cookies and milk. She flew off somewhere. I assumed she was going to start the paperwork.

"Want to tell my parents, Em?"

"Uh, duh! Let's go."

I decided I would time how long it took to get from Em's house to my house, pedaling at an average speed. It took exactly seven minutes, door-to-door. Now I would be able to make a dig at Em and ask her why it took so long if she were ever to make the trip in over seven minutes.

Dad's car was in the driveway, which meant Mom and Dad were home.

"We're in luck… the Green Beast is here, which means both of my parents are probably home!" I said.

When we entered the front door, I heard Mom talking to Dad, and she seemed upset. They turned when they saw us at the kitchen doorway and both got quiet.

"Oh hello, you two!" my dad said. "Don't worry about your mom. It seems Hank Dalton picked a bad day to try to belittle your mother in front of her new friends. All because she hasn't accepted his 'last and very generous offer.' Ember, if rumors start circulating around town about my wife's foul language, I will verify the rumors are all true. She really let Mr. Dalton have it. I guess his bodyguard was scared of Mom, too, because when she started cussing old Hank out, his bodyguard high-tailed it out of the diner, leaving poor Hank to fend for himself. Hank wasn't all that happy about it either. The other ladies all laughed when they saw Mr. Dalton hitting his sidekick with his white cowboy hat as they drove away."

"Well, we want to tell you something that will make your day much better," I said. "Em, can you show them the photos?"

Em held out the phone with the picture of the nest. Mom and Dad, both had quizzical looks on their faces.

"That is the nest of a Short-eared Owl. And it is going to save our property, and Em's property, from Hank Dalton's chubby little fingers."

My parents looked at each other, shaking their heads and still as confused as before.

"The Short-eared Owl is an endangered species in Massachusetts. And we just happen to have one tending to its eggs on Oak Hill… which means the land can't be touched."

It finally clicked with both of them and they started

jumping up and down and hugging each other… and me… and Em. It was slightly embarrassing, but Em seemed to get a kick out of it.

"So do we just show these to the city council?" Mom asked.

Em jumped in, "No… remember how my mom does environmental studies? We just told her the news and she is already getting things going to list the property as a protected area with the state. It sounds like she will be able to submit the application and let the council know it is being reviewed. The city can't do anything related to development on that property while that application is being reviewed. I can't imagine the application will be rejected since there are only 20 to 25 breeding pairs of the owls left in Massachusetts. That's more important than any mall."

"Or parking lot," I added with a smirk at Em.

"And you two found this on Oak Hill?" Dad asked.

"Just downhill from the water tank, in a clearing. It is pretty well protected with thorny bushes and fallen trees, and is far off the normal footpaths," I said.

"I can't wait to see Henry Dalton's face when he hears this news at the council meeting!" Mom said.

"Maybe we can call the protected area 'Dalton's Nature Conservancy' in his honor, just to add a little extra insult to injury?" Dad replied.

We all laughed at that.

I added, "I can just hear him say…. 'Owl' never get my mall now!"

My joke didn't go over as well as Dad's, but I was still

proud of my play on words.

We spent the next 30 minutes talking about the fact that Mr. Dalton's aggression was escalating with Mom and Dad because they had not accepted his offer. It was further proof, in my mind, that he was capable of doing anything or having someone else do anything to get our property. The city council meeting could not come soon enough.

17. SPECIAL DELIVERY

It is going to be a big day... our first shipment of Spores was going out today. I made sure I had set two alarms so I would wake up in time to meet Truffle, Magpie, and the Spore families making their journey to Littleton, Colorado.

I texted Em and told her to park her bike behind our greenhouse and meet me at the hidden room as soon as she could. I had planned ahead and parked my bike there last night.

I cleared out my backpack so I would have space to store the traveling box, got dressed, and ran down the stairs to eat some breakfast.

Unfortunately, Mom and Dad were especially talkative this morning. I kept looking at the clock to make sure I could break out of the conversation, and slip out to the hidden room in time for the pickup.

I let them know I was meeting Em a little earlier than normal, so we could study in the library before school started for our biology test. This seemed to work as they said their normal goodbyes, complete with a big kiss from Mom. Mom and Dad continued talking loudly in the kitchen, which allowed me to use the hallway tunnel entrance without fear of them seeing or hearing me use the secret door.

As I walked down the stairs to the hidden room, I could hear quite a bit of activity and voices coming from down below.

I turned the corner and found Em, Cremini, Truffle, and Magpie already trying to sort the Spore families into compartments in the traveling box we had made. The Spore families looked excited, but also a bit nervous.

As the Spores and their adopted Sporlings got situated into their compartments, I filled out the shipping label, which was to Amanita Muscaria, PO Box 1245, Littleton, Colorado 80120. I made sure I had the $50 bill Cremini gave me to cover the shipping expenses.

It was time to seal the box for their journey.

"Amanita will be there to pick you up at the post office in Colorado. The trip should take a few days. You all have food to eat on the trip, right?" Cremini asked.

The Spore families all looked around their compartments to make sure they each had enough protein pucks and all nodded yes.

"Remember that Olly and Ember have to take you to school with them, and they will drop you off at the post office afterward. Sorry for the inconvenience, but it is the only way they can get you to the post office in time before it closes for the day," said Cremini.

They all nodded again and gave a thumbs-up.

"They're all set to go, Olly and Ember," said Cremini. "I wish you all luck at the new community, and we will hopefully be able to visit once things settle down in both of our Littletons!"

With that, I covered the box, and taped the top on securely, making sure not to cover any of the breathing holes or Truffle's neatly-written "Fragile" signage on the top of the box.

"Sorry about this, but I may need to turn the box on its side to carry you in my backpack. Get ready for the shift here," I told them.

I flipped the box on its side and slipped it slowly into my backpack. I made sure the box was secure inside the pack and unzipped the openings as much as possible for maximum airflow.

"Let's get going, Em. I put my bike near the greenhouse, too, so we can leave through that tunnel door."

We exited the hidden room from behind the wall map and quickly made our way to the greenhouse.

Em and I jumped on our bikes, and made sure we passed by the kitchen window so Mom and Dad would see us together, leaving for school.

We were extra cautious on our way to school, and avoided the normal route, just in case Buzz and Trent had planned to ambush us. We didn't want to get caught with a box full of mythical creatures.

We made it safely to the school, and my locker. Em stood guard as I took the traveling box out of my backpack to place it in the locker.

"Em, we have a slight problem... the box is slightly too big to fit in my locker," I whispered.

"Can you bend it slightly?" she replied.

I whispered to the Spore families as quietly as I could, so that my locker neighbors wouldn't catch me talking to a box.

"Sorry, folks, but it's a bit of a tight squeeze in my locker. I'm going to have to bend the box a bit. Try to stand in the center of your compartments so I don't crush any of you," I said.

Small hands stuck out of a few of the holes, each with a thumbs up.

"Here we go... get ready," I said quietly.

The box creased at the center just enough for me to fit it into the metal frame of the locker. Em's face turned to a wince, as she worried I had bent it too much, but it was the only way to get it to fit.

"Everyone okay?" I asked.

This time, I heard a few of the Spores answer in a hushed "Yes."

"Okay, we'll see you all in a few hours. Hang tight."

The day was pretty uneventful, although Em and I constantly worried about how the Spores were doing. We would stop by the locker as often as possible to check on them. They seemed to be doing okay, and they were able to quietly talk to each other to bide their time.

Em and I joked that "today would be the first time a drug-sniffing dog was brought in to do a locker drug search."

That would be our luck. We weren't sure exactly how we would explain a box full of talking mushrooms to anyone, especially our parents.

We ran to our locker at the final bell, and I pried the box from the locker and quickly put it in my backpack so that curious eyes wouldn't notice. The only close call was when Chase and Kylie walked up and asked what was in the box.

"Just a box of vintage doorknobs that my dad wanted me to take to the post office," I replied, surprised by how quickly I made up that story. Em smiled at me.

We left quickly on our bikes to escape before any more questions could be asked.

We arrived at the post office by 3:30 p.m., and parked our bikes on the side of the building. I pulled the box out of the backpack and straightened it out as best as I could.

"Sorry, you guys look like you went through the wringer already," I laughed.

I held the box upright, and we turned the corner to enter the post office.

"Olly and Ember... what a pleasant surprise!"

I looked up to find Harry Sawyer leaving the post office.

"Oh, hello, Harry!" I greeted him.

"Now that is a familiar sight... your grandfather used to bring boxes just like that into my store all the time. He'd stop in for his customary doughnut and coffee, buy his usual supplies and then head off to the post office. It seemed like an almost-weekly routine. It's nice to see you picking up where he left off. Make sure you take good care of them and keep up the good work, Olly! Nice to see you again, too, Mrs. Fein. Don't be strangers down at the hardware store," Harry winked and then continued toward his hardware store.

"Nice to see you, too, Harry!" I replied, almost at a loss for words.

I am not sure if it was Harry's wink, or him saying to take good care of *THEM*, but I had the feeling that Harry might be in on our secret. The look Em gave me reinforced my suspicion.

"I guess it might be fair to assume Poppy would have entrusted this big secret with his lifelong best friend?" I asked Em.

Em shrugged her shoulders, "I guess we might have one more person to help us out if we ever need it."

We walked into the post office which was empty, aside from an older lady working behind the counter. She had gray curly hair and looked up over her small glasses at us.

"How can I help you two?" she asked.

"We'd like to ship this by... what's it called, Em? I think it's called priority mail. And it's fragile," I said.

Before I could say anything else, the lady grabbed the box and tossed it onto the scale to her left, obviously not caring about the fact that I had just said it was fragile.

She took out a tape measure and turned and flipped the box quickly as she measured each side, then entered the numbers into her computer. Looking over her glasses again, she said, "That'll be $11.20 and it will get there in three days, kids."

I handed her the $50 bill, which she held up to the light, just to make sure it wasn't fake.

"I'll need your name and address for the return label, son," she said as she stared at her computer screen again.

"Oliver Appleton, 25 Oak Ridge Road, Littleton," I replied.

"Appleton... are you related to that crazy old Oren Appleton?" she said with a smile.

A little insulted, I answered, "I wouldn't say crazy, but yes, he was my grandfather... and a great man."

"Sorry, son, didn't mean anything by that. He used to bring boxes like this every few weeks. Always wearing that funny hat made out of weeds. Always struck me as a bit of an odd fellow. Here's your change."

I snapped the change out of her hand and was about to say something rude when she slapped the label on the package hard, right over the words "Fragile" and then tossed the package into the air and into a bin about five feet away.

I just stared at her for a second, and she shrugged at me and said, "Oh, hon, don't be alarmed, it's probably going to see a lot more action than that on its way to Colorado."

Just then a younger worker came in and grabbed the bin and wheeled it into the back room.

I turned to Em, "I guess it's time for a hockey match with our package as the puck."

Em grabbed my arm and pulled me out of the post office before I made any enemies.

It was out of our hands... all we could do now was hope that the package, and the Spore families, made it to Colorado in one piece. I hoped they wouldn't hold it against me that they were being tossed around so badly.

Em and I decided to take Cremini up on his offer to use some of the change for ice cream since we were in town anyway. Ice cream was just about the only thing that could take my mind off the way the postal workers treated my package, and I think Em knew this.

The rest of the week went by quickly, probably because we were excited about the council meeting happening on Thursday.

At school, Chase, Kylie, and Brielle chastised me and Em because we were spending so much time together. It was true… Em and I had spent the week going between school, visiting the owl's nest, and using different secret entrances to visit the Spore village in the grand cavern.

The owl momma seemed happy to see us each time we visited, probably because we would collect beetles for her on the way to the nest, and that seemed to be her favorite snack. She spent most of her time in her nest or taking a break up in the live tree while watching for danger.

Truffle let us know that he asked the coyotes to patrol the perimeter of the clearing, and they agreed to protect her and her eggs in exchange for some of Bella's corn cake. I didn't realize Bella's food was prized in the animal world, too.

Every so often, Em and I would see something running through the bushes and it gave us comfort to know we were all being watched over. Momma owl would swivel her head almost 360 degrees to watch as they ran through the brush around the clearing. It gave her something to do while she waited for her owlets to hatch.

Our visits to the grand cavern gave us a chance to interact with more of the members of the Spore community and their animal friends. Clover and I had become friends, and she hopped over to me every time I entered the village. I think

Magpie started to get jealous that I was getting Clover's attention.

Em seemed to befriend a baby skunk named Flower, of all things. The baby skunk would always find Em and cuddle up next to her. Em would glare at me because she would much rather have a rabbit as a friend. Every time we left the grand cavern I would ask Em if she smelled something 'skunky', which made me laugh, but she would just glare at me and punch me in the arm. My arm started to hurt after a while, so I stopped asking the question.

All we talked about during our Spore village visits was the council meeting and how anxious we all were to get it over with. All of us, especially Cremini, were thinking through other options if our plan didn't work out, but nobody could come up with anything. The owl idea seemed to be our best and last-ditch effort to protect our homes.

18. THE VOTE IS IN

The day of the council meeting had finally arrived. It was odd to be excited about an event that could determine the fate of all of our homes.

Em and I had decided that it would be good for our families to show a united front and all go to the council meeting together. When I asked my dad if it was okay, he got excited because it was another chance for him to show off the Green Beast.

"It's got enough room for Em, her mom, the three of us, and 30 owls!" he proclaimed.

I knew there was no way to avoid going in the wagon, so I made sure to warn Em about the Green Beast and asked her to just ignore the peeling fake leather seats ahead of time.

Mom, Dad, and I jumped in the car and left for the seven-minute journey to Em's house. This was the first time my parents had been to the Fein's house, and they also commented on how close we lived to each other.

"I can see why Hank Dalton needs their property for this mall to go in. Without a parking lot on this side of the road, there will be no way to build a mall," Dad said as we turned into Em's driveway.

Em and her mom were already waiting outside. Mrs. Fein had some large posterboards and a legal binder that looked to be packed with papers. When Dad stopped the car, I got out to help her load everything into the car.

"Well thank you, Olly!" Mrs. Fein said.

"You have a beautiful house… and the gardens are adorable. I may have to get your green thumb over to my house for a proper makeover of our garden. It hasn't been touched since my mother-in-law passed," Mom said.

"I'll trade you some gardening for a hair color and styling," Mrs. Fein replied. "I love gardening as much as I think you love doing hair!"

"It's a deal!" Mom replied.

Dad interrupted when he noticed all of Mrs. Fein's materials that I was stowing into in the hatchback of the Green Beast, "That's quite a bit of stuff. What have we got here?"

Mrs. Fein replied with a big grin on her face, "This is to ensure nobody questions exactly what we have up on Oak Hill. Em and I enlarged some of the photos we took during our site survey. Photos of the nest with the eggs in it, photos of the owl sitting on the nest, and I even took a drone photo showing the clearing and where the nest is situated downhill from the water tower on Oak Hill. I also printed the specific line of text from the Massachusetts Endangered Species Act 10.2: The Delineation of Priority Habitat of State-listed Species. I blew them up as large as I could, just so Henry Dalton can see and read them no matter where he sits at the meeting."

"I can't wait to see his smug face," my mom said.

"Well, let's get going so we can get a good seat at the meeting!" Dad said as he held the door open for Mrs. Fein and Ember.

There was enough room for Mrs. Fein, Em, and me to share the back seat.

"I love this car, Mr. Appleton," Em said with a slight grin directed at me, knowing I would never hear the end of it from my dad later. I could just imagine hearing him say, "I told you that women love this car… just wait until it's yours."

What a nightmare! This is going to be my first car?

I shot a grin back at Em, "Just imagine, Em, when I start driving I'll be able to take you out to Salvatore's Pizza Parlor, or better yet, to the prom in this classic!"

Em laughed, as did Mrs. Fein and my mom. Dad thought I was serious and was beaming with pride.

We pulled up to the town hall, which wasn't a far drive at all from Oak Hill. Pulling into the parking lot, Dad noticed something unusual. At the far end of the parking lot was a large gray Ford F-350. Strangely, it was parked as far away from the main entrance as it could be.

"That's Dalton's truck… and that's Dalton and his big friend sitting in the truck, isn't it?" Dad asked out loud.

Just as we all turned to look, we noticed someone

walking out from the opposite side of the truck, and toward the town hall entrance. He was stuffing something into the inside pocket of his blazer.

"And that's the council president, isn't it?" Dad asked Mrs. Fein.

"Sure as heck is… that is Doug McNabb. I wonder what he was doing with Mr. Dalton?"

"McNabb… is he any relation to that bully Trent that has been giving me and Em a hard time lately?" I asked.

Mrs. Fein snorted back with a quick reply, "The same… Trent is his only son. Doug McNabb and Henry Dalton seem to always share similar viewpoints about local zoning issues… and somehow Doug always seems to be in the right investments at the right time around this town. I've always wondered how certain unpopular zoning decisions were passed in this city council, and I am starting to realize there may be some puppet strings being pulled here."

Mr. McNabb noticed all of us watching him as he passed by the Green Beast, and he shot his eyes to the ground and tried not to make eye contact. He nervously shuffled into the town hall without interacting with anyone else standing outside.

"That was rather odd," Mom said.

"You've got that right, let's get in there and see if he avoids us," Dad responded.

We unpacked the car and started to walk into the town hall when a man's voice bellowed out from behind us. We all turned to find Henry Dalton and his bodyguard Stanley Blackwell a few feet away. Mr. Blackwell stood behind Mr. Dalton with his arms crossed… trying to look tough. His biceps were flexed and he wore a black, short-sleeved shirt in an obvious attempt to let everyone see all of his scary tattoos. I almost laughed out loud at him when I noticed he got his dark black hair shaved off to make way for a mohawk.

"Rebecca and Ronnie, I thought I would see you two here tonight. You are a bit of a surprise, Maisie! I want to give all of you ONE more chance to take my offer. I am a fair person… I would rather buy your land at a fair price than have the city take it away for far less. My mall is inevitably going to be built, so why not make a nice profit instead of fighting me?"

I could sense my dad tensing up, but he remained calm.

"Over my dead body, Hank! But, then again, you've tried that route before and it didn't work, did it?" Dad said stepping toward Mr. Dalton.

Blackwell stepped out from behind Mr. Dalton and got in between him and Dad.

"Don't you think you've experienced enough pain in the last month," Blackwell asked my dad with a serious look on his face.

Mr. Dalton interrupted the tense situation.

"Come, come, Stanley. The Appleton family has been through a lot. They don't want to go down that road again, I am sure. Am I right, Ron?"

Don't want to go down that road again.

I stood in silence, realizing that he just pretty much referred to killing Poppy, without actually admitting it. I could sense my mom and dad caught the meaning behind what Mr. Dalton said, too.

Mom grabbed Dad's arm and pulled him away from the situation.

"I still stand by all of the names I called you last week, Mr. Dalton," Mom said.

Mr. Dalton just grinned as we all turned our backs to him and walked into the town hall.

Sure enough, when the five of us entered council chambers, Mr. McNabb quickly ended his discussion with another council member, walked behind the chamber table, sat down, and pretended to do busy work.

"Interesting," Mrs. Fein said to all of us.

We decided to sit in the middle row on the end seats, so it would be easier for Mrs. Fein to get up and speak. Mrs. Fein had already made sure the big posterboards were facing each other so that nobody could sneak a peek at what was printed on them. Once she had everything organized, she walked up to a small podium in the center of the room and wrote something on a sheet of paper.

She came back and sat down. "I've put my name down to get time to speak on the zoning issue. They have to give citizens time to speak before they can take any votes on the issue. It's in the city charter, and they can't get around that."

The idea of Littleton getting a mall didn't sit well with many of the townsfolk, and it was obvious because the hall filled up quickly. I turned around to see how many people arrived after us and noticed that Buzz Dalton and Trent McNabb had joined Mr. Dalton and Mr. Blackwell who had seated themselves in the back row against a wall. Buzz and Trent caught me staring and both gave me the finger and a look of death. I was glad I wasn't sitting any closer to them and had Em and my family with me as an extra line of defense. With the number of times I was able to avoid their beatings or cause them some kind of harm, I knew they were hankering for some payback.

The meeting was called to order, and a roll call was taken. Mr. McNabb sat in the middle of the council table, with two council members on either side of him. There was also a secretary taking notes at one end of the table.

"I'm going to call this meeting to a start. With the start of the meeting, we closed the sign-in sheet which allows members of the public to voice their opinions. If your name isn't on the list, I'm sorry, but you will not be able to speak at this meeting." Mr. McNabb began.

I could hear some of the public getting upset over not knowing they had to sign the sheet, meaning they wouldn't be able to speak. I was impressed that Em's mom knew how the process worked and was on our side.

Mr. McNabb continued, "The only agenda item for today's special council meeting is the final discussion and a vote on the proposed Dalton Mall. This mall wholly relies on a yes vote for both the eminent domain and the re-zoning of portions of two properties off Oak Hill Road. The two properties up for discussion include a portion of the Oak Hill property, currently owned by Ronald and Rebecca Appleton, and also some adjacent land, owned by Mrs. Maisie Fein. I will open up the floor to the council members first, to hear their opinions before we open it up to those in the general public who have signed the sheet at the podium. Mrs. Stinson, why don't you begin."

Mrs. Stinson was middle-aged and dressed as if she came from a fashion show. She wore long black boots that came to her knees, and a scarf to match. I thought it made her look like Cruella De Vil. She did not dress like the normal Littleton townsfolk I was used to seeing during my short time here.

"While I agree with many of your concerns that Littleton is known for its history and traditional ways, it is beyond time that we start to modernize this town and start competing with neighboring towns. Just as an example, I have to drive over 40 minutes to get to a decent clothing store. I also have two teenagers that would love to have someplace to go after school and on the weekends, other than the fine parks in our city. A mall would be a nice addition to our town," said Mrs. Stinson.

Mr. McNabb then called on the councilman sitting to his left, a Mr. Boswell. His nameplate also listed him as the Financial Manager for the city. It was as if Mr. Boswell knew he was going to be called next because he had started to stand up before Mr. McNabb even called on him.

"After assessing the amount of money the Dalton Mall would bring into our fine city in both sales and income tax, it seems a small sacrifice to take over some of the land through eminent domain to allow it to proceed. By my account, the mall could generate over a half million in tax revenue per year, that being after the tax credits are given to Mr. Dalton for developing the property," Mr. Boswell said and then quickly sat down.

"Tax credits? What tax credits?" my dad blurted out.

The crowd in the hall backed up my dad and started to verbally make their feelings known.

"Order, Order. We will have order. This is not a time for comments or discussion. Those of you who signed the sheet will have a chance to speak. That time is not now. Please hold your comments to yourselves or you will be escorted out by Sheriff McGough," Mr. McNabb said forcefully as he motioned to the sheriff – whom I noticed was standing at the entrance to the hall.

Sheriff McGough shook his head in disagreement as if Mr. McNabb's order to clear the room would NOT be accomplished with his help. He turned and walked further out into the hall to let the crowd know he was in support of them.

Mr. McNabb was angered and turned beet red when he saw the sheriff leave. He didn't want to say anything in front of the crowd, which might have riled them up even more, so he moved on.

"Did the other two council members want to say anything on this matter?" McNabb said without looking at either one.

One of the two shot her head down and decided not to speak her mind. The other shot up instantly.

"I would like to say something," said Mrs. Fredricks, making Mr. McNabb shake his head as though he was hoping she wouldn't speak up. "Throughout this process, we have been bullied by Mr. McNabb into agreeing with this eminent domain and rezoning issue. Mrs. Worthington is afraid to speak because we have been repeatedly bullied to back down from our positions. I do NOT agree with it. Any of it. The mall will destroy the character of this town. I don't care if they are nice stores and will save a little time driving to the next few cities over. As a lifelong resident of Littleton, I am proud to keep our history, heritage and small-town feel. This mall will be the first thing you see when entering the town. Not the beautiful town square, or the Littleton Commons, the library, or our historic railroad station. An ugly mall! I have talked with many of you out on the streets over the last month, and I have not heard one person saying they were in favor of this mall. But Mr. McNabb seems to have some opinion that it will be good for our city. And somehow Mrs. Stinson and Mr. Boswell are the only other two that agree. I will be voting no on this issue, and I am sure Mrs. Worthington will side with me."

"Okay, okay, Nancy… I mean, Mrs. Fredricks. I don't think anyone believes I have strong-armed you in this matter. We have had lively discussions, but let's just say that we disagree on the subject. I have spoken with people in town, too, and there is much support for a mall," said McNabb.

"The only person you have been talking to is your friend Henry Dalton, Mr. McNabb," Mrs. Fredricks snapped back as she sat back down in her chair.

My mom and dad looked at each other and Mom said under her breath, "Way to go, Mrs. Fredricks!"

Mr. McNabb had to bring order back to the room once more, as the crowd was now laughing at Mr. McNabb's obvious discomfort.

I turned to look into the back of the room and noticed Mr. Dalton and Mr. Blackwell sitting against the wall with folded arms and smug smiles on their faces. Trent McNabb looked ashamed and had his head down, embarrassed that his dad was getting roasted. Buzz Dalton noticed me staring and gave me the same smug look his dad had on his face.

Those idiots think they've won already!

"I wonder how much money Mr. Dalton wasted paying off these three council members… it's going to hurt when this doesn't go his way," Dad whispered to all of us.

Mr. McNabb yelled over the crowd, "It looks like the vote will be 3-2 in favor of the eminent domain and rezoning. We will hear from those of you that signed the sheet now."

With that, the secretary at the end of the table, Mrs. Finnian, read out the first name, "Mr. Harry Sawyer, of Sawyer's Hardware, at 222 Great Street. Please come up to the microphone."

None of us had even realized Harry was there, let alone had signed the sheet to speak. Harry entered from a side hallway and walked to the microphone.

"You, and each speaker, have no more than two minutes," Mr. McNabb noted.

After a long pause, Harry stared down Mr. McNab and then spoke, "I'll only need a minute, McNabb."

It was obvious Harry knew Mr. McNabb as McNabb sat back down quickly and didn't make eye contact with Harry.

"A used car dealership that nobody wanted. A landscaping business that forced all others out of the area. Special tax abatements. City-owned property going into the hands of one private citizen in a no-bid scenario. ALL APPROVED by this council, well at least three of the five of them. I've wanted to expand my business, which has been servicing the fine people of this town for over 50 years, and I get rejected every time. I think it is high time this council listens to its citizens and votes no on this deal," Harry slammed his fist on the podium, turned to us, winked, and then walked back to the hallway he came from.

Mr. McNabb didn't look up the entire time. Mrs. Stinson and Mr. Boswell shot a glance at each other and quickly looked down, not making eye contact with the audience – all of which was cheering for Harry.

Mrs. Finnian stood again and called for a Mrs. Perry of Perry's Sports Outfitters, of 520 King Street.

An athletic lady, wearing a blue and gold Littleton High School football sweatshirt approached the podium.

"I've been supplying uniforms and team spirit items to all of the kids and families in Littleton for the last 20 years. Many of you know that I donate items to all of your fundraisers, and agree to cover the costs of uniforms for those kids that are unable to afford them. I have been told that this mall will have a big chain sporting goods store in it. That will kill my business!

And I guarantee that big chain will not give you the same fair pricing I have been offering to all of you. And you know they won't be giving away anything for free. I hope that you three council members voting for this new mall realize all of the other small businesses that will be put out of business if this mall goes in. The smaller, family-owned restaurants, Mrs. Kirklin's vintage clothing store, and Littleton bookstore will be replaced. Some big chain bookstore is going to charge you all an arm and a leg for your school books. Let's keep things local. Go Tigers!" said Mrs. Perry with a hand pump in the air.

The crowd erupted once again. Mrs. Finnian waited for a break in the cheering to speak again.

"The last name on the list is a Mrs. Maisie Fein, of 11 Oak Hill Road," said Mrs. Finnian.

The room quieted down.

It took a bit for Mrs. Fein to gather her presentation items. She motioned to Em to take the posterboards up to the podium. Mrs. Fein then went down the length of the council table and handed each of the council members a packet of papers, each one nicely organized in a colorful folder. She then turned to the crowd to hold up copies.

"These will be available in the back of the room after the meeting if anyone is interested!"

Mr. McNabb seemed perturbed that Mrs. Fein was so prepared. He flipped the colorful folder off to the side of the table as if it were junk mail.

"You have two minutes, ladies," McNabb made sure to remind them.

Mrs. Fein turned to look directly at Mr. Dalton in the back of the room.

"I'll only need a little of your time. Many of you know me, but you may not know what I do for a living. I perform environmental studies as a consultant to the state of Massachusetts. Ember, please hold up the first posterboard."

Em held up a posterboard with our beautiful owl sitting on top of the bird's nest – enlarged and in great detail. It looked like a photo straight out of a *National Geographic Magazine*. Em walked back and forth across the front of the room strutting like Vanna White, showing the council members and the crowd the photo.

"Awwwwwwww...", the crowd all murmured.

"This is a Short-eared Owl. There are only 20 to 25 known breeding pairs in the state of Massachusetts. They are currently listed as an endangered species. Ember, please hold up the other posterboard," Mrs. Fein said.

Em held up a posterboard with the picture of the eggs in the middle of the nest.

Before Mrs. Fein could say anything, there was another warm reaction across the crowd, and I could tell the crowd was already getting personally attached to our owl.

"These are three owlet eggs from that same Short-eared Owl. Cute, right? Ember, next board, please."

Em held up the drone photo of the clearing on Oak Hill, with surrounding landmarks to show where it was, exactly. Em pointed to where the nest sat in the picture.

Mrs. Fein looked at the council members. "This is the location of the owl's nest. On the south side of Oak Hill, in a clearing just below the Water Tower and not far from Oak Hill Road. In the same area that Mr. Dalton wants to clear the land to build his mall."

Mrs. Fein turned back to look at Mr. Dalton, and the crowd followed her gaze. Her antics made Mr. Dalton visually upset.

"I've submitted paperwork, a survey, and photos of the endangered owl and nest to the state of Massachusetts to get this area legally delineated as a priority habitat – to be protected by the state from any proposed development."

The room fell silent, and Mr. Dalton's smile turned to a scowl.

Mr. Dalton jumped out of his seat. "This is a farce. You don't have a right to…"

Mrs. Fein cut him off and turned back to Mr. McNabb, "I believe this is my two minutes, Mr. Dalton, and I would appreciate it if Mr. Dalton would respect that, isn't that correct Mr. McNabb?"

Mr. McNabb just sat and stared down at the papers in front of him.

"Ember, hold up the last posterboard," Mrs. Fein said. Em held up an excerpt from the Massachusetts Endangered Species Act.

"The Massachusetts Endangered Species Act does not allow disturbance of any endangered species, once it is suspected of or being legally delineated a protected habitat. I have spoken to my contacts at the state and they are in the process of reviewing my application. They have assured me that if an endangered species does exist on the land, which it does, it will most definitely be marked a protected habitat. This would mean, Mr. McNabb, that the council will NOT be able to vote on this issue until the state has performed its review of the application and property."

The crowd left their feet and the whole hall jumped with excitement. Mrs. Fein smiled, gathered her presentation items, and walked back to her seat next to us. She and Em hugged, and then they both turned and gave all of us hugs. I looked back to see how Trent and Buzz reacted.

I noticed Mr. Dalton whispering something in Mr. Blackwell's ear. Then Mr. Blackwell grabbed Buzz's elbow to stand him up forcefully. He motioned for Trent to follow and they were pushed out of the hall quickly. Mr. Dalton gathered his hat and stepped over to the far side of the room, as far away from the crowd as he could get.

Mr. McNabb interrupted the crowd, "Well, it seems we need to look into the validity of Mrs. Fein's assertions and check with our legal department. The vote will need to be rescheduled to a future date."

As Mr. McNabb left the table, I noticed Mr. Dalton grabbed him by the arm and pulled him aside. Mr. Dalton seemed rather upset with him, and Mr. McNabb put his hands up as if it wasn't his fault and he didn't have any recourse but to postpone the vote in front of all of these people.

A few of the townsfolks came up and thanked Mrs. Fein, and shook her hand. I could tell Em was very proud of her mom, as were we.

"We would like to celebrate... can we treat you to pizza at Salvatore's, Maisie and Ember?" my mom asked.

"I would love that! Defeating a man like Mr. Dalton makes a girl hungry," laughed Mrs. Fein.

19. FIRED UP

We all packed up the Green Beast and headed over to Salvatore's. News had spread fast, as the owner of Salvatore's greeted us and told us he had heard the good news already. I guess his pizza shop was also threatened by the Dalton Mall.

"I've got a table for our special guests over here by the fireplace," Mr. Salvatore said. "Pizza is on me tonight or any night!"

Em and I both smiled at each other. This offer would make our friends Chase, Kylie, and Brielle very happy as Sal's had become our favorite hangout spot.

We all shared our takes on how the council meeting went and laughed about all of the faces made by the three "yes vote" council members at certain points throughout the presentation. Mrs. Fein talked about how Mr. McNabb had no spine, and couldn't even look her in the eye.

I mentioned how upset Mr. Dalton looked, and how he had forced Mr. Blackwell, Buzz, and Trent to leave right after Mrs. Fein's presentation... I assumed so they wouldn't get into any fights with the cheering crowd. I also mentioned that with Mr. Blackwell leaving in his truck, Mr. Dalton would need to take a taxi back home. We all thought that was a bit odd. Dad said he wished he had known that, as he would have offered Mr. Dalton a ride in the Green Beast.

We wanted to keep celebrating, but as it was a school night, Mom and Dad decided it was best we ended our dinner party at a decent hour. We grabbed our things and walked out of Salvatore's feeling victorious, quite full, and ready for a good night's sleep.

I opened the door for Mrs. Fein and Em and noticed something out of the corner of my eye. In the darkness, I noticed an orange and red flickering glow off in the distance, in the general direction of Oak Hill.

"Do you guys see that?" I asked everyone.

I pointed out toward Oak Hill.

We all stared for a minute, trying to make out what we were seeing.

"Is that a fire?" Dad asked.

"It sure looks like it. Is that on the side of Oak Hill?" Mrs. Fein asked.

"Quick, jump in the car. Rebecca, call the fire department," Dad said as he jumped in the driver's seat and almost took off before we were all settled into our seats.

Dad made record time to the base of Oak Hill. It gave me a little more respect for the Green Beast, and my dad's driving.

Up the hill, we could all see that a fire had reached the top of some of the dead trees on the side of the hill, in the same area where I believed the owl's nest to be.

Em and I both turned to each other with fear in our eyes.

Everything was a blur, but somehow I instantly thought of a plan to save the owl and Oak Hill.

"Dad, let them out at the base of the hill. You and I will take the car up the service road to the water tower. I think there is a cleanout hose we can use to put out the fire. Em… see if you three can get to the nest and save the eggs and the momma," I said.

My dad didn't second-guess me. He let the three out, motioned for me to jump in the passenger seat, and gunned the Green Beast up the service road at full speed before I could even close my door. The Green Beast kicked gravel behind it and lurched forward with surprising speed.

We made it about halfway up the road when the Green Beast started to rock up and down and left to right as we hit the large tree roots that had overgrown the service road. The suspension of the car was taking each hit with a large bounce and a resulting *THUD* on the way down. It sounded like the roots were coming through the floorboards.

The road wasn't well maintained and I knew the wagon wasn't made for off-road driving. I give my dad a lot of credit for taking the Green Beast as far as he had, but the service road was getting worse.

238

"We've got to stop the car, Dad, you'll destroy the Green Beast!" I yelled.

The car slid to a stop and we lurched forward. We both looked off to the left and noticed that the fire was quickly traveling up the hill on the floor of the forest, and it had started creeping up the side of some more of the dead trees. It seemed like it was heading close to where we had created the nest for the momma owl.

In the light of the fire, I saw something that I hoped my dad hadn't. A rabbit ran across the forest floor at top speed, straight toward the brush fires. Against the red and orange flames, I could see the silhouette of two shapes riding on the rabbit's back.

Oh no… it's Truffle and Magpie!

"Get out, we'll go the rest of the way on foot," I yelled to Dad. I was nervous we wouldn't have time to put out the fire, and even more nervous about losing my new friends, Truffle and Magpie, to the fire.

We jumped out of the car and started to run up the service road. Aside from the light cast by the fire lower on the hill, the service road was dark. It was hard to see the big roots jutting out every few feet. Dad and I both tripped a few times, only to help each other up and continue.

We noticed a slight turn ahead on the road and our path became almost pitch black. Any light from the fire was now being blocked by the thick trees behind us.

I squinted to try and make out the edges of the road and was instantly blinded by two bright lights.

Everything happened so fast, I wasn't sure exactly what occurred in the next few moments.

I felt someone tackle me from my right side, hard enough to knock some of the wind out of me. At the same time, the lights passed close by and there was a large metal crushing sound against the tree just to my right. I regained my breath and looked up to see my dad kneeling over me, and patting me down to make sure nothing had been injured. He had pushed me out of the way.

"I'm good, Dad!"

Just behind him, I could make out the front end of a large truck, with its front chrome bumper wrapped around the large oak tree nearest us. I could smell and hear coolant dripping from the engine, but the engine was still running.

As my dad started to pick me up, a shape appeared in the beam of light cast by the last working headlight of the truck.

"Blackwell?" my dad assumed.

The man didn't respond, but I could tell by the silhouette of the mohawk on his head that it had to be Blackwell.

The man yelled to someone in the truck, someone we couldn't see. "Stay back there and get back in the truck. We'll be out of here in two minutes," the man said.

As he started to advance, I could make out that it was Blackwell. I could see that he was bleeding from his eyebrow, and assumed he must have hit his steering wheel when he hit the tree so hard.

"You almost killed us, you idiot," my dad yelled at him.

To my surprise, Blackwell replied, "That was the plan."

I couldn't imagine that this land was worth killing three people over, but Blackwell seemed committed to carrying out his mission.

Blackwell lifted his arm, exposing a crowbar he was gripping with his hand. He advanced toward my dad and took a big swing downward. Luckily, my dad had fast reflexes and stuck out a blocking forearm, which took the brunt of the hit. I could hear the bone in my dad's forearm break, but surprisingly, my dad didn't announce any pain. He must have been relying on adrenaline because he used his other arm to quickly push up off the ground and reach out to grasp the crowbar before Blackwell could recoil into another swing. Blackwell fought to pry my dad's grip from the crowbar.

"You two aren't as easy to kill as your old man, Appleton," Blackwell said loudly.

I don't know where it came from, but I felt a strength I hadn't felt before. I got into a crouching position and pushed myself forward, aiming my head into the crotch of Mr. Blackwell. I knew if I hit him hard enough, it would knock him back a bit, at least enough to give my dad a chance to get free and make a move.

I hit him square in the crotch with the hard part of the top of my head. Blackwell doubled over and I thought I had disabled him enough to create some time to escape.

I was wrong. I seemed to make Blackwell even madder and more committed to killing us. He slowly straightened out and pointed the crowbar directly at me. He raised the crowbar and I thought it was the last sight I would see.

Then came an odd sound.

POP – CLICK CLICK CLICK – BUZZZZZZZZZ

Blackwell gave out a quick groan, completely frozen in the position he was in, and then fell directly toward us, landing between me and Dad, crowbar still firmly in his hand.

In the light where Blackwell had just been standing was Deputy Ostran, with a taser tightly gripped in her outstretched hands.

"You two okay?" she asked as she continued zapping Blackwell with a smile on her face.

"He was trying to kill us," Dad replied.

"Oh, I know, Mr. Appleton. I heard every bit of it as I was making my way over here. I'm sorry I wasn't a little quicker with the tazer, I tripped on a root over there," Deputy Ostran said somewhat out of breath. "I think we can safely say we found your father's killer."

Deputy Ostran straddled Blackwell's back and held the taser in one hand so she could zap Blackwell again if needed. Since she only had one free hand, she asked me to help her to get his other arm behind his back so she could cuff him.

About one minute later, Sheriff McGough stepped into the light behind us.

"Great job, Deputy Ostran. I guess I am not in as good of shape as I once was. I had a hard time keeping up with you, but I see you didn't need my help anyway," the Sheriff said. "Is that Mr. Blackwell?"

Deputy Ostran winked at me and smiled. "Yes, meet Oren Appleton's self-confessed killer. Another case in the books for the Littleton PD. That should make us look good, eh, Sheriff?"

The Sheriff patted her on the shoulder to show his gratitude.

Then he yelled back toward the truck in a stern voice.

"Buzz and Trent, get over here."

Buzz and Trent walked around the front of the truck, all disheveled and with their heads hung low.

"I found these two sitting in the backseat of the truck, all banged up and smelling like gasoline. And, there are two empty cans of gasoline in the bed of the truck. I think we found our little fire starters. Let's get these two and Blackwell down to the station. Olly and Ron, are you two going to be okay?" the Sheriff asked.

"I think I need to head to the hospital. I definitely have a broken arm. But Olly, what about the fire?" Dad asked.

"I can handle it… get to the hospital, Dad! Mom and I will meet you there once the fire is under control. But, I need that crowbar, Deputy Ostran."

Deputy Ostran pried the crowbar from Blackwell's hand, 'accidentally' knocking it into the side of his head as she aggressively snapped it from his grip. "Oops, sorry about that!" she said to Blackwell and then tossed the crowbar to me.

"Fire engines should be at the bottom of the hill by now, Olly!" the Sheriff said.

"I have a plan to help, Sheriff," I said as I turned around and started running toward the water tower.

It was still dark in the woods, but as I got further up the service road, the moon shone down over the water tower, like a guiding light.

I reached the water tower and found the cleanout valve Em and I had discovered during our first adventure on Oak Hill. There was a chain that ran through the turnoff valve handle and around the pipe so vandals couldn't open the valve. I stuck the crowbar into the chain and tried to break it off with everything I had. It just wouldn't budge.

I heard a small voice behind me say, "Let me help with that, Olly!"

It was Cremini.

"Just in time, Cremini. I think Truffle and Magpie are down with the owl, and they might be in danger with this fire. If I can get this chain off, I can run the hose down the hill and slow the fire from above. "

I didn't need to say any more. Cremini jumped onto the pipe, right below where my grip on the crowbar was. He told me to count to three and pull.

"1–2–3, pull!"

The crowbar went tight again, and I struggled to get the chain to break. Just then, Cremini jumped high into the air and came down on the end of the crowbar with enough force to snap the chain.

CLINK

The chain snapped and slipped out of the valve handle. I realized the same chain also went through a bracket that locked the water hose reel, so I unwound the chain from the bracket. I just hoped the length of the hose would be enough to reach the fire down the hill.

I turned the water valve and the hose quickly filled with water pressure. At the end of the hose was a nozzle with a pull handle on it. I pulled the handle back just slightly and a big stream of water shot out the end, knocking Cremini on his butt.

"Sorry about that… I had no idea it had that much power," I said to Cremini.

He laughed, "I needed a shower anyway!"

Together we pulled the hose down the hill toward the light of the flames. The hose became heavier the further down the hill we went. Luckily, Spores could carry much more weight than their body size let on. Without Cremini, I wouldn't have made it to the fire.

The fire had completely encircled the area where the nest was. I could see through the flames that the momma owl was still sitting on her nest, protecting her eggs to the bitter end.

Through the other side of the fire, I could just make out a shape running back and forth.

"Em, is that you?" I shouted out across the two walls of flames.

"Yes, Olly, we couldn't get to her in time. We tried to find an opening but the fire surrounded her. I sent our moms back down the hill to tell the fire department where we are and to tell them we need their help," Em yelled loudly.

It occurred to me that Trent and Buzz must have been slowed down by the fence of dead trees that had encircled the clearing. So, instead of climbing over the trees, they decided to douse the entire surrounding area with gasoline and light it on fire. Luckily, the fire hadn't reached the inside of the fence line just yet, but the wind was blowing and the flames were starting to lick at the brush in the center. It was only a matter of minutes before the flames would jump and completely devour the inside of the clearing.

"Stand back, Em!" I yelled.

Em obviously couldn't hear me because she didn't move. I realized she probably couldn't hear me over the fire which grew louder as it climbed the dead trees on her side.

Oh well, here goes everything…

"Hold onto that hose, Cremini!" I yelled, and then pulled the handle all the way back.

The pressure build-up was so great, the spray knocked me back a few steps and onto my butt. I almost fell directly on top of Cremini. Luckily, he jumped out of the way just in time.

"Sorry about that!" I told him.

"That is NOT the last thing I wanted to see before I died," joked Cremini.

I was able to keep the hose directed by keeping one knee on the ground. I pointed the water toward the wall of flames closest to me, but quickly realized the wind was pushing the wall of fire on the opposite side uphill, and closer to the owl's nest. I redirected the spray to the opposite wall, overshooting just slightly by mistake. I saw Em get hit by the spray and she flew backward and out of sight.

Oops!

The spray seemed to be working at keeping the flames down, but I still noticed smaller fires were reaching into the owl's area, following a path of small brush. I decided the bigger wall of flames could be handled by the fire department once they got up here… I needed to just make sure the fire didn't reach the owl or her nest.

I decided to turn the spray to the ground around the nest. I figured if I could wet the ground around the nest, the fire couldn't spread there.

My plan seemed to be working, and I started spraying a wide circle around the area surrounding the nest, soaking the brush as much as possible. The small fires couldn't continue as they didn't have dry wood or brush to consume. The larger fire wall across the way just seemed to burn up the trees, which didn't concern me as much.

I continued to work my way in from the wide circle and covered the area directly around the owl. As I sprayed more water, the fire created more smoke and it was becoming harder to see the owl and her nest. Eventually, all I could see was the dark smoke from the fires, white smoke and steam from where the water was dousing the fire, and orange and red flames shooting up the dead trees in the background. The fires in front of where I was spraying were out, and I kept spraying a lane between me and where I thought the owl's nest was. From my left, I saw Em running toward us. She was completely covered in soot, and her hair and clothes were dripping wet.

"I'm not letting you anywhere near my Green Beast looking like that, Em," I joked.

Em was glaring at me with her hands on her hips.

"You aim that hose as well as you ride a bike, Appleton!" Em chided back.

I placed a few more big sprays in the direction of the nest just to be safe. I could see the outline of the firemen setting up their hoses on the far side of the fire, getting ready to beat the large wall of flames.

"I think Truffle and Magpie are in there, Em. We have to get them out before the fire department douses them, or worst, discovers them," I said. "And the eggs. I think momma owl is staying to protect them."

I turned off the hose and dropped it. I told Cremini to stay behind, just in case any other humans came around. We didn't want to reveal their secret, and Em and I were able to go in and save Truffle and Magpie without him risking it.

We ran through the crackling ash and gray smoke, to find the land starting to resemble a green forest floor again, only doused in water. There in the center of a wet 15-foot circle was the nest. The momma owl was dripping wet and had her wings spread out as far as they would go, covering the entire nest. Her head was facing down, protecting her eyes from the bright flames that were only about 25 feet away.

Em and I were nervous because the owl wasn't moving at all.

I hoped the smoke hadn't killed her, or worst yet, me spraying her with a strong blast of water from the hose.

We slowly walked up to the nest. When we got within five feet, the owl popped her head up and screeched loudly. It startled me and Em because it was so loud.

When the owl looked at me, she recognized me, but then turned to Em and cocked her head sideways, as if she was trying to figure out who Em was.

"I guess you look a little different with the wet look!" I said.

As Em got closer, the owl seemed to begin to recognize her. Hesitantly, the owl pulled in her wings, stood up, and stepped aside. The owl looked down into the nest with a proud look.

Em and I bent over to see how the eggs fared through the fire.

"Awwwwwwwwwww, you have three beautiful, fluffy babies!" Em let out with a tear in her eye.

I have to admit, I was tearing up as well.

The owl lifted and dropped her legs a few times like she

was dancing. I took that to mean she was proud of her accomplishment.

"I hope this means Truffle and Magpie made it out safely," I said.

Just as it came out of my mouth, two of the owlets wiggled aside and Truffle and Magpie popped their heads up. Both had smiles on their faces, and they shuffled toward Em and I with open arms.

"The owl protected us and the owlets. She was going to stay here until the very end if she needed to," said Truffle.

Em continued to tear up.

"Magpie – tell momma owl that we will take her owlets to a safe place until the fire department does their thing. We will reunite them with her tomorrow or the next day, when we can guarantee the fire and smoke are all gone, and we can make her nest dry again," I said.

Magpie walked up to the owl, stroked her chest feathers, and whispered my message to her.

The Owl looked at me, then at her babies, and flew off with a big push. The water from her wings sprayed all of us, and we watched her fly off in the direction of Bumblebee Meadows.

Em picked up two of the owlets, and I picked up the third one. They were like carrying balls of soft feathers, and they barely moved as we held them.

"Your father is going to be very happy to see you two," I told Truffle and Magpie. "I saw you running into the fire on Clover's back. Did she head home already?" I asked.

Truffle and Magpie turned to each other with frightened looks.

"There is no way she could have... the fire had formed a circle completely around us right when she dropped us off at the nest. I thought she was going to stay near the nest as we did. You didn't see her leaving when you came in?" Truffle responded with a look of worry on his face.

"Em, hold this little one," I said as I handed my owlet to Em. "You three take the owlets out and back to the cavern. I don't want anyone to see you. I am going to search for Clover." I didn't give them a choice.

I ran along the inside of the circle closest to where the flames were starting to die down already. I could hear the fire department spraying the downhill side of the fire. Some of their spray was hitting me, and the water was bone-chilling, but I didn't care. I had to find Clover and make sure she was safe.

That's when I saw her.

Clover's body was lying under a layer of ash, motionless, just near the edge of where the fire had ended.

Uh-oh, she's not moving...

She had risked her life for Magpie and Truffle, and didn't make it out in time. It looked like she tried to run around the circle, trying to find an exit, but couldn't escape the smoke and ash.

I started to tear up.

Then I saw her leg move, just slightly.

"Clover!"

I picked her up and brushed all of the soot off her. Her eyes were half-closed and she was listless and barely breathing. Each breath sounded like a wheeze as if she was breathing through a straw. Every so often I would see her leg twitch as if she was trying to run.

I could hear the firemen and they were getting close to where I was. I don't think they knew I was on the other side of the fire they were putting out.

I held Clover close to my chest and made a run toward where I last saw Cremini. Exiting the fire circle, I saw the water hose. I followed the water hose uphill and found Cremini, Truffle, Magpie, Em, and the three owlets all hugging near the water tower. They turned when they heard someone running toward them. They must not have recognized me in the dark and I realized I must look like Em with all of the soot and water dripping down my face and arms.

"It's just me, Olly," I yelled. You could see the relief on their faces. Until they realized I was carrying a lifeless rabbit against my chest.

"No, not Clover!" screamed Truffle.

Magpie ran over to my feet and motioned for me to bend down. She stroked Clover's forehead and pressed her head against it. She whispered something to Clover, which made Clover kick one of her feet.

Clover was fighting for her life.

Magpie pointed to the ground, motioning for me to set Clover down. Magpie turned uphill and whistled the same tune she had whistled in Bumblebee Meadows. Then, without hesitation, she reached into a small bag, similar to my satchel but much smaller, and pulled out some of the blue moss that usually hung in the grand cavern. Magpie whispered into the blue moss, and the blue moss started to pulse slowly. She whispered again, and the blue moss started to pulse more quickly.

Magpie started tearing pieces of the moss off and gently placing them into Clover's mouth. Clover attempted a few chews, still not opening her eyes fully. It was obvious Clover just didn't have the energy to chew the moss. Her breathing was becoming more sporadic.

Magpie turned to me and held out the remainder of the blue moss, with a desperate look on her face. She motioned from the moss to her mouth and then pointed to me. I quickly realized that she needed me to chew the moss for Clover. Without hesitation, I grabbed the small clump of blue moss and threw it into my mouth.

The moss was warm, and tasted a little bit like the seaweed paper they wrap sushi in. A little bit earthy, but sweet and salty at the same time. I found it hard at first to build up enough saliva to start chewing it, just because I wasn't sure about the taste of it. But the more I chewed, the more the taste grew on me. I noticed that, as I chewed, the moss felt like it was pulsing in my mouth, and it got warmer.

I was so distracted by this new experience that I didn't notice Magpie was motioning for me to quickly place it into Clover's mouth.

I looked around, and everyone was staring at me and Clover in silence, obviously afraid that Clover wasn't going to make it. I pulled the wad of moss out of my mouth and gently fed it to Clover as Magpie held her mouth open for me. Clover seemed like she had a little more energy now, and she was able to chew the moss a few times. Her eyes opened and, although still listless, she began to seem more alert. Magpie rested her forehead against Clover's again, and Clover blinked at her and continued chewing.

Just then, I heard a noise coming up behind Em and the Spores.

Oh no, our secret is going to be exposed.

There stood one of the large coyotes that helped us in Bumblebee Meadows. The coyote got down on all fours, and slowly crawled over to where Magpie and I were. Magpie motioned for me to put Clover across the coyote's back.

Truffle jumped up on the coyote's back, too, and helped pull Magpie up. Cremini joined them. Truffle wrapped his arms around Clover to keep her on the coyote's back.

"We're going to take Clover back to the cavern to get her the help she needs. Are you two okay?" Cremini asked.

Em and I shook our heads yes and watched as the three escorted Clover home on the back of the coyote.

Em turned to me, holding the three owlets in her arms, leaned forward, and kissed me quickly on the lips.

"I'm going to consider today our first official date as boyfriend and girlfriend. Is that alright with you, Olly?"

I was smiling and blushing and before I could respond, Mrs. Fein and my mom yelled for us. "Olly, Em, where are you?"

"Up here!" I yelled back.

Our moms hugged both of us, being careful not to squish the baby owlets in Ember's arms.

"Mom, Dad broke his…" I started.

"I know, I know… I saw him on our way back up the hill. He is heading to the hospital in an ambulance. He told me you protected him from that Blackwell guy, Olly?"

I blushed a little. "Well, we protected each other."

20. PEACE AT LAST

The week after the "Great Oak Hill Fire of 2022" (as it was already being called in the local paper), Em and I were able to place the baby owlets back into a cleaned and improved nest. Momma owl quickly returned to raise her family safely protected by the Spore community and soon the state of Massachusetts. Magpie was already out and about recruiting more Short-eared Owls to come and live on Oak Hill.

Cremini invited me and Em to attend another harvest ceremony, which we both thought was rather odd because we thought they only happened twice a year. When we arrived at the grand cavern for the party it was very dark and unusually quiet. We thought maybe we had the date wrong. When the blue moss lit up, and the cavern lights flickered on, we were humbled to find it was a surprise party for me, Em, Truffle, and

Magpie. They wanted to thank us for the work we did to save their Spore Community.

When we sat down for another great dinner by Bella, we were presented with another surprise. Clover, a little slower than she was before the fire, hopped over to me and curled up next to me for the entire party. It was nice to see that she had almost completely healed. Em, of course, had her baby skunk friend, Flower, to keep her company.

At the end of the party, Em and I both expressed our thanks and our desire to continue helping the Spore Community in any way we could. We both felt like we were part of two communities now.

After everything that had happened since we moved to Oak Hill and Littleton, it was nice to finally be able to just hang out with friends without worrying about Buzz Dalton or Trent McNabb anymore. Both were charged with arson and were sent away to a juvenile detention center for a year. We had a feeling the McNabb and Dalton families would not be around Littleton much longer anyway.

The shame of what Trent did forced Doug McNabb to resign his seat on the council. The candidates running to replace him all let it be known that there would be no way that a mall was going into Littleton, as whoever won the election would be the deciding vote – even though it wouldn't matter because the state had already started the process of designating Oak Hill a priority habitat.

Sheriff McGough and Deputy Ostran stopped by the house to let us know they got a full confession out of Stanley Blackwell, on condition of testifying against Mr. Dalton. In return for his testimony, he would get a choice of which prison he would spend the rest of his life in. But even though Blackwell pointed the finger at Henry Dalton as the one who told him to murder Poppy, Mr. Dalton's lawyer said this was all a lie and just hearsay, and there was no proof. It looked like the next year would be filled with trials and lawyers for Mr. Blackwell and Mr. Dalton. In our mind, we had already beaten Mr. Dalton, because he quickly shuttered all of his businesses in Littleton. It didn't seem to matter because townspeople made a pact to no longer support any of his businesses.

Harry Sawyer surprised my parents with a celebration of life ceremony he put together for my grandfather down at the town square. The whole town was there to honor Poppy. To our surprise, the townspeople all pitched in for the city to create a rabbit habitat in his honor, to be built down on the Bumblebee Meadows property. They named it "Oren's Rabbitry." I laughed because it seemed a convenient way for the townspeople to get rid of any rabbits they found on their properties and 'donate' them while avoiding any curses. My dad said Harry would make a nice fortune selling rabbit traps to all of them, which made me happy. I know Poppy would have been happy, as well.

The State of Massachusetts was so impressed by the work Mrs. Fein did on the Oak Hill environmental study, they hired her on as a full-time employee in all things related to endangered species.

Our takedown of Mr. Dalton and Mr. Blackwell, and our work in stopping the mall, made us local celebrities. My mom opened a hair salon just down the road from Oren's Rabbitry, aptly named "Hair, Hare." She was doing well with the business and had to hire three more stylists to keep up with demand.

My dad continued helping Harry run and grow the hardware store business. With Harry getting close to retirement, and without any heirs, he felt it only appropriate to offer the business to my dad to carry on the store's success. Harry decided to allow him to buy the store out over time, at a very fair price.

Em and I let our friends know that we were officially boyfriend and girlfriend now, and we both promised to spend more time hanging out with them. We spent a great deal of time eating free pizza at Salvatore's. The boyfriend/girlfriend situation also allowed Em to hang around my house more often, making it easier to visit the Spore Community together.

21. LITTLETON, COLORADO

November came, and Mom, Dad, and I were sitting at the dinner table when the doorbell rang. I jumped up, thinking it was Em, but it turned out to be Mr. Carell, the mail carrier.

"I've got another certified package for your family, Oliver. All the way from Littleton, Colorado," said Mr. Carell.

The package was one of those bubble packs, letter-sized, and it seemed heavy for its size.

I signed for the package and thanked Mr. Carell, then returned to the dining table.

"Who was it," Mom asked.

"It was Mr. Carell from the post office. It's a package

addressed to you two," I said.

I handed the package to Dad, who smiled at Mom, and then ripped into it like a child on Christmas day. In his fervor to open the package, the contents flew onto the dining room table.

Five large gold nuggets and a few papers scattered out across the table.

Mom gathered the nuggets into one hand, with an amazed look on her face, and held them out to get a sense of how much they weighed.

"This has to be about 10 ounces... that's about $16,000 of gold in my hand," Mom said.

Mom grabbed the torn package and turned it over to see who had sent the package.

"It's from the same person that sent the last delivery of gold to your dad just before he passed," Mom said. "It's from an A. Muscaria, from Littleton, Colorado. But it is addressed to us this time."

Dad picked up a letter from the table and read it aloud.

Amanita Muscaria
PO Box 1245
Littleton, Colorado
80120

Monday, November 1, 2022

Dearest Ronald and Rebecca,

It was with great sadness that I heard of Oren's passing, and the terrible events surrounding his death. I was very good friends with Oren (we grew up together in

Littleton). He was always there when I needed him, especially during my move from Massachusetts to Littleton, Colorado. He was like family to me and mine. He shared many stories with me – of his wife, Mary, the both of you, and especially his adventures with Olly (who I can't wait to meet!).

You are probably asking yourselves why I am sending this gold to you. While it may seem like it is quite a bit of gold, it is nothing compared to what I owe Oren for his friendship and support of our community out here in Colorado.

You may not know this, but before Oren's death, he purchased land and a cabin on an abandoned gold mine named Sapphire Creek. It's just outside Littleton, Colorado, on Santa Fe Mountain. I have enclosed the deed to the property, which is fully paid for and is now assigned to the two of you as his heirs.

I have also enclosed a letter agreement that Oren and I signed, allowing me to mine for gold on the property. A portion of the profit allows me to support my community, and the remainder goes to Oren's estate, which I will send to you monthly. As I am retired, the mining is a hobby that keeps my mind busy and is a nice way for me to feel like I am doing something good for others.

I would love for you three to come out to meet me and, of course, see the property (it's beautiful). I have included my contact information below. I look forward to meeting all of you very soon!

Sincerely,
Amanita Muscaria (303-867-5301)

----- end -----

Dad folded the letter and looked at the deed and the letter agreement. "I can't believe this," he said.

Mom turned to me and said, "Looks like we are going to be taking a trip out to Colorado!"

WILL YOU SHARE A FEW STARS?

Please know... your reviews **feed my soul** and **encourage me** to keep creating. I would be honored to earn your review wherever you purchased this book. I read all reviews… many times, in fact! I even place the great ones on my fridge like a proud parent.

 You can scan this code to leave a review on Amazon, even if you didn't purchase there.

To learn more about me, upcoming releases, and to watch videos of me creating the book art, visit:

Author's Blog: GlennSomodi.com
TikTok and Instagram: @ollyandthespores
YouTube: @GlennSomodi
Facebook: /gsomodi

AND DON'T FORGET TO SUBSCRIBE & WIN!

I randomly pick winners from my subscriber list to receive some really cool items. Subscribe at www.GlennSomodi.com and you will be automatically entered into all drawings.

ABOUT THE AUTHOR

Glenn Somodi is an American author who writes his stories in the short space between lying down and dreaming. The stories are written over many nights, replayed, and rewritten in his head for enjoyment. His mission is to find anyone who enjoys reading his stories as much as he enjoys creating them.

He is a proud graduate of the E.W. Scripps School of Journalism at Ohio University in Athens, Ohio. His paying job is as a partner at EYEMG.com, LLC in Akron, Ohio, a website development company.

He was born in New Brunswick, New Jersey, raised by a schoolteacher and a mechanical engineer in Olmsted Falls, Ohio, and has resided in Brunswick, Ohio, for most of his adult life.

He has a patient wife whom he met at Ohio University in 1989. He also has three beautiful children that are his favorite creations. His coworkers include three cats and a dog – a Siamese tabby named Nala, a Chantilly-Tiffany cat named Coco, a Maine Coon named Josie, and the loudest coworker is Beckham, a Yorkshire Terrier. All five share office space for the entire workday.

Made in the USA
Middletown, DE
27 April 2024